ANTICHRIST RISING

END TIMES CHRONICLES SEASON 3
EPISODE 1

J. A. BOUMA

CHAPTER 1

ALEXANDER ZARRUQ HUGGED THE COLD, slick concrete wall pockmarked by decay and neglect as if his life depended on it. Because it very well did, or at least the one whom they were after. Even then, if he fell, and he was caught, him and his teammates, it was all over.

The bristles of his close-cropped dark hair brushed against the ceiling, its roughness scraping against his skin. He was already hunched, his back aching from the awkward position shuffling down the narrow ledge that lined the underground sewer system beneath the target, his feet barely finding purchase. Several paces back, he had finally found his center of gravity, letting his weight and height do most of the work keeping him from descending into the murky, toxic depths below.

The darkness was all-consuming—as was the smell, the pungent excrements cloying and clinging to the inside of his nose compounded by the rot of vegetables and sour, spoiled meat. That wasn't even touching on the bloody water that had infected the underground channel, the apocalyptic consequences of the second and third celestial trumpets that sent a sanguine cesspool clotting on toward the body of water that surrounded the tiny island. The stench was made all the worse by the oppressive heat, temperatures hovering near ninety even in the waning evening, and with the sun having dimmed from the onset of the apocalypse.

The sharp tang of bile had pushed high at the back of the throat an hour ago and never let up. His stomach clenched tight from his abdominal muscles both aiding his journey and threatening to retch from the overwhelming stench of human waste and bitter water.

Was any wonder Alexander hadn't turned back and swam for home! But he had a job to do. They all did. And their target depended on them staying the course. Hunched, aching, smelling of urine and feces.

A line of sweat wound down his forehead, tickling his skin and screaming for him to wipe it away. He couldn't spare a hand, and the crawling sensation rose to a fevered, needling pitch at his brain. Instead, he concentrated on his footsteps.

One step, two step, three step, four—

His left foot slid on a sludgy slick spot that escaped his sight, nearly sending him sliding into the rushing waters just beyond his feet.

"Watch it, homefry," John Mark Ford said from the back, his Noramericana twang extra sharp. "It's a right wicked plunge to the bottom."

"Right stinky plunge methinks!" Sasha Pavlovich said before adding a string of Muscovia in his native Ukrainski tongue.

Alexander chuckled at his good buddy, the pair of them roommates from back in Britannia at Oxford. They had become instant friends by nature of their shared name, Sasha being a diminutive form of Aleksander. Not only were they about as opposite of people as you could be—Sasha the life of the party and outgoing while also incredibly bookish;

Alexander much shyer and introverted but competing on the collegiate soccer team as a wicked goalkeeper and a mean long-distance runner.

The pair had also pursued about as opposite of a career path as two people could take: Sasha's was a world of atoms and quantum physics and string theory, combined with wackadoodle ideas about the time-space continuum—or rather, the space-time continuum as his good friend would surely correct. He had vowed to crack it and pave the way for traveling back in time. And he'd done it too, not only solving the scientific riddle but manufacturing a traveling device, an actual time-travel belt that could rend a rift in reality itself to carry its user back in time.

Which Alexander himself, along with others from the team, had leveraged to keep Ichthus's head above water the past few years, retrieving from the memory of the Church's past to contend for the once-for-all faith in the future present, preserving the remnant Christian community.

Time travel...

Alexander smirked and shook his head, continuing his careful steps in the suffocating darkness, clothes clinging to him and making him itch all over. All of it was positively preposterous, and he would've thought someone bloomin' mad in the head for speaking of such things—had thought Sasha himself was bloomin' mad in the head for speaking of such things, usually after several shots of his friend's favorite Ukrainski vodka. But he'd done it. The crazy lad had done it.

He, on the other hand, had pursued about as opposite of a career as one could from the sciences: the Church of Jesus Christ. Perhaps to be expected as the only child of a regional north Alkebulanan bishop who'd risen through the Ministerium ranks as a cardinal before apostatizing. Regardless, he had loved his studies and cherished his time with Father James Ferraro, his academic mentor who had instilled in him a deep and profound understanding of the Holy Scriptures, along with kindling a love for theology and doctrine, particularly its formation through history.

Had nearly thrown in the towel halfway through the four required semesters of ancient Greek and Hebrew, the Bible's original languages. But Father Jim had cheered him on, gifting him small bars of dark chocolate to keep his spirits high and then treating him to a round of pints at The Eagle and Child—a meeting place made famous by two other Christian patrons, C. S. Lewis and J. R. R. Tolkien.

Another smirk and more careful stepping. Father Jim. He was the reason he was inching along that bloody sewer canal to begin with!

Three years ago—had it been that long?—the cardinal and Ministerium Master had sent along a messenger with a dispatch calling him to a conclave of fellow priests and bishops and other ecclesial figures in the Church. The Fidelium they were, the faithful ones keeping the faith from fraying in the face of a rising apostasy. Little did they know what awaited them—the darkness and destruction, the struggle and suffering.

Little did *he* know...

How different things would have been had Alexander not heeded Father Jim's invitation. Strike that: How different things would have been had he chosen a different profession! Something sensible like accounting or practical like engineering. Instead, his path had taken him home again, shepherding his childhood parish as a simple, small-town priest. Sasha had found his name in lights—literally, appearing on OneWorld News. Alexander's name, unknown and unmentioned.

Truth is, he couldn't imagine doing anything other than serving as Christ's undershepherd, caring for the sheep of his pasture. It was as the Apostle Paul himself said, recorded in the Book of Acts, when he was beckoned to Ephesus: *'I consider my life worth nothing to me; my only aim is to finish the race and complete the task the Lord Jesus has given me—the task of testifying to the good news of God's grace.'*

Same for Alexander. Now, more than ever.

Because while apostasy had risen within Ichthus and the complete dismantling of Christianity had been bad enough, Solterra had been embroiled in the apocalypse the past year. As was Ichthus, enduring the Great Tribulation foretold in the Book of Revelation.

A year ago, the scrolls had given way to the trumpets; the general chaotic groans of a world consumed by sin—with all of the political, economic, civilizational violence that has marked and marred the world for ten millennia—had ratcheted to a fever pitch with the unfolding of God's judgment. The sun and moon had dimmed, the rivers and seas had turned bloody and bitter, the land had been consumed by fire and ash, and the fallen ones of the Unseen Realm had been unleashed against humanity, the demonic horde inflicting horrifying terrors upon the polis.

With the Church of Jesus Christ in the middle of it all.

It had all bloomed into a terrifying climax with the revelation that one of their own—a former colleague of Alexander's in the Ministerium, a priest from Germania—had been possessed by the power of the dark side.

Alexander could still see the face of Apollos Nicolai in the suffocating darkness, the one that had appeared in the night-time sky announcing the Republic's salvation with a Voice sounding not of this world. Guttural and growly and edged by a hawkish call, he'd sounded eerily like the snorty, roary, chittering screech that had come from the demon riders and their horde that had descended upon Solterra from the Unseen Realm.

"Babylon the Great," he had called himself, or at least the Voice within had.

Alexander had instantly understood what that meant. The moment they had been waiting for months was beginning to unfold. The Antichrist had begun to rise.

Apollos had promised he would have more to say in the coming days, with a pledge for the Republic's tri-part promise of peace, prosperity, and progress, invoking the name of the Dragon, the Beast, and the Prophet—the Satanic Trinity of the Book of Revelation. Boy, did he ever have more to say.

The Purge had ratcheted up to a terrifying degree, ravaging church communities across Solterra. Countless Christian brothers and sisters had been snatched in the middle of the night, black bags slipped over their heads and dragged away to reprogramming camps where Christ only knew what was happening. In fact, one of their own had been snatched by Enforcers last year—one of Alexander's own. A remnant of the religious order he was Master over, the Order of Thaddeus, Kareema Salam, a sturdy woman who had been instrumental in reconstituting the ancient defenders of the faith stretching back to the earliest apostles.

Now she was imprisoned inside the Enforcer outpost, which they were infiltrating through the bloody sewer. At least that's what the intelligence had suggested. It's what he hoped. Because if this stinky, sweaty, slogging journey to a speck of dust in a Canadian sea didn't show results—he might turn over his medallion that christened him Order Master and take up his last job scrubbing fishing hydrocrafts in southern Roma!

Their plodding continued, Sasha striking up a lowly conversation with Junia Kaminski now, his fellow Ukrainski who had joined them a year ago. The faint purple glow from that wicked Scythe weapon of hers was their only light, the electrical tendrils barely making purchase in the suffocating darkness.

He was thankful Nia was on their side, her skills and spunk sharp and exacting. Just what Ichthus needed during these dark days. Same for the others—John Mark Ford, the Ministerium's trusty head of operations; his fellow Noramericanan, Ryder Reeves, the Order Remnant they'd picked up a year ago, same as Kareema; Luciana Jane and Rebekah Kony waiting for them in their hydrocraft, along with Jin Sung.

That is, if they made it out alive...

Alexander came up to a bend in the sewer canal, the wall disappearing to his right, laughter floating his way along with a hot breath of rotting meat and excrements. They must still be on the right course of things, but it also meant a maneuver he didn't know if he could manage.

Moment of truth...

Stretching his leg farther down the edge, he cast off his other foot from around the corner with a powerful shove— edging around the other side with a wobble that sent his stomach doing cartwheels. But—

He made it.

Wanted to take a deep breath but forewent the lungful of air.

Faint yellow light floated down from somewhere farther on. They were close.

A small landing sat a few feet away with a set of stairs. Looked like a service door entrance but missing any handle or lock on their side. Which meant a no-go on that front.

He made for it anyway, reaching it as the others made their own harrowing leap into the void.

First Nia, the woman handing off her Scythe to Alexander as she made her way around the edge.

He held his breath and held her Scythe high for all the light she needed, the purply electric charge bouncing off from the concrete marked by decay and disrepair. In one motion, she completed the turn, joining Alexander and taking back her weapon.

"*Spasibo,*" she said, a relieved sigh escaping her. "Now for the rest."

Alexander said, "I'm not too worried about Ford. He's managed worse. Same for Reeves, given his experience with the Order."

"I'm not either. I wasn't referring to the cowboys."

As if on cue, Sasha threw up an expected complaint: "Oh, I am not knowing about this..."

"Take off your granny panties, son," Ford said from behind, "and hop to it!" Reeves stifled a giggle but left it alone.

Sasha muttered something under his breath before slipping a hand around the corner. Then a foot. The left side of his face was next, that nest of tight blond curls gleaming purple in Nia's light.

Just a few more steps...

And—

"*Aiya!*" he exclaimed, sliding down the corner and slipping his legs into the rushing current of toxic sludge.

Hands caught the concrete edge, but it was all over after that. Half of Sasha was submerged in the rushing sewage, his other half was scrambling just to breathe!

"*I am dying! I am dying!*" he screeched, legs kicking and hands scrambling to right himself but making no progress.

"*Idiot...*" Nia muttered under her breath as she handed off her Scythe again and knelt to help. Needed no translation on that one!

For Alexander's part, he held her Scythe aloft to aid in his friend's recovery. Reeves just laughed; a real help he was.

"Keep it down!" Ford spat, the pair of them easing Sasha back to the ledge. "You wanna get us killed, lug nut?"

Voices instantly silenced them. Through a faint curtain of light parting the darkness—down the way, from above.

Sasha calmed enough for Reeves and Ford to hoist him back to safety, but Alexander was petrified they'd been heard, their cover blown.

He left them to contend with Sasha's recovery while he shimmied farther along, a landing coming into view, along with a thick metal grate anchored above in the ceiling.

They'd arrived.

Alexander glanced behind, Sasha back to plodding with Nia taking point, Reeves behind her. Ford glared at him from the rear in the faint purple light with a finger pressed to his lips before passing along the message to Sasha.

He got it, loud and clear.

"Ya catch the game last night, Charlie?" a voice echoed from above, deep and growly.

"Sure did!" another voice sounded, high and heady. *"Germania creamed Catalonia in the last quarter! Can you believe it? Germania!"*

Deep Voice snorted a laugh. *"Don't you know it. And wouldn't you know I had a hundred merca credits riding on that game!"*

"Oof. That's gotta hurt."

"Sure does. Especially since the missus found out and cut off my allowance!"

"Double oof."

A *clomp-clomp-clomp* reverberated from above, then: *"Why don't you finish up here, then we can tap into my stash of merca credits and bet on Britannia and Tripolitania!"*

Alexander snorted his own laugh. No way was his home country going to lose to the British Isles!

A distant *clomp-clomp-clomp* indicated Deep Voice was heading out, while the *swish-swish-swish* of a broom or mop confirmed the other man left behind was finishing up—whatever that meant.

A gloopy, gloppy pile fell with a sudden plop from the grate, slapping the concrete stairs below and oozing down into the flowing river of detritus—before a hose turned on and even more garbage rained down from above.

Alexander stepped away, as did the others, water and thick glop pouring down from above. And—

"What was that being?" Sasha asked on a shaky breath.

The light caught the detritus just right—triggering an instant rise in bile.

A finger, with long, filed nails and painted candy apple red, bobbed on the sludge. Another surfaced, then one more, joined by a mashy hash of matter that looked like ground beef. Didn't even want to think about what the heck had been discarded from above.

Clomping feet were joined shortly by a clanging shudder, then the *whoosh* of a heavy door on cranky hinges followed by a resounding slam.

The last hostile had left, opening the window of opportunity to infiltrate the Enforcer outpost—the reprogramming camp Ford promised held Kareema.

Nia snatched back her weapons and quickly got to work, swinging around that Scythe of hers. The head glowed an otherworldly purple, an electric charge sparking from a point that promised entrance.

As she worked, her instrument of resistance cutting through the metal, a sharp, sour tang tickled the back of Alexander's throat, and his gut clenched tight before a shuddering wave wound its way through his abdomen. His mouth began to salivate as well, a stream of cold liquid readying the hatch for what was to come, joined by a cold sweat washing over his skin—from his forehead down his face and from his armpits down his back.

He heaved a breath, trying to stem the retching tide, the noxious smell of toxic stew beneath almost jettisoning the contents of his stomach, then and there.

This was not happening...

It was all he could do to keep from losing it. Someone else did the losing for him.

A belch, followed by a retching, rushing stream was thrown up from Sasha, the man doubled over with both hands on his knees and a spray of chunky puke flying from his mouth again. He heaved a breath, choking and coughing, then sank against the wall, muttering in his foreign Muscovia tongue.

Poor guy. His mate had certainly been through the wringer. Alexander went to cross behind Nia, when she suddenly stepped back and jutted out a hand.

"*Ostorozhno!*" she shouted.

Right before a square object fell from the ceiling with a clattering clang, the metal grate from above bounding down the stairs and splashing into the toxic rush.

The light was blinding, a spotlight of white from the ceiling casting down into the darkened void.

The group held their stance. Waiting, intuiting, discerning if anyone from above heard the ruckus.

No one came.

Ford turned to Alexander and jerked a thumb toward the ceiling.

"You first, homefry."

He crouched and cupped his hands together, offering a

foothold. Nia joined him, getting on one knee and offering her joined hands.

Swallowing, Alexander nodded, stepping a foot into the crook of Ford's hands and bracing a hand against his shoulder before shoving off into the void.

Nia quickly lent him her own support, Alexander putting his other foot in her hold as he reached for the opening. She and Ford lifted him up with a grunting push, and he clasped the edge with ease.

The surface was cold and wet. The air was cool against his face, and smelled sweet. Of cleaning agents and alcohol, joined by the trace scent of something burning, like steak or chicken. He wasn't far enough through to catch a glimpse of what lay beyond, and the light above still shone down with a blinding brilliance.

"On three..." Ford said lowly, readying for the final push. "One, two—"

On three Alexander was lifted high, and he pulled himself through the portal. It was a tight squeeze, his shoulders aching from the contortion and arms rubbed raw, but he scrambled inside.

Heaving a breath, the air blessedly pure and free from rank refuse, he couldn't help but smile and sigh with relief.

He'd made it. Inside the belly of the beast!

Catching his breath, he allowed his eyes to adjust and revel in his success.

A whistle drew his attention back to the void below—as well as the rest of the room.

He was not prepared for what he found.

Not in the slightest...

CHAPTER 2

John Mark Ford was as nervous as a teenage boy in a Noramericana revival tent service—complete with singing and dancing, hootin' and hollerin' Jesus' name, a preacher bringing down the gospel funk from heaven on high. The convicting power of the Holy Spirit tended to have such an effect on teenagers with too much time on their hands.

Which Ford had in spades growing up on that peanut farm of his in Deep South Noramericana. Which led to the nervous discomfort of the Almighty attending those jumpin'-jivin' church services a time or twelve thanks to a meemaw with a pincer grip that would give an earwig a run for its money. And had sweated to beat the band every time—not only because temperatures in them southern parts of the former U.S. of A. reached near a hundo every summer, but also because of the threat of hell's fire and damnation.

Never did take, not until a few years ago, but flashes of those childhood Jesus powwows were throwing up the same nervous sweats and heebie-jeebie willies as when he'd walked into those religious meetings—and for good reason.

Because just as Ford had felt the weight of conviction for sinning against the Lord Almighty stepping into his churchy turf, he felt the same weight of sinning against the Republic standing in the bowels of its own territory.

Not only was he an Unfit, the designation Solterra Republic had given Christians, labeling them as blights on society—threats even, their allegiance to a King and Kingdom that was not of this world a menacing risk to all the Patron had built, all the Republic held dear. He was also a Defector, a former elite Enforcer Purifier who had fled the Legion after finding who he had been waiting for his whole life, Jesus Christ, only later to find himself in a reprogramming camp before escaping. Because once in the Legion, it was impossible to get out; you were married to the Patron whether you liked it or not, till death you departed.

Ironically, it had happened on the complete opposite kind of an operation than the one he was on right now: Instead of infiltrating an Enforcer outpost, he'd raided a monastery of Benedictine monks to drag them Christians to a reprogramming camp before that was officially a thing.

He'd sinned against the Patron himself by abandoning his sworn duty to protect the Republic from all designated threats against the peace, prosperity, and progress of the one-world civilization that had risen from the ashes of a world gone berserk. And now he was busting back into the Patron's little shop of horrors—to rescue, yes, but more to atone for his screwup.

Hence the nerves that threatened his bowels to unloose then and there in the Republic sewer!

Ford had set out with his Resistance companions the day before last from Blake Ridge Outpost, a deep sea submergence station Ichthus had commandeered years ago that was serving as one of several forward operation centers for the Church's mission at the climax of the Great Tribulation.

Was as shocked as anyone he and all his other bros and

broads in the faith were neck deep in apocalyptic mayhem. Bet Meemaw was too, Ford's granny feeding him a healthy dose of end-times theology built on the back of some 20th century Bible-belt fiction series—and for good reason. If those revival services didn't take, she thought scaring the hell out of him would! Only one problem: The temptations of this present world had a stronger pull on Ford's heart than the promises of the future one—both of eternal life and everlasting damnation.

Irregardless, Ichthus had been through the wringer the past few years as Solterra broke and went bonkers from those blasted trumpets, well, blasting! One right after another, followed by all manner of apocalyptic mayhem—including those alien demon hordes descending from space in those massive chrome cigars like a Stephen Spielberg fever dream. And who did the Patron and his newest lackey Apollos Nicolai blame? Yeah, that's right: Ichthus, the Church.

No surprise on that front. Christians had been blamed before when the shiznit hit the fan back in the Roman world after Pax Romana turned out to be a thin disguise for the naked emperor. Same for Pax Solterra, the Patron as bare-skinned as a bare-naked bear in a berry patch, which ratcheted the persecution of the Church to the nth degree beyond the initial wave of the Purge that led them to that Enforcer outpost to begin with.

"What the..." Alexander echoed from above.

"What is it homefry?" Ford asked, standing and peering into the void. Junia did the same, raising that Scythe staff thingy of hers up for a visual.

Alexander's head peeped through the hole, his head hallowed by the light above and face lit purple and creased with worry. Or was that terror, panic? Whatever it was told him all he needed to know.

Not good, Johnny Mark.

"What's the dealio?" Ford asked.

Alexander swallowed and heaved a breath. "You better get up top. This isn't good."

"Stop with the drama, *bratishka*," Nia said.

"It's worse than we imagined, this place—" Alexander stood and spun, continuing in an echoey mumble that did no one good.

Huffing a sigh, Ford went back to his knees and motioned to their resident Ukrainski physicist. "You're up next, doc."

Sasha went to protest but Nia mumbled something in their Muscovia tongue that stayed his complaint. Good girl.

The quintet was on a crucial operation that held the promise of hope for retrieving one of their own, Kareema Salam, as well as unraveling a vital piece of intelligence for the rest of Ichthus, the Remnant followers of Jesus Christ during these last days.

The woman had been captured by a platoon of Enforcers in Tunisia after returning from capturing the memory of Cyprian of Carthage. She and Ford had jumped phases back in time to AD 256 to retrieve the Church's experience through the Great Cyprian Plague that had ravaged the known world. Father James Ferraro had believed it offered Ichthus a prime example of how to bear witness to Jesus when the Lord himself unleashed the full wrath of judgment upon Solterra—with all of its suffering and misery and death— inspiring the Church to care for the polis and lead them to repentance.

Their journey back in time started out rocky, being discovered by the Republic before they made the jump. When they returned, the Legion was waiting for them and managed to capture Kareema, whisking her away in a Queller aerialcraft and giving the Republic a major propaganda get: an Order

Remnant. One of the few remaining members of an ancient religious order tasked with contending for and preserving the once-for-all faith, the Order of Thaddeus.

Ford hadn't forgiven himself.

Had spent months tracking her down, going deep underground in the backwater corners of Solterra sussing out any intel that might shed light on her whereabouts. Even took up a part-time gig tending bar at a local watering hole just outside one of the few reprogramming camps Ford knew of.

His, the one he'd been stationed at for a stint after Defecting. Vowed he'd never return, the scars on his back pulsing in the humid darkness—brought about not only from his salty sweat soaking his undershirt, but also from the memory of how he'd gotten them in those specific, torturous ways.

The haunting image of the Rack sent the synapses in his noggin firing on all cylinders now, a new flashback surfacing that terminated in his throat.

Threatening to snatch his consciousness!

The all-consuming darkness made it all the worse, as well as the oppressive heat and suffocating stench. As if a rag doused in piss had been shoved down his throat, cutting off all breath, leading to—

The Grip...

Ford's mouth was drier than the Yazoo-Mississippi Delta, tasting of chalk and those old-world pennies. He tried to generate some saliva, moving his tongue this way and that, swallowing hard and repeating, but it was no use—his adrenaline was bucking something fierce.

He cursed himself for his weakness, hated how he got when the pressure mounted, pressing in and tightening around his chest like a vice grip and flaring without warning.

The Grip, he called it, had stretched back to boyhood. Ever since those days on his family peanut farm in Noramericana, he had a rough time keeping it together under pressure. Sports had helped some, having to learn to just plow through the offensive line without a care for the cornerback running his ass down. But the same dry mouth and constricted feeling in the chest would take hold of him without warning something fierce. Then he'd fumble and get a beating from his daddy, and the whole damn feeling would rinse and repeat.

Had learned to manage it well enough through basic training, and during the start of his service with the Legion he'd heard nary a word from the Grip. Mostly thanks to Grandpappy's moonshine recipe. But the deeper he went with Solterra's military, and the further he walked down his particular assignment and specialty rounding up those the Republic wanted to quietly reprogram—the Unfits, they called 'em—the harder he had keeping the Grip in check.

Especially after he Defected and took on his new identity, John Mark. A throwback to his dead grandpappy's middle name. Needed the *nom de plume* once he was on the run. The ghost from his past was always one klick away from spottin' him, nabbin' him, then draggin' his backside into a reprogramming camp—just as he had done with all of those Unfits he had hunted for the Republic.

And now the familiar haunting chill blew its icy breath up his neck, the fear that Solterra would find him a constant worry. Now more than ever, given Solterra's Purge campaign against Ichthus.

'Get a grip, ya spineless sissy...'

The voice of dear old Dad rising from the grave, somewhere at the borderland of Americana and Noramericana. His final resting place during the Second Civil War a few months before the Reckoning brought the bloody conflict to an end.

"What is this place anyway, cowboy?" Sasha said, shaking

him from spiraling any further and drawing his attention back to the moment, Alexander having slipped beyond view of the portal up top.

Ford swallowed and heaved a desperate breath, praying to the good Lord he didn't crack, that he'd stay the Grip's hand.

"Mackinac Island," Ford grunted as the Ukrainski finally hopped to it.

The doc shuffled to the same footholds he and Nia had offered Alexander—his pants still soaked with Lord only knew what. But he didn't complain about it. No use. Instead, he held his tongue and held his breath, which Ford figured a first. Don't say you can't teach a hound dog new tricks!

"What is this Mackynacky—"

"Mackinac, doc," Ford said, the physicist wobbling in his hold and climbing onto his head before steadying himself with a foot on his face. "Pronounced with a dubbya at the end."

"*Khorosho*, but what is it being?"

"Back in the day, it'd been a pivotal 18th and 19th century fortress for both the British and French colonies, swapping hands through a few battles, one of which was the War of 1812. It eventually became the property of the United States, back when there was such a thing. The French Canadians retook the island during the Reckoning."

"The French..." Sasha sputtered his lips and spat before reaching high for the hole in the ceiling. "Cursed Canadians!"

"Don't disagree, partner."

"And now," Nia added, "it is being an Enforcer outpost."

On two, the pair lifted Sasha farther into the void.

"Not just an outpost," Ford explained. "A reprogramming camp."

"*Bozhe moy!*" Sasha startled with a muffled echo above. "You were not telling me that—"

A sudden echoey cry sounded from Alexander's best friend. A cross between a startled gasp and a horrified moan.

Ford leaped to his feet again. Same for Nia, raising that wicked stick of hers and both craning for a viewing.

Sasha had disappeared, Alexander pulling him through before that high and heady rush of Muscovia, his cry growing panicked and pained.

Not good, Johnny Mark.

"You just better be right about this," Nia growled, "that is all I am having to be saying. Because if we came all this way, and your friend—"

"*Our* friend," Ford corrected, eyes narrowed. "Our sister in Christ and comrade in the Resistance."

"*Khorosho*, forgive me. You are being right. I am just hoping that we did not come all this way for *nothingk*."

Irritation at her second-guessing wound up his back. But the way she pronounced nothing, with a K, reminded him she was just a person who was as freaked as he was at the prospect of diving headlong through the Legion looking glass.

"Believe me, I am." Ford gestured up top. "And if those pair are offering any indication, it's worse than I feared."

Looked like she was gonna keep at it, but instead she nodded and poked that Scythe thing of hers into the void before gesturing toward Ryder Reeves.

"*Idti!* You go, then send me up."

Reeves nodded. "Sure thing, chicken wing."

The pair knelt and easily sent the man sailing into the portal of doom.

Once inside, Ford called, "Hey, fellas, incoming!"

Took a beat, but Alexander appeared, reaching a hand down to help.

Kneeling again, Ford cupped his hands for the alley-oop. Setting down her weapon, Nia stepped a foot inside. She steadied herself while he pushed her toward the ceiling, then grabbed onto Alexander and was pulled up top.

"Hand me my weapon," Nia said.

He did, then he readied to jump—back into the lion's den.

As a Defector...

Heaving a breath as she and Alexander reached down for his jump, Ford leaped for their arms and grabbed tight, the pair gripping him and yanking him through the void.

First thing he noticed was the smell of the joint. The sharp tang of cleaning agents and alcohol, both the medical kind and the whiskey kind. These fellas were well versed in sanitizing both the floors and their livers! Which did a decent job of masking the rank stank of a mule's backside—not quite as bad as the Republic sewer below, but almost there.

He knew why as his eyes adjusted.

Because what his peepers peeped made him want to crawl back down into that portal of doom and take his chances with the piss and poo he saw floating past on their journey. It also made crystal clear why he'd peeped those floaters from earlier.

The finger floaters.

For strapped to a table at the far end was the body of a woman Ford couldn't bear to identify.

Her skin wasn't dark. More ashen than anything. Long hair draped behind the back of the table, wavy and black and—

Except. Wait, no. It couldn't be...

His peepers couldn't believe what his brain instinctively told him he was peeping.

"I did this..." Ford muttered, the past rushing from long-buried history fighting for the Legion rounding up Unfits with the Purifier battalion and getting into firefights with Resisters.

More than that, terrorizing said Resisters—torturing them.

Architecting their torture, even.

All of which were nothing short of demonic.

Demons Ford had been confessing for years. Ones he never could seem to escape.

Especially the other thing—the one main thing!—his peepers couldn't believe they were peeping. The one maneuver he'd perfected from that damned movie that had been Daddy's fave family feature, pizza and soda and booze and all.

The Hannibal maneuver.

So-named after the creepy cannibal antihero of 20th century movies who performed a craniotomy on one of his victims while he was alive—removing parts of his skull and cutting away his brain and sizzling it on a cast iron skillet.

Though fava beans and a nice Chianti were the farthest thing from this joint.

"I-I-Is that what I am thinking that is being?" Sasha said on a horrified breath.

Ford gave no answer, though he certainly had one.

"That poor *zhenshchina*..." Nia whispered, hand covering her mouth.

"She's missing part of her skull," Alexander said matter-of-factly.

Yes, yes she was.

Ford took a careful step, then another, holding his breath in his burning lungs and his hope out to the poor soul strapped to the bloody table.

Prayed like he'd never prayed before it wasn't the woman they had sought.

"Is it Kareema?" someone said from behind.

Alexander, shaking voice barely above a whisper.

Didn't pay him any mind. Couldn't. Head swam with dizziness, Ford's conscious part denying the possibility while the back of his lizard brain began reckoning with the probability. Because knowing Purity, the elite Enforcer unit he'd helped devise, the only kind of Unfit these torturous interrogation techniques were used on were high-value subjects. The kind the Republic wanted to extract vital intel from, the kind the Patron hated with a passion that burned bright and strong.

The kind he himself used to hunt...

Nia was a pace behind now, following on hesitant steps with her Scythe held high, its purple light falling across the way in wicked shadows that revealed all.

That held breath escaped, all hope going with it. Bowels almost joined it in the world below, but Ford held it together, that dizziness blooming into a sparkly darkness that gripped him tight and threatened to send him overboard—his mouth chalky and coppery, the adrenaline coursing through him screaming at him to get out of Dodge and run. From the Republic. From his past.

But he stayed put and stayed the course—hiking up his big-boy pants and facing the truth of the matter.

Then forced himself to look.

CHAPTER 3

Alexander thought he was going to pass out. From his held breath, from the overwhelming stench drilling into his head through his nostrils, from the stuffiness of the room and cramped space.

From waiting for a positive identification of the body...

He didn't want to look. Couldn't. The quest to find Kareema had taken weeks of careful work and even more to put together the operation to rescue her. Even he himself had trained for it, Ford putting him through the wringer with proper Neutralizer training and hand-to-hand combat, giving him a workout plan to bulk up his frame that was far more adept at desk work and preaching than the sort of special operation he now found himself in.

Retrieving Kareema's body was not the plan; rescuing her was. So to think it had all gone to waste, their planning and preparations, that the life of one of his own—a Remnant of the Order of Thaddeus over which he was Master—had been lost...

It was all too much to contemplate, too much to behold inside the three pounds of brain matter that had already beheld so much over the past few years. Especially with the instruments of torture he couldn't bear to look at, not to mention the blood and fluids smeared across the floor.

And waiting for the word from Ford—now Alexander really did think he was going to pass out!

Another beat, then a breath from his companion and Ford grunted a sigh, as if being punched in the gut by the sight.

Alexander faltered a step, bracing himself against Sasha's shoulder.

Lord, have mercy...

"It's not her," he announced, then spun around and raced to the hole they'd come through, the poor guy retching up a thin stream of vomit.

"*Slava Bogu,*" Nia sighed, joined by the same from Sasha, which Alexander interpreted as a heavenly thanksgiving.

"Praise the Lawd Almighty," Reeves said in his Noramericana twang.

Alexander sighed, swallowing back rising emotion. Praise the Lord Almighty indeed.

He and Reeves embraced, as did Nia and Sasha. Then the four formed a group hug while Ford recovered.

"Hey, cowboy," Nia said, "I thought you said Kareema was being in this cell."

Ford sauntered over, wiping his mouth on the backside of his hand, face whiter than Alexander's best *thawb* ankle-length dress robe from back home.

"Appears I was mistaken."

"Glad you were," Alexander said, clasping Ford's shoulder. The man offered a faint smile. Face falling, he continued, "Only one problem..."

Clenching his jaw with recognition, Ford nodded. "Where the hot Hades is our gal?"

"I am being on it," Sasha said, shuffling to a workstation mounted to a desk at the far end.

It was a laptop of sorts, the display larger than the Republic-issued slate devices granted to the polis for an awareness of the goings on across Solterra. He and others just thought it was the Patron's way of spying on his citizens. Rather than a slab of sapphire the size of a sheet of paper that illuminated into a display, this was more like a coffee table book, with an illuminated key panel at the bottom and folding in two.

Sasha got to work, fingering away on the device and gaining entry. Knew better than to interrupt him whilst he worked, so he watched in silence as he moved through layers of windows and data in search of Kareema Salam, their sister in Christ and his Order Remnant.

Reeves shuddered, shifting on uncertain feet and glancing around. "Really drives home what we're up against, don't it?"

"What does?" Alexander asked.

"All the blood and gore, the thingamabobs inflicting untold horror."

Another shudder before the man crossed himself and began whispering with closed eyes.

He understood the feeling. Hadn't truly understood the depths of the Republic's Purge campaign until now, as well as their depravity and the lengths they would go to persecute Ichthus, to make them suffer.

Alexander nodded. "I can't help but recall the words of Saint Peter in his first letter: *'Dear friends, do not be surprised at the fiery ordeal that has come on you to test you, as though something strange were happening to you.'* This sort of persecution has been long promised—every era of Christian persecution has."

"Suppose that's true," said Ford. "What did Christ himself say? *'If the world hates you, keep in mind that it hated me first. If you belonged to the world, it would love you as its own.'*"

"That's right, from John's Gospel. And it is precisely that

we do not belong to Solterra Republic—chosen in Christ as citizens of a different Kingdom, in service of a different King— that it hates us. But Jesus reminds us what he told his disciples: '*If they persecuted me, they will persecute you also…They will treat you this way because of my name, for they do not know the one who sent me.*'"

"'*They will treat you this way…*'" Ford mumbled, glancing across the instruments of torture.

"'*But rejoice inasmuch,*'" Reeves said, "'*as you participate in the sufferings of Christ, so that you may be overjoyed when his glory is revealed. If you are insulted because of the name of Christ, you are blessed, for the Spirit of glory and of God rests on you.*'"

Alexander smiled. "The rest of Saint Peter's letter."

"Right-o."

Sasha whistled and pointed at his device, a slight satisfied smile playing across his face. "I am finding our *sestrenka*, Kareema Salam. Prisoner 527149117."

Ford sighed, leaning in. "Praise the Lord with trumpets. Where is she?"

He looked up, frowning. "She is being on this level, as you suspected. But she is being on the entirely other side of the prison."

"Shucky ducky…"

Nia stepped over. "Where exactly?"

Sasha worked on the display device, flashing his index fingers across the illuminated sapphire display in sync, zooming and twisting along a map that traced the route.

Reeves said, "We won't make it ten paces looking like this in these black special-ops getups."

"He's right," Ford agreed. "There is a strict protocol surrounding codes of uniform conduct while on a reprogramming camp premises. One of the ways they keep Unfits from escaping with ease, creating instant recognition between the help and the prisoners."

"Then what's the play here, chief?"

The room fell silent, the soft slide of Sasha's fingers across the glass all that was evident.

Until—

"Hold up," Ford said, leaning over Sasha's shoulders. "Let me see something…"

He began doing what Sasha was doing, using his fingers to manipulate the floor map, moving it this way and that.

"What do you have?" Alexander asked, curious and holding out hope.

"Back in the day—"

Nia interrupted, "When you were a Purifier, you mean?"

The woman clearly still harbored resentment for Ford's previous life as an enforcement arm of the Republic. Something they did not need.

He stopped his manipulating, glancing back with fingers still pressed against the display before returning to his work.

Ford went on, "Back in the day, every level had an armory for easy access to enforcement goods."

"Neutralizers you are meaning?" Nia asked.

"And Disruptor grenades, if need be." He jammed a finger at the sapphire glass and threw up a successful cry, standing with crossed arms. "There we are, just what the doc ordered."

"I am being sorry," she said, "but while an extra Neutralizer and even a dozen Disruptors would be coming in handy, we still have the same problem as before. We cannot be looking like this."

"Good thing the armory also carries an assortment of uniforms. And we've got one just down the hallway."

"*Vpechatlyayushchiy,* cowboy."

He leaned toward Sasha. "What's she saying, doc?"

"She is saying you are impressive."

"But don't let it go to your head," Nia added, raising her Scythe before spinning toward the door. "*Poydem!*"

Alexander caught a grin playing across Ford's face before he steeled his jaw and joined her. He chuckled to himself and shook his head, glad they were getting along enough to get moving.

But that was part of the problem. Because while they had a plan now to retrieve Kareema, that plan wasn't even half the battle. First up was looking the part.

Ford approached the door and grasped the burnished steel handle, an odd sight given the Republic's panache for chrome and titanium. He pressed his ear against the smooth surface and stood still.

Alexander came up to his side. "Anything?"

"Sealed tighter than a nun's girdle," he muttered. "No telling what's out there."

Besides Nia's Scythe, they had each brought a side arm. Peashooters, really, as Ford called them. Not Neutralizer strength, but the Blastguns would do the job, if it came to it.

Ford withdrew his weapon from behind his back, joined by Reeves. Sasha had snagged the Republic workstation and had it wedged under his arm. He also wore a frown and furrowed brow that signaled clear displeasure at the turn. Understood the feeling, mate.

Alexander reluctantly reached inside his jacket and slipped his own weapon out from his waist. Clenched its grip fast and nodded for Ford to get to it. No time to waste while one of their own was still held captive—

He glanced at the body resting peacefully in the corner.

—and undergoing all manner of torturous horrors.

The door opened inside the cell, so Ford held up an opened fist and counted down his fingers to close.

Five. Four. Three. Two—

On *one*, he wrenched the handle down, then swung the door open.

Flooding the cell with white light from beyond the threshold.

A bright, bland hallway greeted them, familiar chrome edging the ceiling and floor, the Republic's architectural calling card that added to the gleaming glow. Never understood the fascination with building in the gleaming material, along with glass and titanium. Far too ultramodern for Alexander's tastes, but perhaps that was the point. It was an easy way to erase and sanitize the past, the cultural and regional distinctions from history in all their varied forms of expressing beauty replaced with functional sterility.

The walls themselves looked like they were made of concrete or perhaps brick, which would have been a holdover from pre-Reckoning days and made sense based on Ford's description of the reprogramming camp's history. They were painted white, and gleamed whiter than Rebekah's lovely teeth and almost blindingly so after coming out of the dark, dank cell.

Smelled of cleaning agents and a summer storm, like ionized air and the faint scent of bleach. Blessedly, no more of those rotting corpses and spoiled fluids.

And blessedly no one was around.

Ford waved them on, the quintet stiff and ready as they shuffled through the corridor, their boots throwing up pounding squeaks Alexander feared would give them away.

The hallway ran in an arc, slowly snaking right around the central courtyard. There were no prison cells in this wing, the room they had come out of some sort of interrogation room. Blank walls, joined by white floor tiles, funneled them along the corridor, its clean, sanitary nature betraying the dark desecration unfolding elsewhere in the reprogramming camp.

Alexander's heart was beating a mean beat now in sync with every footfall, his blood pulsing in his ears in sync with his breath. He tried moderating his diaphragm, pulling in calming breaths to ease his rising anxiety, but it was no use. Had heard plenty of tales from Ford over the years about the nature of these compounds, with all of their security that ensured no chance of escape, with all of their brainwashing techniques to reprogram the minds and bodies of designated Unfits in subservient service to the Patron and the Republic.

Now with the Antichrist's impending arrival and the persecution of Ichthus rising to a fever pitch, and him and his teammates launching an unguarded incursion into the belly of the beast, no chance would his body and mind quiet themselves before—

Ford suddenly skidded to a halting stop, raising a fist and edging to the wall.

Alexander nearly plowed into him, and Nia into him. But they held firm, with Sasha and Reeves making up the back and joining them at the wall.

Glancing behind, Ford pointed at his eyes before waving them down the corridor.

The angle wasn't helpful, but the faint outline of a dark entrance stood stark against the white walls.

Their target.

Alexander whispered the upcoming door to Nia, who passed it along quickly down the queue.

Ford counted off another five fingers before launching back down the hallway.

He quickly reached the portal, Alexander coming to his side with Nia at the other, Sasha and Reeves taking the rear again.

Grasping the burnished steel handle, Ford whispered, "On three."

Certainly wasn't wasting any time, even though they hadn't a clue what was on the other side. Not that they had any choice in the matter. Their time was running out standing in their dark tactical clothes better suited for the sewers and Solterran streets than a reprogramming camp. Would be a dead giveaway should some Enforcer stumble upon them.

Kareema's time was even shorter. He just hoped she held out a bit longer for their arrival.

Lord Jesus Christ, Son of God, may she hold out a bit longer for their arrival...

Ford whispered, "Three. Two. One—"

Moment of truth...

In one motion, he wrenched the handle down and shoved inside.

Where three men were sitting in their boxers and T-shirts playing cards around a small circular chrome table. No doubt Enforcers taking a break, with a dozen Neutralizers stowed away, and their armor lying beside them.

But no protection from the sudden intrusion of hostiles.

Took only a few seconds for Alexander and the rest to file inside, then Reeves slammed the door shut and they opened fire on the unsuspecting men.

For their operation, yes, but it was more than that.

It was for Kareema.

Sure, vengeance was the Lord's. But Alexander was learning that sometimes justice was served at the end of a Blastgun.

Especially when one of their own was involved.

All three Enforcers tried leaping for their weapons, but it was no use. It was over before it started, the faint tang of particle beams and death lacing the air.

"Are you thinking someone was hearing us?" Sasha squeaked, moving to the door and pressing an ear against it.

"Not a chance," Ford said. "Those doors are as thick as my skull. Which is saying a lot."

He flashed Nia a wink, who chuckled and regarded the room.

"I am not seeing enough armor, cowboy," she observed.

She was right. Only suits were the ones the three men had left. Plenty of weapons, but it didn't matter if they couldn't use them.

"Got an idea." Ford reached into one of the lockers and withdrew two black bags and a pair of titanium cuffs. He handed them to Alexander and Nia.

Alexander licked his lips, a ping of adrenaline jolting his heart forward with recognition. "Please tell me you're not—"

"Only way, homefry," Ford said, already starting in on a pair of crimson pants. "This armor here will fit me and Sasha and Reeves. You and Nia are our prisoners."

"You have got to be kidding me!" She scoffed, holding the cuffs like a dead rat. "You think I am going to be wearing these?"

Ford slipped the shirt over his head and shrugged. "No other choice."

Finishing, he tossed Reeves a charcoal outfit, same for Sasha. "Don't forget to take that workstation device along, doc."

Alexander flashed Sasha a glance, who was holding the two pieces to his charcoal Legion costume with a downcast face. Looked positively terrorized by the prospect of posing as an Enforcer, his eyes wide and face pale. Or maybe he was simply projecting his own terror.

"Hold out your hands," Ford directed. Alexander did, the cuffs slipping easily around his wrists and clicking into place.

Another click followed, joined by a faint protest from his fellow prisoner, laced with a hint of worry.

Nia muttered another Muscovia complaint but followed Alexander's lead, handing off her Scythe to Ford for safe-keeping and snapping at Reeves to get on with it.

Ford secured her weapon around his shoulders and grabbed hold of Alexander's arm. "Now for the hard part..."

Alexander took a breath, and he slipped the bag over his head, the constricted darkness all consuming.

Ford guided him several paces, then the door opened with a shudder and out he went.

With a Neutralizer at his back and flying blind.

CHAPTER 4

DIDN'T EXPECT to be wearing one of these getups again, that's for sure! The tight-fitting uniform all scratchy and constricting, the crimson material marking him as a Purifier. Just as he'd been when he was one of the Patron's lackeys.

But there Ford was—standing in someone else's threads with a hot and humid helmet on his noggin. The dude before him must've eaten something with lots of onions, because it reeked something fierce.

On the flip side, it was nice having an instant digital read on the inside visor for the weather, directional bearing, and heat signatures if that was your thing. It also shielded his face from any recognition from any Enforcers that might be roaming about.

And now he was readying to shove back out into the hallway of blinding white light that brought back way too many memories from his last go around in a reprogramming camp—both as a Purifier interrogating Unfits and as a guest after Defecting.

Ford shivered at the thought, remembering what it was like standing in both of those feet, suffering at the hands of the Republic and doling it out on others.

Couldn't worry about that now—who he'd been, who he was. All he could do was trust who the good Lord above said he was was true: a child of God, who was chosen and set free. He'd also need to trust the good Lord above to carry him through—because it was about to get real.

Heaving a breath, he opened the door and jammed his Neutralizer into Alexander's back. The poor fella shuffled through with the Shroud covering his noggin, the hood effectively leaving the guest sensory deprived, shrouded in an otherworldly state that rendered them more cooperative, malleable, reprogrammable. Was a specially crafted piece of interrogatory ingenuity that blocked out all sound and light, even temperature beyond what his body regulated.

A piece of interrogatory ingenuity specially crafted by yours truly.

Which he'd slipped over his teammate's head as part of a cockamamie plan to salvage their operation blown to hot Hades. Didn't really have a choice, given the mistake—*his* mistake!—in mapping Kareema's location.

Must've read the intel wrong. Probably upside down, too, knowing his grasp on reality. And probably during one of his stupid drunken stupors after she'd been nabbed. Had a rough go of it for several months drowning his embarrassment and self-hatred in moonshine for letting one of his own get snatched by the Republic under his watch. Grandpappy's recipe was good for more than keeping the Grip at bay.

Now it was time to snatch her back, to make amends for all of the wickedness he had crafted for the Republic.

Just hoped it wasn't too late...

Shoving into the hallway, he held his breath—waiting for the Patron himself to come trotting toward him with a platoon of the Republic's finest. Or worse.

Oscar Campbell, his old commanding officer with the

Purifiers from back in the day! With that face pockmarked by a bad bout of adolescent acne and that rancid breath that smelled like the backend of a camel—which his pals during basic training had joked about, calling him Colonel Camel behind his back.

Couldn't think about that now. And no way would Fate hand him a run-in with his former CO a second go around after what had happened a year ago at the former headquarters for the Order of Thaddeus. Prayed not, anyway.

Alexander played his part well, the poor man bound and hooded but throwing up not a peep. Same for Nia, handled by Reeves, though Ford thought he caught her mumbling grumbly Muscovia complaints. Sasha was sandwiched between them, handling that workstation doohickey of his. It was folded in half backwards, the display part with their map of the facility at the ready.

Ford led the group several yards down the corridor, the hallway bending right as it channeled them around the circular prison. Kept at it for several beats before he was comfortable chancing a glance behind. As it looked, they were just a merry band of Legion jarheads transporting newly minted guests to their freshly prepared quarters for the rest of their Solterran existence. Stopping might draw attention if anybody were to pass by, but his brain was screaming for him to make sure they were good to go.

So, putting a hand on Alexander's shoulder, he pulled back on the reins and threw his peepers over his shoulder.

There was Sasha, looking ridiculous in his costume bearing that workstation at his arms. Right behind him was Nia, head bowed and bagged with hands clipped at her waist, guarded by Reeves, who threw him a knowing nod.

All quiet on the Western Front, and clear of any Legion jarheads.

Ford sighed a breath he didn't know he was holding, then whipped his head back to the course ahead. Same story: just them and the low HVAC hum of the ventilation doing its ventilating thing and those blindingly bright white LED lights doing their blinding bright thing. Just the way he liked it, although no way they could hide in these parts if things got hinky, that's for sure.

"*Oo-oo,*" Sasha said before adding, "this is not being good..."

Ford spun around. "What's not being good?"

Cradling the workstation, he pointed at the display. "There is being a warning indicator on this floor."

"What indicator? Indicating what?"

"Indicating us!" he hissed, gesturing wildly around the group, then jammed a pointer at the device screen. "*Smotret.*"

Ford obliged, seeing five orbs pulsing an angry red all huddled down a corridor on the bottom level.

Just like them!

"Is that us," Reeves said, craning over Sasha's shoulder, "the Legion fingering us as hostiles?"

Sasha nodded. "*Da.* That is what I am thinking."

"But how can they know that?"

"I am guessing perhaps the Enforcers and prisoners are outfitted with tracking devices that are indicating an authorized presence. And we are not being that."

Dread bloomed in Ford's head, sinking fast down his gullet and hitting his stomach hard. He glanced around, thinking that chrome trim edging the ceiling and floor weren't just for decoration. Apparently the Legion had upgraded their security protocols since last he was in their care.

Grateful for no alarms—yet. But once they were noticed by someone who cared about that sort of thing, they were in deep shucky ducky.

Ford said, "Can you shut this down, somehow mask our identity as bona fides?"

Sasha licked his lips and brought the workstation around, then started tapping away on the display. His fingers raced across it, typing in command lines and zooming in and out of windows. He and Reeves shifted on uncertain feet, glancing behind and around for signs of trouble and waiting for the Patron's hammer to fall. Nia and Alexander just stood there, oblivious to the danger, given their complete sensory deprivation. Ford wished for a hood right about then.

The seconds ticked by mercilessly fast, without any resolution.

"How's it com—"

Sasha interrupted Ford with a raised pointer and pursed lips before returning to the task.

Wanted to huff a frustrated sigh but knew the doc was only asking for patience. Patience that was quickly running out.

Almost went to Plan B, hustling down the corridor with Neutralizers ready for anything, when the pulsing red-warning orbs blinked to nothing but nothing.

There one second, gone the next.

"*Khorosho*," Sasha said, smiling with pride, "we are being back in business."

"Like a boss, doc," Reeves said. "Like a boss!"

Ford clenched a grateful hand on Sasha's shoulder, giving it a squeeze and easing out a held breath.

Cheated the Republic once again. For now.

Carrying on, doors came into view farther down, black things set starkly against the white walls, the group edging into the cell-block sector of the reprogramming camp. Which meant they were getting close, thank the good Lord above! Didn't know how much more his ticker could take of this.

Tiny windows anchored to the outside gave a window into the world beyond. He didn't want to look. Didn't need to. Knew exactly what was behind those doors personally. In more ways than one.

Ford needed to get a clearer lay of the land, so he brought her to a standstill and leaned toward Sasha, taking a gander at that map.

"You have a sense of where we are, doc?"

"*Da.* We are being right here—" Sasha gestured to a spot about a quarter turn "—and need to be getting to here." He pinch-zoomed then followed the arc of the prison to Kareema's cell. Not too bad, about twenty-three doors to go, but also not close enough.

Nodding, he got back to it, counting down to the LZ.

Twenty-one, twenty, nineteen.

Then on toward *fifteen, fourteen, thirteen—*

When a pair of Enforcers and a desk came into view.

His breath seized in his chest, and he nearly choked on the unlucky number.

What the hot Hades was this?

He faltered a step, slowing but not stopping. Any weird movements or hesitations would throw up all kinds of ugly question marks they didn't need.

"What the tarnation is this?" Reeves said lowly from behind.

Now Ford did stop, leaning against the outer wall butting against the inner courtyard ring. He waved his free hand back and pulled on Alexander's shoulder with the other.

The group slowly retreated, quietly and out of sight, the Enforcer goons none the wiser, it seemed. A real shame the Legion had lost its standards, but a real boon for them!

Satisfied, Ford turned to Sasha. "Why didn't you mention a checkpoint?"

"Because it is not being—"

He shushed him and glanced back down the hall.

Still quiet on the Western Front.

Sighing, he leaned in closer. "What's the dealio, doc? What are you saying?"

Sasha swallowed. "There is no checkpoint being on the map, that is what I am saying. It must be a recent addition."

Not good, Johnny Mark...

Except, fake it till you make it had been something of a life mantra. Especially after being called up to duty with the Ministerium and then when all the crazy started going down —from traveling back in time to the Republic opening up a can of whoop-ass on Ichthus. Heck, to even the good Lord Almighty opening up a can of whoop-ass on the world after launching the apocalypse!

No reason he couldn't put that same mindset to good use with a couple of Enforcer jarheads, hiking up his big-boy pants and hustling toward destiny.

So hike he did, whispering lowly, "Keep your heads on straight, cats and kittens. Follow my lead."

Grasping his Neutralizer by the snout with one hand, the other by its waist, in one motion, he whacked it into Alexander's back.

"Move it, Resistance scum!"

Alexander stumbled forward, nearly biting it on the tile floor. He recovered all right and shuffled forward, glancing back.

Heart was strumming a mean beat now, a cold dread spreading through every limb and nerve and hair follicle, head swirling with the pressure of the possibilities of how the next few seconds would play out.

Either Ford and his crew would glide along the bright white tile floor on toward destiny, or—

The alternative wasn't even something he wanted to contemplate.

A Defector like him, who had left the Legion when he decided to follow Christ, only later to find himself in a reprogramming camp before escaping—he was toast if those whack jobs anchored at the checkpoint found out who he was.

That wasn't even touching on what would happen to his crew of Unfits—those declared to be unpersons by the Republic, the detritus of Solterra fit for nothing more than canceling or reprogramming. They'd even handed themselves on a silver platter to the Republic, waltzing right into a reprogramming camp! Could hardly breathe at the thought of what fate would await them.

Him!

Just a few more paces, a few more seconds...

The two Enforcer goons barely paid him a passing glance on their approach—one tall, skinny dude playing with a yo-yo and leaning against the wall; the other, short and squat, sitting on a stool like he was laying a deuce and reading a magazine he swore looked like *Humanoid Hustler*, a dirty rag filled with naked androids doing all manner of nasty.

Not that he had any familiarity with the thing—anymore...

"Halt!" String Bean said, raising a hand and stuffing that yo-yo of his in his pocket.

Which activated Pork Belly in an instant.

Ford smirked. Tweedle Dumb and Tweedle Dumber, they were. This would be a walk on Lunattica.

Rolling the humanoid porno and stuffing it at his back, Pork Belly waved them forward—retrieving a slate device Ford hadn't noticed before resting on the desk. He fiddled with it as Ford and the others arrived.

Clearing his throat and jamming his Neutralizer into

Alexander's back for added believability (sorry, partner!), he said, "Prisoner transport to cell block 1138."

"Prisoner transport..." The goon fiddled with his slate, the rolls in that pudgy face growing with concentration. "I don't have that in the relocation inbox. What's your designation?"

Ford sucked in a breath riding high on his ticker jolting into a gallop.

Shucky ducky...

By designation, the Enforcer meant his Purifier credentials. The ones that gave him authority for his cockamamie prisoner-transport plan.

Took every ounce of energy to hold it together, to keep the Grip from rising and grabbing his throat and squeezing till his balls fell out.

Was as familiar with his Purifier designation number as he was with his own nose. But Ford hesitated, taking a breath.

Should he or shouldn't he?

The goon cleared his throat, those Basset Hound jowls sinking with irritation.

"Haven't got all day, pal," he grunted, eyeing Reeves and Sasha now, who shrank some from his stare.

So Ford widened his stance, squared his shoulders, and let the skunk out of the bag.

"438052381," he said.

"That sounds like an older call-sign."

Fake it till you make it, Ford!

"Yup. I'm old," he replied without missing a beat.

"And prisoner transport, you say?"

"That's right." He gestured down the hallway. "To 11—"

"38. Yes, you said that. Except I don't have that on my manifest. I'm going to have to call this in."

The Enforcer set down his slate device with a clatter and reached for a comm unit, the moment slipping away.

Fake it till you make it, Ford!

"Just you wait, Mister Cocky Pants, these Unfits were nabbed out of Blake Ridge and we don't have time to waste on this bureaucratic bulldookie."

Now String Bean got in on the action. "Blake Ridge? Really?"

Ford regarded him, standing straighter and throwing back his shoulders. "That's right. On an operation sanctioned by the Sacradi himself."

"Right, understood. Seems so soon..." Now String Bean picked up the slate device and started flipping a finger across the surface.

Seems so soon. Odd response, with a confusing meaning.

Temperature was really cranking now. And on top of it, Ford really had to pee!

"Whatever," the Enforcer mumbled. "Go on and get them settled. Then check back here once you're through to sort through this mess."

Nodding, he carried on, shoving Alexander extra hard, the butt of his Neutralizer jamming into his spine with a *smack.*

Sorry, partner!

Didn't take long before they'd flashed by doors *eight, seven,* and *six* before picking up the pace to numero zero—cell 1138.

The LZ. Kareema's landing zone.

Just as the cell door shuddered open and out stepped a large Purifier, bald and all neck. Nearly plowed into the group, shouting a curse to watch their bleepin' steps.

Ford apologized and kept his gaze trained ahead, leading the group past as the goon sealed the door shut and sauntered the other direction, the coppery scent of blood ripe along with body odor from a workout trailing him back toward Tweedle Dumb and Tweedle Dumber.

Satisfied they were alone, and with time running out, Ford withdrew a key to the titanium cuffs, edged close to Alexander, and unlocked the restraints, then he slipped the bag off from his head.

Alexander gasped a breath and blinked rapidly, working his jaw to moderate his hearing again while gulping down more air.

Ford said, "Understand the disorienting feeling, homefry. We're here."

He glanced down the hallway past the group. Ford did the same, satisfied they were alone and throwing a nod at Nia, who was also free and clear of restraint. He handed off her Scythe; she snatched it and offered a curt smile before thanking him for keeping it safe.

Nodding, Ford said to Sasha, "You got the key code to this cell?"

"*Khorosho.* Let me just..." The doc rapped on that device of his, taking far too long for Ford's liking, but he eventually surfaced with the goods.

"1138 is being code."

Ford frowned. "Same as the room number?"

Sasha just shrugged. "I am guessing the Republic is not as smart as we are assuming."

"Guess not." Ford punched in the code, gears turning inside to unlock the cell. "Let me go first. Make sure the coast is clear."

The group agreed.

Glancing down the hallway, then the other direction, he swallowed hard and shoved through the steel portal and into the unknown.

Room was no bigger than a Noramericana garage, the one his folks had stowed that vintage Corvette Pops had wasted so much of his time on as a child. Was the last of the gas guzzling type before Chevrolet shifted their whole fleet to electric engines.

Ford cursed himself for his brain spinning out memories that mattered not a lick! Last thing he needed was his noggin distracted, so he shook it and forced himself to do a quick look-see before the others ushered inside.

First thing he noticed was the smell. Same as the first room they'd crawled up inside. The sharp tang of cleaning agents and alcohol. More of that medical kind and whiskey kind. Purifiers like he'd been, the kind that interrogated Unfits to purify them of their wrongthink, had always held their alcohol well. He'd always held *his* alcohol well. In fact—

There went his brain again!

Focus, Johnny Mark...

Was too dark at first, the inside cell back to that putrid dark brown and only illuminated by the blinding white LED light from the hallway. Found a switch by the door and flipped it.

Then instantly regretted his decision.

A chair sat in the center of the room, under a bright spot-light. The kind he himself had used to interrogate high-value targets.

Memories from those days sent his stomach lurching for a way out.

Strapped to the chair was the body of a woman, slumped forward with her head lolled toward her chest. Skin was a grayish hue. Not only because she was clearly dead—and clearly a she, given her shape. But also because she was from a part of the world where the melanin was olive. Even a yellowish tint to it. Smooth too, real smooth. And long wavy hair falling over her face.

Ford took a careful step, then another, holding his breath

in his burning lungs and his hope out to the poor soul strapped to the bloody chair.

Praying, discerning, praying, intuiting, praying some more that it wasn't Kareema Salam—the sweet-and-spicy soul who had nearly whooped his ass and fought like hell for the Church.

And yet—

And yet he knew. The back of his lizard brain had screamed at him the answer the second he'd stepped into the room.

Reaching the subject, he knelt and parted her hair, then sighed.

"It's her," Ford simply said.

The bile came quick and sudden.

CHAPTER 5

A BREATH ALEXANDER didn't know he was holding escaped him. An icy dread flooded his veins, and his bowels went watery with horrified disbelief.

It's her.

That's what Ford said. And he knew what that meant.

It was Kareema Salam.

One of their own—one of *his* own, a member of the Order of Thaddeus over which he was Master, ancient defender and protector of the Christian faith. Tortured and dead.

He stood still and stiff, dread churning in his belly at what he would find while whispered conversations of disbelief swirled around him. They were muffled, unattended to by his consciousness, his attention only trained on the sound of his heart throbbing in his ears and the squeaking of his boots on the wet tiles beneath his shifting feet. It was soaked in blood and matter, the remnants of flayed skin and coiled hair littering the floor. The only saving grace was the sharp scent of cleaning agents—pine and chlorine bleach, the smell of home, in fact, after a thunderstorm rolled across Tripolitania.

Alexander wanted nothing more than to run back to that former life in his simple single-level, two-room parsonage. The life preparing sermons and counseling his people in the ways of Christ and caring for those good, simple people of his parish alongside his associate Zakaria. A life of reading, dabbling with poetry, strumming his guitar. Where Saturdays were spent playing soccer with a local league in Tripolitania reviving his college goalkeeper position, and then getting supplies for the week at the local market and running errands. Hosting dinners with his friends and staying up all night cheering and booing the latest Solterra soccer match on the broadcaster. To tend his garden and make another vintage wine from those berries that grew along the bluff overlooking the Mediterranean Sea.

Of course, all of that was gone. Blown to smithereens, literally by that terrorist with the ancient Nous organization, his parish reduced to rubble and his community murdered. His life had been a simple one, filled with simple pleasures and simple people and simple tasks. And he missed it.

Instead, he was staring down the barrel of an operation he was the farthest fit to lead with an end that spelled tragedy for one of their own—his own!—and very well doom for him and his teammates.

The overhead light glowed yellow from above but focused at the center, with the edges shrouded in shadows. The source of interrogation for Kareema, the point of her suffering horrors too imaginable to contemplate.

Behind her sat a DiviNet workstation terminal, like the one Sasha had swiped from the other cell. Another chair rested in the corner, and anchored in front was a Republic-issued slate device strapped to a tripod. It was angled for a viewing of the chair, a cord snaking to the workstation.

Facing him, over Ford's shoulders, was a chrome chair glistening a purply hue from Nia's outstretched Scythe weapon underneath the woman they had come for.

She was naked, her dignity denied along with her life stolen, and barely recognizable. Aside from her still-intact features was a recognizable faded tattoo. An anchor, ringed by Greek characters, marked her as a Remnant of the Order of Thaddeus, with those words from the founding Master, Jude Thaddeus, testifying to her devotion—'*contend for the faith that was once for all entrusted to God's holy people*'—no doubt the Republic's *raison d'etre* for their torturous display.

The one side of her face was missing an eye, the void oozing brown with infection and dark crimson. Her nose had been wrenched off as well. Not severed or torn, but bent with a straining twist that had to have been agonizing. As expected, several fingers and toes were severed; some were contorted at ungodly angles. The worst of it was the woman's head, whose skull had been sawed open with a portion removed. Brain matter showed through, gray and purple, with unholy probes sticking out at wicked angles.

It was a shop of horrors, the room still pulsing with a wickedness that smacked of Satan himself. Surely she suffered the hellish depths of dreadful agony and terrific torment.

Various instruments of torture were still strewn about the room—probes and wired clamps; a rack for stretching victims beyond their means, with another compressing and contorting them in the other direction; wrenches meant to tear away fingernails, scalpels meant to cut away pieces of flesh, irons meant to sizzle and sear the vulnerable parts of the body.

That wasn't even touching on the blood smeared across the floor and pieces of flesh scattered about with disinterest, the spent body fluids that added to the stench. The horrifying memory of what had transpired in that room still hung like a phantom.

Alexander swallowed back a rising tide of bile at the sight and thought of all Kareema had endured, the sour sludge tangy at the back of his throat and threatening to send him retching with disgust.

But no, he wouldn't. Wouldn't show weakness in the face of such wickedness, wouldn't disrespect her memory that way.

Had never known anyone personally who had been snatched as an Unfit and secreted away to a reprogramming camp—interrogated and tortured, brainwashed and indoctrinated. By the look of it, in Kareema's case he supposed it was the former rather than the latter, the woman paying for her steadfast resolve with her life.

The world was not worthy of her, as the author of Hebrews had said of the faithful who were persecuted and mistreated for their faith. Not worthy of Kareema Salam.

The first of many, he feared.

"*Bozhe moy...*" Sasha groaned before turning back and running to the other side of the room where he vomited, the throaty belch and liquidy splash threatening to trigger the same response in Alexander.

For her part, Nia stood stiff, arm extended with her Scythe held high. As if standing at attention, paying her respects to the woman who had suffered for her faith.

And paid for it with her life.

A sudden voice rose up from behind. A deep baritone starting in a hum before crescendoing into a series of lyrics.

"Swing low, sweet chariot. Coming for to carry me home. Swing low, sweet chariot. Coming for to carry me home."

It was Ryder Reeves, the other Order Remnant they had connected with a year ago. A black man from deep in Noramericana who had not only survived the Purge and an Enforcer raid on his apartment. He was also one of the few remaining agents of the Order of Thaddeus, a fellow Order Remnant, same as Kareema had been.

Had been...

"I looked over Jordan and what do I see," the man continued, his voice low and resonant. "A band of angels coming after me. Coming for to carry me home."

Reeves repeated the first set of lyrics, a beautiful song Alexander had never heard before, then again: "Swing low, sweet chariot. Coming for to carry me home."

The room stood still, unmoving, as if one of those angels Reeves just sang about had descended in their midst, bearing a revelation from the throne of God himself.

"If you get there before I do. Coming for to carry me home. Tell all my friends I'm coming too. Coming for to carry me home."

Then that resonant verse again, clearly aimed at memorializing Kareema: "Swing low, sweet chariot. Coming for to carry me home. Swing low, sweet chariot. Coming for to carry me home."

Reeves repeated that stanza another three times, voice dimming to a strained whisper before silence filled the painful void.

"That was beautiful, *bratishka*," Sasha whispered.

"*Da*, Ryder," Nia agreed. "What was it being?"

Alexander nodded, still taken by the tune. "Yes, I've never heard of this particular song before. It was magisterial."

Reeves sniffed and swatted at his eyes before ending up at his nose.

"An old negro spiritual it is," he replied. "From back in the days before the First Civil War from the former Younighted States. Sung at homegoing services it is, the words referring to the Old Testament account of Elijah ascending into Heaven by chariot. Figured it appropriate for the occasion."

"Certainly was," Alexander said, throat growing thick with a rise in emotion. He swallowed hard and cleared it, adding: "We should find something we can use to gather her remains. Do you see anything that might—"

"Sonofa—"

Ford slammed his hand against the wall, cutting off Alexander and throwing up an echoey clang that resounded far louder than the quintet needed!

"Would you be quiet!" Nia hissed, spinning around and making for the closed door.

"It's all my fault..." Ford cried, falling to his knees and burying his head in his hands, muttering again with a muffled yell: "*All my fault!*"

The man shook. His shoulders heaved and fell, then again, a moaning groan coming from those hands clenched against his face. Ford was weeping, and Alexander didn't have a clue why.

Neither did Nia, who was still at the door, mouth wide as if in a question. Same for Reeves, who had crossed his arms and was shifting on uncertain feet.

"What is being your fault, cowboy?" Sasha asked, taking a step toward the man.

Alexander joined him. Wanted to put a hand on his shoulder, something reassuring, something that signaled solidarity with whatever was happening inside the man.

Instead, he asked, "What are you going on about, John Mark? What's wrong?"

Took a beat, then another before Ford let his hands drop to his side. His face was blotchy and wet with emotion. He remained on the floor, spent and silent.

Had never seen him like this before, so overcome with emotion, so despondent. It must be bad.

Ford brought a trembling hand to his forehead, then wetted his lips and swallowed. He finally answered, "I'm a man of history, you see."

Not what Alexander was expecting.

"And here I thought," Nia said, "you were just being a Legion jarhead slinging it for the Republic."

"Au contraire, sassafras," Ford said with a chuckle, the man's jovial nature returning some. "Before I became an Enforcer, I was a history major at Ole Miss. Go Landsharks!" He gave a quiet hoot and raised a fist of solidarity before letting it fall to his lap. "Anyhoo, was right fascinated with 20th century history. Mostly when the Great War consumed Europa, with all of its totalizing, terrorizing mechanisms of controlling a polis that so willingly bowed before the State. Wanted to be a history teacher, I did. High school, maybe college."

He fell silent again, his face darkening with narrowed eyes reflecting his quiet contemplation. The room waited with him, letting him have his moment.

Clearing his throat, he sniffed away the memory. "At any rate, my scholarly dreams were cut short when I signed up with the Legion. Because, hey, that's what all the cool kids did back home in Noramericana after the Great Reckoning. Was almost finished with my degree, too, but Patron's call and Pop's death had sent me down a different course. One that would leverage all I'd learned for the Republic Legion."

"Leveraged?" Nia said with a start. "What is this...leveraged business?"

"Forty years of interrogatory torture," Ford went on, ignoring her, "practiced in Muscovia—erm, Russia, as it was known back in the day. Anyhoo, they'd perfected the art of what would later become the Purifier playbook. All of which came in handy when I was tapped as an Enforcer, rising through the ranks on that history degree of mine to perfect the Republic's encouragement tactics, as they were called—drawn from the Great Bear with no one none the wiser. Because by that point, history was history, and all the muckety-mucks at the top of the Legion food chain cared about were results, no matter where or how they were plagiarized. *My* playbook, the one I'd used to parlay that Noramericana brain of mine into a successful career that promised untold riches and power."

He put his face back into his hands, going silent with shame.

Alexander's heart pounded in his chest and brain bloomed with the implications of what Ford was going on about. It was a confession, wasn't it? Of what he had done, of who he had been.

He glanced at the mutilated body still resting on that chrome chair of the Republic.

A confession to crafting the very course of action that had led to Kareema's torturous death.

A tingly rage raced up his spine and spread through his body. Ford had told the truth, hadn't he? This was his fault. Kareema had suffered and died because of his horrifying designs!

He clenched his fists and heaved a breath, steadying himself. He wanted to lay into Ford, letting that tingly anger unleash a raging, lashing blow into the man with an admonition that would bring emotional relief from the freighted weight of what they all were facing—their comrade tortured to death and left to rot.

More than that: These were the weapons of interrogation that were being used against all of their brothers and sisters of Ichthus across Solterra—the ones that would be used against them if they weren't careful.

Against Alexander...

Yet alongside that disgust, that revulsion, was a simple truth, one from the depths of the heart of God himself.

This is who Ford *had been*, not who he was now.

In the blink of an eye, sandwiched between the truth in that chair and the truth of Jesus' good news, a passage from the Holy Scriptures surfaced.

Clearing his throat, Alexander quoted from 1 Corinthians, chapter 6: "'*Do not be deceived: Neither the sexually immoral nor idolaters nor adulterers nor men who have sex with men nor thieves nor the greedy nor drunkards nor slanderers nor swindlers will inherit the kingdom of God.*'"

Ford eased his face from his hands and sat upright, face white and glistening with a wetness Alexander figured was self-loathing emotion.

Alexander knew he himself had been what the Apostle Paul had written about, that and so much more. But then there was the kicker, the part of Scripture that had meant the world to him, and he imagined to Ford himself.

He continued, "'*And that is what some of you were. But you were washed, you were sanctified, you were justified in the name of the Lord Jesus Christ and by the Spirit of our God.*'"

Emotion raced to Ford's eyes before he managed a grinning chuckle. "Something Brother Benedict had drilled into my noggin a time or twelve. From good ol' Saint Paul, his first letter to the Corinthians. Meant the world to me back then, after he led me to Christ all proper like."

"That's right," Alexander said, nodding and smiling with the same emotion. "Still means the world to you—the fact you've been washed of those sins from your days with the Republic, purified and sanctified from the unholy wickedness of your past, declared not guilty for your sins."

Ford heaved a breath, huffing a sigh and batting at his eyes. "That truth from God's Word was about the only thing that kept me from ending up in a pile of self-pity back in the day. About the only thing now..."

The room fell silent, the HVAC hum and a set of beeping

command lines from a workstation terminal the only soundtrack.

Ford stood and went to Alexander, offering him his hand. "Thanks, partner. For the reminder of who I was."

He took it before embracing his brother in Christ. "It's also a reminder of who you are now."

Ending their show of solidarity, Ford nodded.

Alexander heaved a breath and took a parting glance at Kareema, then scanned the chamber. "Now what?"

"I don't know, partner. What do you think?"

"Is it being any question?" snorted Sasha. "Leave before we are being tortured like poor *sestrenka!*"

Reeves added, "Getting out of Dodge ain't such a bad idea."

"*Da*, I am agreeing," Nia said, turning to Alexander, "but what about the others? Surely there are more prisoners awaiting reprogramming."

Good question. Good point.

Alexander sighed and shook his head, then turned to Ford. "What do you think?"

"Don't ask me, homefry! You're the Order Master."

"That is being true, Alexander," Nia agreed. "What is being next?"

"And you're the head," Alexander replied, "of Resistance security, Ford. So why don't—"

"What do you reckon," Reeves said from behind, cutting off Alexander's biting reply, "this here contraption is all about?"

He was standing next to the corner metal folding chair with his hands on his hips. He gestured to the slate device on a tripod planted in front of it and rubbed his chin.

Earlier, Alexander had given it a passing glance with all

the other—unmentionable devices of torture. He went to him, then to the chair and tripod.

He eyed the Republic-issued slate device mounted on top. The mandatory kind required of the polis to get news and register all manner of life in and with the Republic.

Nia joined him. "That is being a good question, Reeves. What indeed is this about?"

"Perhaps," Sasha said, pointing to the workstation in the corner, "it might be having something to do with this."

Alexander leaned in for a closer look. Somehow he had logged in, rummaging around the server and opening a file. Not surprised in the slightest, given both his technological chops and penchant for nosiness.

"What's this, doc?" Ford asked.

"It is looking like a video," Sasha replied. He glanced at Alexander. "Of our poor *sestrenka*."

Took a beat to catch his meaning. Then he did.

"Of Kareema Salam?" Nia asked, echoing his own understanding.

"What, like a last confession?" Reeves asked.

Sasha nodded. "*Da.* It is looking like something those bastard Republic Purifiers were extracting from her."

Ford gasped; Alexander echoed him, disbelief and confusion winding through him.

"Play it," Alexander said.

Sasha threw him a glance. "Are you being sure, *bratishka*?"

Alexander frowned. Not really. But they needed to face whatever headwinds Kareema had left them.

He nodded, leaning in for a viewing.

Sasha tapped the screen, then Kareema began to speak from the grave.

CHAPTER 6

Ford's heart was rapping a mean beat against his ribs as Sasha set the video a playin'. Didn't take long before the workstation display faded to a familiar scene.

The metal chair, set in the middle of the room under that bright center light, with a beautiful woman with olive skin and long dark hair hunched on top—clothes tattered and drooping from her gaunt frame, face bruised and bloodied, body shivering from untold harm he was all-too familiar with.

There she was, Kareema Salam.

But for the shivers, she was still, unmoving. Her head had not yet been messed with, her skull still intact and brain tucked nice and tight inside her noggin. The rest of her face... that was a different story entirely.

That eyeball was removed clear from its socket; they were always the first to go. Part of the Purifier playbook. His playbook.

The thought sent a cold regret skating down his spine. His chest tightened at not only the painful memory, but at the sight that sprang from it—what was left of that beautiful face of hers; the void hissing something fierce where her nose had been, like air easing out of a balloon; the trembling hand missing the thumb and pinkie wiping away a line of sweat beading at her forehead; the burn marks pockmarking her cheeks and lips.

"*Now, Kareema Salam,*" a voice suddenly rose from the workstation, gruff and growly and off-camera, "*let us hear your confession.*"

Nia and Sasha whispered to one another in their foreign tongue. Reeves started humming again. Probably another one of those negro spirituals that had gotten his distant ancestors through their own torturous past.

"We were right," Alexander said, shifting and crossing his arms. "They were indeed extracting a confession."

"This should be interesting," Nia said, widening her stance.

Ford swallowed, his throat raw like sandpaper. He was not sure he was ready for this.

A cough thrown up from the workstation punctured the silent void that had filled the space where Kareema had once sat—where she had once *lived.* Then nothing but the HVAC hum and Ford's rapping heart for the longest time.

Then Kareema stiffened, the picture zooming for her face and coming in and out of focus. That poor, poor face, the one good eye glistening with emotion now even as the blackened void oozed dark crimson.

Her quivering lips parted, and the voice of an angel— trembling and uncertain—began with a whisper, "*I confess that I have sinned against the Patron—in thought, word, and deed.*"

Ford sucked in a breath, furrowing his brow and craning for a better hearing.

What the hot Hades was she doing? Confessing, to the Patron? That she had sinned?

Again: What the hot Hades!

"*Louder,*" that gruff, growly voice commanded again. "*So the Patron himself can hear you.*"

She took a breath, then a beat, swallowing with a painful wince and face twisting with weariness. "*By what I have done and what I have left undone.*"

Alexander gasped. "I recognize what this is."

"What's that, homefry?" Ford asked.

He turned to him, eyes wide. "A confession, mirroring the one I myself had used to guide my parishioners through in my Tripolitania church for years—in congregational settings, in confessional booths. The same one Christians across the millennia themselves had used."

"That's right," Reeves added. "From the Anglican *Book of Common Prayer.*"

"*Kakogo cherta,*" Nia said, spitting to the side. "What the heck is she doing?"

That gruff voice off-camera returned, commanding her to continue.

Supposed they were about to find out.

Kareema shifted, wincing again before she continued: "*I have not served the Republic with my whole heart, I have sought to undermine Solterra with my false beliefs.*"

Her lower lip trembled something fierce now, that one remaining eye overflowing with emotion, a line of tears trailing down her cheek. She slumped forward, her head dipping and a few of those tears glistening with sorrowful drops down to her lap.

"*Confess!*" the voice off-camera boomed, jolting her upright. She quickly nodded her obedience.

"*O my Patron,*" she continued, head snapping back to attention, "*with all my heart I am heartily sorry for having offended you, and I detest all my sins.*" Her throat was strained and pained, sounding mousy and meek. Not at all the woman

Ford had known the past few years. Supposed that's what a torturous extraction did to a person. *"In choosing to do wrong and failing to do good, I have offended you whom I should serve above all things. I firmly intend, with your help, to do penance, to offend you no more, and to avoid whatever leads me in offending the Authority."*

She cried, burying her face in her hands before an arm appeared and wrenched her head back.

Alexander said, "Now there is an element of Catholic Orthodoxy to her confession."

"That's right," Reeves agreed. "A page from the Act of Contrition."

Kareema cried out but continued on, *"I am truly sorry and I humbly repent. For the sake of the polis, have mercy on me, Patron. So that I may delight in your will and walk in your ways."* Then she raised an arm, the one missing the thumb and pinkie, her middle three digits jutting out and palm flat. *"For Humanity!"*

Gasps sounded from Nia and Sasha before they conferred with one another in their Muscovia tongue—no doubt voicing the same surprise Ford had.

There it was, the Republic's anthem cry. The motto that bound the polis to the Regime, discarding personal interests and beliefs with full allegiances to Solterra Republic, to the Patron.

To hear Kareema repeating it like that, alongside that confession—too weird for words.

And scary...

The picture zoomed out, and a different figure came into view. Just a head, bulbous and bald, leaning down toward the poor woman. She shrank back, closing her eyes and whimpering softly.

Leaning back, the voice growled off-camera, *"Now, you*

will tell me everything you know about the Order of Thaddeus."

There was the slightest flinch of recognition, then: *"The... what? What are you—"*

"Don't play dumb with me, Kareema Salam. We know all. And you will tell all."

A sudden screech sounded from behind Kareema before ratcheting into a grinding whine. Like a motor or a drill or a—

"Saw..." Alexander said on a shaky breath, bringing a hand to his mouth.

He was right. Light glinted off from a spinning blade, the whirly sound tinny and menacing coming from the workstation. Reminded Ford of getting a root canal, and the sound it made when the tiny drill connected with his tooth. The thought was revolting, knowing where the script to this horror flick went.

That blade connecting with Kareema's skull!

"Please, I don't know anything!" she whimpered, throwing up her stumpy hands, what little fingers she had wiggling like frightened worms.

"You will tell me everything you know," the voice commanded, *"the easy way or the hard way. Your choice."*

She shrank from the blade coming into a sharper—no pun intended—view. *"Please, no..."*

Another hand grabbed for her hair from behind, yanking back her head with a violent jerk, the blade swooping for her skull.

Kareema screamed. Then, in a panicked rush: *"No! I don't—"*

Before the video cut to nothing but nothing.

Kareema Salam was no more.

"That is being all..." Sasha said quietly.

Silence filled the void. Even the HVAC hum wound

down to zero, the Republic conserving energy or forgetting to pay their wind farm bill. Ford wished for the AC to come roaring back, even the furnace. Anything to distract his heart thwapping a mean beat against his ribcage and throbbing in his head setting his brain a buzzin'!

"That was crazier than a one-legged jackrabbit," Reeves said. A bit uncouth, but that was Noramericana for you. Was thankful someone voiced what he wanted to say.

"Yeah, it was," Ford said. About all he thought to say.

"What I am wondering is," Nia said, turning toward him and Alexander, "what is it meaning?"

Ford turned to her. "What is what meaning, sister?"

She gestured to the workstation. "The confession. You were hearing what I was hearing. She recanted her faith. Pledged her fealty to the Patron."

"Under torture!" he boomed, his anger at her insinuations echoing. Didn't care a lick.

"No thanks to you!" she boomed back.

That smarted. But he deserved it.

"Whoa whoa whoa..." Alexander stepped between them, face furrowed and pained with surprise. "What's in the past is in the past. All that matters is the now. What happened in this room, in that chair. What happened—"

He stopped short, swallowing hard. Thought he was about to gesture at Kareema's body. Instead, he waved a hand at the workstation display before sweeping past the chair and tripod-mounted slate device.

"All that matters is what happened in Kareema's head."

"I am not sure," Sasha said, staring at Nia, "that I would be any stronger in the face of a spinning hacksaw."

"I would." Nia slammed her Scythe stick thingy down hard with a smack. "I will never recant my faith. Never confess disobedience to the Patron. Never voice fealty to his reign!"

"But is that what she did though?" Reeves said. "We don't know what was going on in that heart and head of hers. Only what came from her mouth."

"The mouth speaks what the heart believes."

"Even under pain of torture?"

"*Da.* Especially under pain of torture. And especially when *Iisus Khristos* is concerned. The one who remains faithful until the end is the one who is victorious. That is what the Revelation of John is teaching." She went silent, eyes casting down and face softening. Then she snapped her eyes back to Ford's own peepers. "That is what my own family taught me when they were—"

A muffled voice cut her off. At the door, just outside in the hallway.

Everyone pivoted toward the entrance, stepping back and shifting in defense.

Not good, Johnny Mark.

"What is that being?" Sasha squeaked.

Ford heaved a breath. "Company."

Then: The faint beeping of a keypad verifying its user before the gears of security unlocked the door and the massive slab of steel swung open.

With an equally massive Purifier at the threshold. Tall and commanding, a bulbous, bald head mounted on wide shoulders. He was all neck and wearing the crimson getup Ford himself had donned, along with wires jutting and tubes winding—marking him as an Auger, one of the elite of the elites who were augmented with genetic and AI algorithmic enhancements. Just as he had been.

Ford and the jarhead locked eyes; time slowed as recognition dawned.

Right before the goon reached for his back.

Shucky ducky...

Knew what was back there. Neutralizer. The weapon of choice for Legion jarheads. Had his own stuffed behind, but time wasn't on his side.

Didn't think twice about what was needed in the moment. Because if they didn't want their backsides canceled, then he'd have to get his twinkle-toes a movin'!

So he did, rushing the man. Head down, arms out, and barreling like a magnarail for the entrance.

Ford threw up a berserker yawp just as the Auger swung that Neutralizer around for action.

Moment of truth...

He slammed into the goon's chest, like a pumpkin against a brick wall, shoving the souped-up Purifier stumbling back into the outside corridor and cinching his hands around the black barrel of the weapon.

But not before the jarhead discharged the weapon with a deafening *chew-chew-chew-chew*.

Electric blue blobs sailed uselessly down the bright hallway. Thankful they didn't strike any of his crew—or him for that matter! But the ruckus would certainly draw the attention of the Purifier's comrades, those Enforcer goons they'd passed earlier.

Not good, Johnny Mark.

Didn't have time for a struggle, so Ford reached deep into his arsenal of ninja-fighting tricks hammered and honed over the years.

Stepping back, he brought his leg up and let it sail for the Auger's gonads—hitting pay dirt.

A cheatin' low blow, that's for sure. Literally. But Ford didn't care. No use pussyfooting around when an operation starts to come off the rails.

The goon grunted and coughed, reaching for the family jewels with one hand on instinct. Which gave Ford the window to finish the job.

Snatching the Neutralizer from his distracted grip, he pinched off a *one-two* punch that set the jarhead on fire—those familiar blobs smacking into him before wrapping their electric tendrils around his body. Sent another one smacking into his head for good measure. It was over, just like that.

Until an alarm sounded—cranky and piercing and begging for attention.

And livid crimson lights flashed in the corridor, undulating with warning and calling out who knew how many other Enforcer whack jobs from the shadows.

"Shucky ducky," Ford cursed, pointing the Neutralizer down the corridor pulsing angry red. "Why do things always get worse?"

"Which way?" Alexander asked, snapping his head this way and that.

He handed off the Auger's Neutralizer to the priest and shook his head, retrieving his own weapon and switching its settings to kill, but taking a step stage right.

Several more doors lined the concrete corridor. Big, heavy steel things with tiny glass windows like their own—no doubt more cells hiding more Unfits suffering the same terrifying torture one of their own had endured.

"It is being this way!" Nia started stage left, the opposite way Ford had figured.

Ford spun around, miffed she was taking the leader baton and running with it. "Says who, sassafras?"

She didn't turn back. "Woman's intuition. *Idti!* Let us get going."

Went to retort when Alexander gave him not-now eyes and threw a hushing finger against his lips. He huffed a sigh.

Whatever. As long as they made it out of Dodge alive, he didn't care if it was the Easter Bunny guiding them with a rainbow from his backside.

"What about the body?" Reeves asked, his own Neutralizer ready for action while yanking his free thumb back inside the cell.

"Never leave a fallen comrade behind," Ford said, making for the cell again.

"Good motto," Alexander said with a nod. "One of the Legion's creeds?"

He planted a thumb at his chest. "It's one of my creeds." Then slipped inside, Reeves joining him.

"How are we going to be taking that woman?" Nia asked in a huff outside.

Ford ignored her, finding a single body bag folded in a cupboard above the workstation. Probably the last of several. The thought soured his stomach.

Reeves snatched one end of the bag and helped him lay it on the wet floor. Ford zipped it open, then the two got to work carefully retrieving Kareema's body and lying it inside. Didn't even think about what he was doing, all that mattered—

A sudden *chew-chew-chew* erupted outside, followed by another *one-two-three-four* blasts of a Neutralizer.

—was giving her a proper burial.

That is, if they made it out alive themselves!

"Incoming!" Nia shouted, slipping into the cell as blue electric blobs sailed past.

"You heard the woman, homefry," Ford said, glaring at Alexander. "Hop to it!"

Had to give it to the man. He didn't flinch. Stepped right up to the plate and offered his own *chew-chew-chew* rejoinder, then another trio.

"Go help him out," Reeves said, finishing with the bag. "I've got it."

Ford hesitated, but nodded. Man was brawny enough, and he needed to help Alexander.

More Neutralizer fire sailed past, an electrified blob smacking mighty close to Alexander's head. He skipped back and cursed, apologizing.

The weapon fire wound down to zero, but heavy footfalls echoing their way replaced the sound of Neutralizer fire.

Incoming was right.

"Alex, Nia," Ford said, "you ready to lay the funk down on these Enforcer bastards?"

"*Da.*" Nia nodded and gripped her Scythe. "Let us get to it."

"Show the way," Alexander agreed.

Ford did. Wasting no time, he raced to the entrance, took a breath, then a beat, then—

Moment of truth...

—he leaped into the hallway, facing stage right, the way he'd intended to go.

With nothing but no one staring him down.

Supposed that meant Junia Kaminski was right after all.

Which also meant the platoon of Enforcers were hot on his backside!

Confirmed by an eruption of Neutralizer fire from behind.

CHAPTER 7

Ford threw himself against the wall for cover.

But Alexander was the one squeezing the trigger to his Neutralizer on a pair of charcoal-clad goons taken by surprise.

Hated guns, and hated that he had to use them. As a former priest and a current order Master tasked with protecting Ichthus and the Christian faith, he could hardly reconcile the violence with the teachings of Christ. However, they were in the middle of things, and it was either his death and his companions or the Church's sworn enemies.

He trusted the Lord Almighty would understand.

The Enforcers folded like used bathrobes, shuddering on the floor wrapped in blue tendrils, a sight he was far too accustomed to seeing given the past few years of things.

Nia threw up a Ukrainski shout and put her Scythe to work, bringing it down hard on another Enforcer's head, that purply tip smashing through the black visor and sizzling its face with a menacing electric glow.

He had been quite pleased she was on the Church's side of things, especially this past year. She had more than proven herself in protecting the interests of Ichthus.

Two more Enforcers were left, letting their own weapons unload in a dangerous *chew-chew-chew* response that could've ended wickedly.

Almost did, too, one of the electric blobs nearly chewing through Nia before landing with a smack at the ceiling above his shoulder! But she sidestepped just in time and Alexander dropped to his knees, outstretching his Neutralizer and lining up the perfect shot.

He sent a *one-two* punch sailing down the corridor and smacking into one of the goons.

The single remaining Enforcer had the same idea, dropping to his knees and taking aim.

Ford growled from behind, "Not a chance in hot Hades, pal..."

He pulled the trigger of his own Neutralizer—but nothing came of it.

Empty.

"Shucky ducky..." he complained, tossing it to the floor with a clatter.

"Don't worry," Alexander said, "I've got your back."

Neutralizer fire went sailing past them both far down the corridor, a racing heat letting him know that was a close call. He followed it up by popping off three shots that sent the final Enforcer to Saint Pete's pearlies. Or Lucifer's, more like it.

"Nice shooting, partner," Ford said.

He heaved a breath. "Thanks. Suppose my father was good for something growing up."

"Your old man taught you to shoot?"

"That's right. Hated going with him, but it was about the only thing he cared to share with me, his love of the rifle range."

Ford clamped a hand on his shoulder and gave it a

squeeze. "And we're lucky he did. So is the Church, given the stakes."

Reeves emerged from the cell with an oversized black bag draped across his back. The sight of Kareema's lifeless body sent a shiver ratcheting down Alexander's spine, driving home the truth of those stakes.

Sasha rushed past him and joined Nia. "We better be getting a move on. The Republic won't be sleeping for long."

Ford gestured down the hallway from whence those Enforcers had emerged. "Suppose thataway is the way to go."

Nia smirked. "You mean the way I was going, the way opposite of your way?"

"Yeah, whatever."

"Like I said. Woman's—"

"Intuition and all that jazz," Ford interrupted, shoving past. "Got it."

"*Podozhdat*," Nia said, kneeling next to the first Purifier Ford had taken out. The Auger, as they were known, who had been Kareema's torturer.

"What are you doing?" Alexander asked.

"Getting supplies."

"What suppli—"

The sparking sizzle of Nia's Scythe cut him off, the purple tip slicing through that Auger's wrist and severing his hand.

Ford exclaimed, "What the hot Hades was that for, sassafras!"

"This is our way out," she said, holding up the severed hand. "Our key."

Alexander grimaced, same for Sasha, the pair of them twisting their faces in disgust on the same wavelength.

"Suppose you've got a point there," Ford said, taking a handkerchief out from his back pocket and handing it over to Nia.

"*Spasibo.*" Snatching the piece of cloth, she wrapped the bloody, stubby end.

Alexander looked away, bile threatening to rise. They weren't out of the woods yet. Or reprogramming camp, as was their case. Not by a long shot. Perhaps the Lord had given them a lifeline.

Ford knelt beside one of the downed Enforcers and retrieved his Neutralizer, then jerked a thumb down the way. "We better scram before reinforcements arrive."

He led the way with Nia close behind. Reeves made up the rear carrying Kareema's body, with Alexander and Sasha sandwiched in between as they raced down the long, bright concrete corridor.

The electrical discharge from the firefight hung like a midsummer Tripolitanian storm, sweet and salty and full of the promise of rain. However, in their case, it was the promise of death, a reminder of the stakes. As were the shuddered cell doors and lifeless tiny windows hiding their prisoners within.

Images of the cell they'd come from—the blood-washed floors, the bits of matter and flesh and hair, the pieces that had been swept aside down the drain at their arrival; the desecration of Kareema's body with torturous ruin, with the missing eye and nose and fingers, with her skull cut apart and those probes sticking out of her brain.

Those probes...

What were they for? To administer a shocking pain, to extract vital intel Kareema had refused to give up about the Order of Thaddeus through ultramodern means?

Alexander didn't want to know.

The corridor was a long one, shuttling the quintet past a few dozen doorways beneath crimson-pulsing lights and curving around the perimeter of the prison, a panopticonic nightmare bending inward with a single guardhouse at the center courtyard keeping watch. Alexander could see the guard station through narrow slits in the concrete wall from the bottom floor, the darkened world splintering through a slapping rain thundering outside now.

It was not supposed to be like this. They were supposed to extract Kareema, intact, through the sewer and rendezvous with Lucy and Rebekah keeping watch out at sea just beyond the prison island. Logistical preparations did not include breaking out of the reprogramming camp because they knew it couldn't be done. Not with the design that ensured maximum security and the levels and layers of security. He just hoped Nia's instincts were correct, that the dead Auger would lend them a helping hand—literally! Otherwise, as Ford would say, they were screwed.

A door at the far end appeared, this time guarded by a keypad at the right, rather than a key code panel.

They raced for it, Nia pushing past Ford and wielding the hand, while the others hustled behind in wait.

The last in the long line of cells awaited them, the tiny window peering into the darkened void of wicked, menacing restraint. Waiting, Alexander wondered who, if anyone, was within. This cell was guarded by a similar keypad as the door, instead of the simple key code panel like Kareema's cell. Must be a high-value prisoner for such reinforced security measures.

"*Nu zhe...*" Nia said, positioning the hand and its fingers upon a plate of darkened glass. "Come on! Why isn't this working?"

"Let me try," Ford offered. Nia hesitated, but handed over the key.

He set about wrenching the hand into place, positioning and repositioning the severed appendage. It wasn't working, and the seconds were ticking by like a metronome, aided by the continued angry alarm, until they were caught and dragged into one of the cells.

Alexander couldn't bear to watch, so he took a glance at the cell door window—

When a face appeared in full view!

Wrinkled and gaunt, with cheek bones jutting at wicked angles between a curtain of silver hair.

He let out a startled scream, falling back against the wall and pointing at the door.

"There's someone in there!"

"What?" Sasha said, glancing at the cell before scurrying to Alexander's side with a frightened yelp.

"Someone is being in there!"

Ford glanced at them, then at the door. "What are you talking about?"

Heaving a steadying breath, Alexander swallowed. "I saw a face."

"Me too!" Sasha agreed.

Reeves walked over to investigate, then Nia and Ford—the trio stepping back at the same sight.

A man peering at them with pleading eyes and a fist pounding against the thick glass with a muffled petition for rescue.

"We have to do something," Alexander said.

"Do what?" Nia asked.

"Help him, that's what!"

"*Nyet*," she growled, then went back to the keypad for another go of it.

Ford turned his back on the cell. "Ukrainski chickadee is right. We've got an operation to complete. Which doesn't entail rescuing civilians."

Alexander raced a frustrated hand across his close-cropped hair. "That's no civilian! He's one of us. An Unfit. Probably a brother in Christ. We have to save him."

"Bullfeathers!" he cursed. "There's gotta be a hundo more of his kind. Can't save 'em all."

"We haven't saved anyone, the least of all one of our own!"

Ford's face fell, and regret churned in Alexander's belly.

The man sighed, returning to the keypad. "No, we can't save them all."

"But we can save one!" Alexander exclaimed. "And that's enough for me. We can't possibly leave—"

The keypad finally sent up a hopeful ping before it turned green. Gears turned inside the wall and the door shuddered open.

Ford whipped his Neutralizer around and made for the door, ignoring Alexander's plea and handing off the appendage back to Nia.

Alexander looked behind at the window, that pained face still visible, eyes red and rimmed by glistening emotion.

He knew what he had to do.

Shoving past Sasha, he put a hand on Nia's shoulder and jerked her back, then snatched the hand from her and slapped it against the keypad standing guard to the cell.

"*Chto delayesh?*" she protested, sounding ticked to high heaven.

He didn't care. No way would he leave this man behind. Not after losing one of their own to the Republic.

But the keypad didn't take.

He grunted his frustration, repositioning the hand and fingers—when a hand clenched his wrist.

It was Ford, face hard and eyes on fire. "Leave it, homefry! That's an order."

Alexander jammed his shoulder into his chest, shaking him free and pivoting to block any further apprehension.

"What the hot Hades do you think—"

Another ping of success sounded, followed by an affirming green keypad. Then a set of gears turned, and the door unlocked, swinging open.

"Now you are doing it, *bratishka*," Sasha complained.

An updraft of putrid air came riding out of the cell on a hot, humid breath—rancid and rank, smelling of excrements and body odor and coagulating blood.

Smelling of death...

While the others threw an arm across their nose to shield themselves. Alexander took a careful step toward the darkened void, the flashing crimson light offering enough visual to glimpse what lay inside.

There stood a rail-thin man a head shorter than Alexander, skin pale and sagging from bony shoulders and jutting ribs, like an oversized shirt dripping from his frame. He was naked, bruised and beaten, with burn marks dotting his chest and an infected gash oozing green pus. He reminded Alexander of Father Jim.

"We've gotta go, homefry," Ford said, turning back to the exit. "So do your thing."

Alexander nodded and stretched out his hand. "We're here to help. Can you walk? Can you understand me?"

His hand was suddenly seized, the grip clammy and cold, but firm and insistent.

"*Da*," he said, voice hoarse and low and echoing the Vostokanan tongue of their companions. "I am understanding, and I am grateful."

Alexander took off his jacket and helped the man inside. "Come along. I'll help you."

The man nodded his thanks and slipped a spindly arm

inside, then the other. The jacket looked positively dreadful on the man, oversized and ill-fitting, as if a child slipped into his father's navy blazer. But it did offer a modicum of dignity, for which he looked grateful.

"Homefry..." Ford said from the doorway, holding it open after the others had already filed through.

While Alexander ushered the man through the exit, the others following, Ford whipped out his mobile device and sent Lucy a mayday text message, instructing her to bring their fish around into open seas. Not sure how, but their rescue plans had taken a drastic turn for the cray-to-the-Z.

Finishing, he followed his crew into a hallway connected to a stairwell, the other end leading into what appeared to be another wing of the reprogramming camp. They were at the very bottom of the Republic's wicked well, so only way was up —a mawing, spiraling void leading to who knew where flashing like the flaming fires of hell.

Thunder rumbled with a muffle high above—grumbly, foreboding, speaking of ill intent.

Which was quickly drowned out by the clomping of boots on metal, another Enforcer wave descending to intercept the threat.

To intercept them!

"We've got company," Nia growled, spinning her Scythe and waiting for no one.

She took the stairs by twos, Ford close behind and aiming up the well spinning ever upward. Sasha took aim as well, his Neutralizer shuddering within his shaking hands. Reeves was useless, standing behind with Kareema still slumped over his shoulders, keeping the mystery man company.

Alexander raced to join Ford, the pulsing crimson lights of warning and the swelling sound of boots-on-metal growing like a gathering wave before crashing ashore.

Except Nia was the first to strike, two floors up. Her *Hi-yah!* cry joined by the slicing *smack* of that electrified head of her Scythe connecting with an Enforcer—a cry of pain, of death, confirming the kill.

Right before Ford's Neutralizer opened up, the *chew-chew-chew* of his own weapon connecting and sending his victim stumbling against another Enforcer, adding to the kill count for the one—

And opening up the window for Alexander to finish off the other.

Score three for the Remnant! Or the Order of Thaddeus, even the Resistance—though Father Jim would have his hide for such talk. Either way, they may not have had the high-ground advantage, but it did seem they had momentum on their side.

He just prayed it lasted.

A blue blob smacked against the concrete just above his head—electric tendrils sparking and spreading across the wall.

From below!

Then another, Sasha crying out as Reeves and the mystery man raced past for cover between the pair keeping the ceiling of descending Enforcers from caving in on them and the rising tide of reinforcements from sweeping them away.

They were sandwiched between two forces—a vice grip coming in for the kill!

"Shucky ducky..." Ford muttered, spinning around and joining the renewed assault.

The threat above seemed to have abated, the three Enforcers neutralized, which opened the window for safer passage farther up for Reeves and their new comrade.

Nia led them, the purply glow of her Scythe lighting the way through the maw of darkened steel and concrete. No chrome and glass and titanium in these parts, the Republic's building elements of choice. Which meant this facility was real old, and far outside the purview of normal Republic concern. The end of the world, really, the last place before death, already buried several stories beneath earth. Or a reprogrammed existence lived in numbed servitude to the Patron, which was a kind of death in and of itself.

All Alexander knew was that they needed to get up and out. Recalled the sewer system they had come through was connected by a series of canals and levels deep underneath the compound, running under the main town and out into the open sea. They had waded through several switchback twists and turns, the water swirling past and cascading down into larger tributaries of rancid waste. Now they needed to ascend far above to sea level if they had any chance of making it out alive.

Where he hoped their chariot awaited to extract them!

He helped, bringing up the rear as the battle raged below, Ford and Sasha holding back the rising tide of Enforcers while—

A door swung open, and a pair of Purifiers—crimson-clad in thick, bulbous armor—were waiting. Looked about as stunned as Alexander did!

But Alexander was quick on the draw—and quicker.

A *one-two-three* punch sent the elite Enforcer unit staggering back into his companion.

Who let off an instinctive *chew-chew-chew* that grazed Alexander's shoulder.

The electrified blue blob blazing past was enough to shock his arm and send it into numbed uselessness. Like a lead pipe had smacked his funny bone.

Except this was the farthest thing from funny, his arm tingling and failing in his hour of need.

Another Enforcer appeared as the other two went down,

the bulky, hulking brute in charcoal armor raising his Neutralizer for the kill.

Right as his arm threatened to drop his Neutralizer, the tingly numbness spreading down his limb and into his shoulders. But his one good one snatched it before it fell—just not in time.

The Enforcer raised his arm, took aim—

Dread flooded Alexander's veins. This was it. The end.

—and fired.

A livid *chew-chew-chew-chew-chew* resounded in his ears —sending a shuddering jolt through him from the sudden turn.

And flattening the Enforcer flat on his backside.

Alexander clutched his chest on instinct, checking himself before twisting for a look.

It was Sasha, come to rescue his own backside!

"Thanks, mate," he sighed. "I owe you one."

"Just be giving me a big glass of Stolichnaya when this is being over!"

"I'll give you a case of Stoli when this is over!"

He laughed, a roiling rumble of thunder intercepting any further reply.

From the doorway, leading out into a darkened world still sparking with the echo of white thunderbolts and flooded by rain.

Rain!

Massive watery pellets sheeting from the heavens and soaking the ground and now the floor.

Which meant one thing.

Freedom...

"This way!" Alexander shouted, gesturing to his comrades and running into the nighttime downpour.

Except...

This wasn't right.

Not at all where he expected them to be.

"*Bozhe moy,*" Sasha moaned, throwing a frightened hand on his waterlogged head.

My God was right...

CHAPTER 8

FORD RACED AFTER ALEXANDER, hardly believing their luck. They rise through the portal of doom as a pod of Enforcers busts in on them, opening the way into the great outdoors? What are the odds?

Although, he understood odds and luck had nothing to do with it, not in his latest line of work anyway. It was the good Lord above giving them a helping hand. Just hoped he was feeling generous that evening, because they were not out of the woods yet—or the reprogramming camp, as was their case!

A frigid volley slapped Ford clear across his mug, the kind of rain that hurts your face and your feelings. But they'd made it. By golly, they'd made it!

Took a bit to get oriented where they were. By his calculations they should be near the entrance to the cray-cray compound. But the sound of the deluge rushing across the grounds spread out from behind and assaulting the high walls was disorienting, as well as that feelings-hurting rain.

More lightning raced across the sky, a thick canopy of engorged storm clouds low and threatening. He slapped at his eyes for a clearer picture of things, water splashing up his nose and in his mouth.

"*Smotret!*" Nia complained, pointing that Scythe thingy of hers into the darkness, Alexander and Sasha and the others gathering around.

His breath left him the moment his peepers peeped the problem.

They were nowhere near the entrance! Instead, a long, wide promenade stretched before them, with basketball hoops at one end and benches at another, the reprogramming camp rising all around like that ancient Colosseum amphitheater in the center of Roma's great city with a menacing guard tower smack dab in the middle.

And with them as chum for the Enforcer gladiator sharks.

"Shucky ducky!" he cried out barely above the roar of the swirling storm around them.

Wouldn't take long before the entire reprogramming camp knew where they were. At least they'd taken out eight of the Legion's goons. How many were left was anyone's guess. Standard op when he ran his own camp way back when was five guests per Enforcer. Yeah, that's right. Guests. Code for the Unfits shackled in their reprogramming cells, as if recipients of the Patron's beneficent blessings. So, in a place the size of this one, three more levels to the three they'd already ascended —had to be well over a hundo Unfits holed up in these parts.

Which meant a whole helluva lot of Enforcers.

"Now what?" Alexander asked on a shaky breath.

The splashing splat of something sailing from on high intercepted his call.

Then a crying scream.

From their new lackey!

He was on the ground clutching his right foot, the last bit of electric charge from a Neutralizer blast winding down to zero where he'd been standing. Didn't take a genius to know what was what. Lucky it hadn't been a direct hit.

Or providential, those helping hands giving them protection right when they needed it.

Yet Ford knew about the other side of that equation: The Lord helps those who help themselves. Never could find that maxim in the Good Book, but Meemaw always said it, so he believed it.

And lived by it.

"We run, that's what!" he yelled, more Neutralizer blasts zipping past and splattering in the soggy courtyard.

"You are hearing the man," Nia said. "*Bezhat!*"

His exhortation to run sounded more convincing in Muscovia. The group took off, sloshing through mud puddles and slipping on rain-slick grass. A lighted void in the far wall looked like the way out.

They made for it, on the double.

Alexander helped the old man hobble along with his one good arm thrown around his back and bolted for the entrance. Like the champ he was, Reeves adjusted his hold on Kareema and kept pace with Ford and Nia who were leading the pack, with Sasha at his side.

Until he bit it in a pothole and landed on his face.

He threw up something Ford interpreted as a not-nice Muscovia word on par with shucky ducky, pushing off the ground as blobby Neutralizer blasts splashed on either side in all their menacing blue-electric glory.

"Let me lend a hand, doc." Ford hooked a hand under his arm and hoisted him back to his feet—

Just as Nia shouted something he had no cotton-pickin' clue what.

Motivating Sasha to scram, shouting another *Der'mo!* curse for good measure.

In the split second Nia called her warning to scram and he recognized what was whistling their way—Disruptor grenade!—Ford managed a few steps toward some semblance of safety, those benches he'd spotted looking pretty good.

A sudden menacing blast stopped him in his tracks, fire and fury blooming from behind.

And tossing him like a rag doll, light and heat and soggy sod washing over him—

Before darkness threatened to consume him, the crown of his head throbbing with injury and pain lancing through his cranium, joined by the twinkle of twilight's stars.

But he didn't fade—wouldn't fade, not when they were so close.

Confusion engulfed him, his ringing ears and starlight eyes made all the worse by the mawing darkness and deluge of both rain and Neutralizer blobs from up on high.

Relief came when everyone was alive and accounted for and rushing for the other end and making progress for the entrance.

Heaving a stabilizing breath and hiking up his big-boy pants, he scrambled from the slick ground and joined them, weapon fire fading as the group reached the lighted entrance.

A stout security checkpoint of that chrome and glass and titanium sat like an underworked and overstuffed guard snacking on donuts and coffee all day at the center of a massive stone arch, the darkened sky and faint city lights about the only thing his peepers peeped.

Didn't take any chances, though, none of them did—with him and Alexander and Sasha aiming with their locked-and-loaded Neutralizers, Nia beside with her purply Scythe ready to strike.

No movement, no sign of life, no nothing.

Ford snorted a laugh. "That was eas—"

He skidded to a halt just beyond the checkpoint, cursing

under his breath and quickly revising his opinion on the matter.

No, not easy.

Dumb. Stupid dumb.

Because they'd run right into a trap of Ford's own making.

The reprogramming camp was perched up on a massive bluff overlooking the raging sea of blood and water below. Knew that much when he planned the mission, but the view from up there made it all far more treacherous.

And iffy.

Because that perch had to be a thousand feet from the mainland below. The bloody sea water crashed against the base of the cliff, which was a real shame. Because back in the day, before Mother Nature's water broke and birthed Armageddon—an apt name for the climactic climate change that had wreaked the world and sparked the Great Reckoning at the turn of the century—a tourist town stuck in the 19th century lay strewn below. With fudge shops and horse-drawn carriages and hotels his family had visited a few times when he was a boy.

Now all that was left was a gleaming checkpoint at the end of a long road spread out before them that led to what was left of the old town and docks, a seawall towering at the end holding the sea at bay.

Lights were whirling and twirling red and white, angry and livid in the downpour. No doubt with a contingent of Enforcers waiting for them with their own locked-and-loaded Neutralizers ready for their arrival and probably some Raycannons to boot! That, joined with the forces raining down the funk just inside those walls, and, well—

They'd need a heaping helping of the good Lord's helping hands if they were gonna have any hope of getting out of their sticky wicket alive!

"Why are things always getting worse!" Sasha complained.

Ford smirked. "What'd you expect, a field of tulips to tiptoe through?"

"Well, *da!* After all we've been through, I was hoping God would be sparing us a *merca* or two."

He ran a shaky hand through his hair, the Grip threatening to take over now. So he heaved a breath and swallowed, sending up a prayer for providential intervention.

Somewhere out there was their hydrocraft, Lucy and Rebekah bringing her around from the backside of the island for the extraction. Just hoped they made it in time!

Alexander offered, "We ought to give Rebekah and Lucy a heads up. I imagine however we get out of this, they'll need to be standing by to whisk us out of here."

"Already did," Ford said. "Back when we were scrambling out of Dante's Inferno!"

"Where are they planning on being then?" Nia asked, searching down below.

"The docks, straight ahead." Ford pointed down past the checkpoint, a long drive paved in cracked blacktop their only way out.

"*Nyet.*" She shook her head and waved that Scythe of hers overboard, the purply head casting a haunting glow over the cliff down to the roiling, boiling waters below. "We jump. That is being only option."

"Jump? Are you crazy, sister ma-gister?"

Alexander peered over, Neutralizer fire starting up from back inside the compound, the blue blobs sailing past and smacking into the checkpoint—putting an exclamation point on the urgency.

Several more Enforcers were coming their way up the drive from stage right, weapons drawn and shouting commands to surrender. Even had a Destroyer, a Raycannon mounted on top glowing green and ready to evaporate their asses if they didn't surrender.

A light suddenly flooded them, bright and white like a prison-yard beacon searching for an escapee. Which pretty much fit the scenario of the hour!

Except—

It was angled all wrong. From the side and from below.

"*Come on!*" a voice split through the night, faint but there.

And from the side and from below!

"Did you hear something?" Alexander asked, eyes wide with hope.

Ford grinned. "Sure did, homefry!"

He raced to the edge of the cliff, careful not to misplace a step. Alexander was at his side, then Nia at his other.

There was indeed a spotlight shining bright from the churning waters below—with two women waving their arms and calling for their names.

First a blonde from California: "*John Mark!*"

Then an Alkebulana beauty: "*Alex Zarruq!*"

Ford smiled at the latter and appreciated the former: His gal, Lucy, was calling for his name; same for Alexander, his African Queen screaming for him to jump now.

Their women had come to their rescue!

But, man, quite the jump. One wrong move, not enough oomph and you'd be chopped liver. Or, rather, crushed human on those rocks down there!

"*Jump!*" the women said in unison.

"*Pryzhok?*" Sasha yelled. "Are they crazy in the head?"

"It is a long way down," Reeves said, Kareema still firmly on his back. "Suppose it's plenty deep with the hydrocraft butting up against the cliff like that."

"*Jump!*" the women repeated, a squall of wind and rain

churning the waters beneath something fierce. Was right dangerous, but what choice did they have?

"*Khorosho,*" Nia said, strapping her Scythe to her back and readying for the plunge.

Alexander conferred with their newcomer, making a plan for them to plunge into the waters together.

The sudden *chaw-chaw-chaw* from a Raycannon down the way put an exclamation point on the urgency of the matter.

"*JUMP!*" Ford yelled, waving his arms for the group to hop to it while launching a *chew-chew-chew-chew* volley as a proper response. All shots went high and wide, and he added another *one-two-three* blast for good measure. Same for Alexander and Sasha, the trio opening up on the pack at the end.

The others renewed their assault now from just inside the prison. If it wasn't for the guardhouse, they'd be goners. They didn't have much time.

Nia was first, the woman leaping into the churning water and plunging down deep. Took a few beats, but she emerged, swimming to the hydrocraft bobbing in the roiling, boiling lake.

Sasha followed—sort of, edging to the cliff's lip before adding a nervous: "Oh, I am not knowing about—"

Ford gave him a shove, the man throwing up a screech before bringing his limbs in for the cannonball plunge. Good man.

He turned around and unleashed his Neutralizer down the causeway again, another *chaw-chaw-chaw* his reply—

Right before a phantasmic show of sizzling greenish-yellow fire and fury exploded at the roof of the guardhouse.

Setting it ablaze!

Alexander sheltered the older fella with his one good arm, the other still limp at his side from the Neutralizer graze. Ford yelled for Reeves and motioned for him to hop to it.

Hiking Kareema's body over his shoulders, he took a running leap off the edge, and down he went.

Just as several blasting spits of Neutralizer fire came from behind—smacking into the blazing guardhouse and sailing past them over the cliff. Which was joined by the hustling rush of a squad of six Enforcers storming up the gangway with that Destroyer rumbling between.

Could've almost seen the whites of their eyes, too, had they not been shielded by bulbous black helmets. That old Revolutionary maxim from Old General Putman would've normally sent Ford into action, but they had to get a movin'.

Another *chaw-chaw-chaw* sailed past with wicked speed, exploding in that greenish-yellow firelight again against the side of the rising prison behind.

Another near miss!

Either the Legion had gotten real rusty with their shots since he'd Defected, or they were just pussyfooting about until they got close enough to take them alive.

Or maybe they were holding back to take their man-o-mystery alive. The thought pinged the back of Ford's lizard brain, throwing up a bazillion question marks about who they'd nabbed.

Either way, over his dead body...

"Zarruq!" Ford yelled, "hippity-hoppity, let's go!"

"He's petrified of heights," Alexander said, face drawn with worry. The guy had really taken to the older fella.

"Go with him, then." He spun around, blasting his Neutralizer back into the reprogramming camp void.

Until it fizzled to a hissing nothing but nothing.

Shucky ducky...

Ford tossed it aside. "Go on, scram!"

Alexander nodded, handing off his own Neutralizer and readying to leap.

He snatched it and spun back, homefry and the old man edging with clasped hands to make the jump—

When one of those pesky Enforcers got the jump on 'em and nailed the cliff with a blue blob—the ground erupting in an electrified blast that chewed away the edge.

And sent the newcomer slipping from Alexander's grip as Alexander himself began falling away.

Ford clenched his wrist just in time, but he didn't have a third to lend a helping hand.

Down the older fella went, tumbling head over heels into the rain-soaked air with a faint splash down below.

With Ford and Alexander falling back onto the ground.

And that damned squad of Enforcers bearing down on them!

"NO!" Alexander cried out, scrambling for the edge for a look-see.

Just as a Neutralizer blast exploded at the edge with another chomp.

They were trapped and down like dogs.

Not good, Johnny Mark...

Alexander skittered back. "Where's a time-travel belt when you need one!"

Ford glanced behind, boots flashing closer, emerging from the mawing darkness of the reprogramming camp inner court. Then he glanced right, catching a glimpse of something he could use to turn the tide.

"Don't got no time-travel belt, homefry," Ford said, readying his Neutralizer for the shot he prayed to the good Lord above worked. "But I've got something better."

Alexander turned to him, eyes wide. "What's that?"

A breath, then a beat, then: "A lemonade maker."

Because if you can't make the Noramericana good stuff with the crate of lemons life deals you, then whatcha good for?

"What are you—"

Ford's blasting Neutralizer cut him off, a double *chew-chew* sailing down the sloping drive toward destiny.

Destiny being a weak spot Ford knew about on those Destroyer crafts the Legion was so high on. Had experienced the flaw firsthand once on a mission in the heart of Canadia, of all places, sussing out a pack of Quebecian rebels refusing to cooperate with the Republic's language requirements. Always were more beholden to the *lingua franca* of their Frenchie ancestors than the *lingua franca* of the Republic. Wouldn't you know it, a well-placed shot from one of those rascals had sent his ride up in flames. Something about a low-lying pipe at the undercarriage that connected straight to the main engine.

Didn't get it; didn't need to. All that mattered was having the same luck this go around.

Moment of truth...

The first shot slammed into the front end of the Destroyer, erupting in a brilliant show rivaling any Noramericana summer storm. Lightning shows in them parts were wicked cool!

Now for the second—

Which Ford didn't even get to enjoy because the entire middle part of the road erupted in a phantasmic show of fire and fury. No Noramericana summer storm there! Just a big ball of fiery ugly that washed hot and acrid over him and Alexander.

Giving them the window they needed to—

"*JUMP!*" Ford said, scrambling from the road.

"Don't have to tell me twice," Alexander said, doing the same.

Just as Neutralizers erupted from behind.

Didn't matter a lick. They were sailing toward the murky depths below and plunging beneath the angry dark water in *three-two—*

One came far quicker than Ford expected—bitter and biting and smacking his chest before he could catch a breath.

But he managed to stay with it and reach for the surface, the hydrocraft a few strokes away. Reaching it, strong arms pulled him up top the slippery submarine.

He fell against the yellow surface trying to bring a leg up top, smacking his jaw with a clatter. It hurt something fierce, but he'd live. He'd *lived,* several times over after enough brushes with death to last a lifetime after escaping that damned reprogramming camp.

Twice over now!

Deserved a medal is what he deserved.

That could wait. What couldn't were the blasts sailing down into the water from on high.

"Go!" Ford yelled, Alexander leading the charge scrambling into a narrow circular hatch and down a red ladder into the belly of the fish—a cramped, narrow space of dim LED lighting and steel girding that extended back to front before splitting into a T at the rear.

Seats ran along the sides, with a functional tin-colored aesthetic punctuated by navy. The steady hum of engines and fans filled the aural void.

Jin Sung was at the controls, with Lucy taking the second chair.

Ford smiled. Thata girl.

The others were flopped on the furniture and catching

their breaths as the fish descended below the surface and sped out into open water.

He sighed, flopping down into one of those seats himself, the plastic throwing up a squeaking complaint.

They'd made it. They were safe.

For now.

CHAPTER 9

SOMEWHERE IN THE ATLANTIC OCEAN.

ANOTHER SUBMARINE, another outpost. Seemed to be Ford's lot in life ever since joining the Ministerium as head of security. Now that was defunct, a Resistance rising in its place, and he was still puttering about in an Ichthus-issued personal submergence vehicle twenty thousand leagues under the sea.

Not that he was complaining. He'd signed up with the Legion because that's what all the kids did back home in Noramericana after the Great Reckoning, but the Republic Classis seafarers was where his heart had truly been. Much more of a fish than a fox, so zooming around the underwater world in hydrocrafts that would knock ol' Jules Verne's socks off was definitely childhood wish fulfillment. *Twenty Thousand Leagues Under the Sea* had nothing on the Republic's watery world!

And all of it was his oyster. At least in service of the Ministerium and Ichthus, and the whole Resistance movement against Solterra. Especially safely navigating his crew through the Great Lakes and back out into the Atlantic Ocean. Thought they'd bite the big one motoring through Montreal and then Quebec City, given their trespasses against the Republic in that other part of Canada, but it was smooth sailing. The rising oceans had given them plenty of places to hide along the way through the Saint Lawrence River on their way to the gulf.

Ford had taken over for their fearless operational support guru, Jin Sung, after breaking for the Atlantic. The man had motored them to that blasted reprogramming camp to begin with, then had the endurance to wait out their infiltration and extraction before navigating them out of Dodge. Was Ford's turn to man the controls and bring the fish to port while the others got some shuteye.

Shouldn't be long before they reached their particular deep submergence station, Phoenix One, the main operational center for a renewed Order of Thaddeus, headlined by none other than their own Alexander Zarruq, along with another outfit Ford wasn't too keen on—the Ichthus Resistance.

Thought the whole Phoenix One name was a funny designation, but apparently there was some history to it, the churchy kind. Came from the mythical desert firebird that cyclically regenerates itself from the ashes of its predecessors every five hundred years. Apparently, the emblem had been a symbol of Christianity. Not only because of the cyclical nature of the Church—which had regenerated itself every five hundred years or so—but because for the early Church, the phoenix represented the resurrection, the bringing of new life.

Which was exactly what the former Blake Ridge Outpost was all about. Had been a former deep ocean station for hiring mercenaries and dealing in black-market thingamajigs and exchanging the latest gossip or top-secret intel among the Republic's elite. But after Ichthus got ahold of it years ago, it became the central hub for the Resistance, led by none other than Commander Joshua Kaminski, Nia's son from another lifetime ago.

First impressions was he was too cocksure and swaggery.

That black fedora and cape didn't help matters. But the past year he'd proven himself more than capable of organizing the Church's response to the Republic's Purge campaign, keeping Christian communities scattered across the Republic safe during these last apocalyptic days—and even sticking it to the Patron when it was warranted.

Father Jim wasn't too pleased about it all, believing it wasn't the Church's place to resist but instead to evangelize as a Remnant, preserving the gospel. To jump in with both feet and preach the good news Jesus himself had preached: *'The kingdom of God has come near. Repent and believe the good news.'*

Come near is right! The good Lord's kingdom come was right pounding on the door and ready to barge in in no time flat. Which made the urgency of Ichthus's witness that the more potent, the necessity of the Church's evangelizing efforts that the more necessary. Saw the fruits of that urgency last year when Sasha's parents were mauled to death by that alien demon horde, those fallen ones tearing through Ma and Pa Pavlovich—who weren't believers. The same fate was coming for the rest of Solterra if Ichthus didn't suit up and move out to make one final eleventh-hour plea for salvation.

Only problem was, some had other ideas. Like Commander Joshie, who was swiping a playbook from some long-lost ecclesial entity of the Order of Thaddeus called SEPIO. Apparently the project had been something of a para-military arm of the organization back in the day, launching over a century ago to give some more muscular, intentional attention to defending the Christian faith in the face of growing hostility during the 20th and 21st centuries. But then there had been trouble, the group going rogue and later disappearing altogether, as these things seemed to go.

Now they'd been resurrected a year ago, going on a

crusade across Solterra to help brothers and sisters in the faith survive the Republic's Purge campaign. Which seemed to conflict with Scripture's teachings about vengeance being the Lord's. Although Kareema had schooled them that the Knights Templar Christian Order arose precisely to attend to the same matters as SEPIO during these dark times, protecting Christian pilgrims from the Mohammedan hordes. SEPIO was those Templars rising for a new millennium.

Didn't know what to make of it all, what to make of a resurgent SEPIO, not in the slightest. The prideful side of Ford was irritated to beat the band the new kid on the block was swaggering onto his turf. The more Christian side of him was unnerved by division and discord and a rogue leader of rogue Christians exacting revenge. Didn't seem right. Didn't seem at all what Ichthus stood for.

And yet...part of him was conflicted. He understood more than most the power of the Republic—the power of the Purge to rid Solterra of Unfits, and using truly medieval means. Wasn't Master of the Order like Alexander was, who was responsible for caretaking the once-for-all faith entrusted to God's holy people by Christ himself. But Ford had been chief of Ministerium operations for a spell when it was still functioning, organizing their response to the Republic's rising threat against the Church. Now they were in the middle of an apocalypse, with the Republic rounding up Christians, so he understood the impulse for muscular defense.

Especially since only one more trumpet was left until the bowls of judgment tipped over. One more breath away from the Antichrist storming onto the stage all proper like after that wackadoodle Apollos Nicolai announced the arrival of the Authority, his mug flashing across the Solterran sky like Big Brother himself from that authoritarian rag that had scared him crapless as a teenager. That's right, *Nineteen Eighty-Four.*

Gave Georgie Orwell a run for his money, that's for darn tootin'!

All of it was a big ball of ugly confusion. The past year made it all the more confusing with Commander Joshie and his tattooed band of Christian crusader Resisters waging war against the Republic for the sake of the Church's persecuted, dying brothers and sisters. Father Jim had said it wasn't the way of Ichthus, a Resistance. Instead it was as a Remnant, preserved during this time by the Holy Spirit and Christ himself to offer the world one last chance before all hell broke loose.

Ford leaned back and closed his eyes. Resistance or Remnant. Which side of the coin was he on? Which was he fighting for?

A *bring-brong* suddenly sounded from the dashboard, one of those irritating indicator lights indicating, well, something of indication he had no patience for. His feet were barking something fierce, muscles he didn't even know he had ached to beat the band, and he needed a dose of pineal-gland love with some melatonin giving him juice for dreamland. Jin could handle the fish for a spell until he—

"Uh, Commander Ford..."

Ford huffed a sigh, not only at that silliness Jin insisted on calling him, but also at the disturbance. Couldn't a man catch some Zs for one second without—

That *bring-brong* turned into an ornery *honkity-honk* now that meant nothing good.

Snapping his eyes open, he went to ask what the hot Hades all the ruckus was about when his peepers peeped the problem straight away.

A jumbo cherry was racing across their radar, indicating trouble.

Republic-size trouble.

He scrambled for the display panel, his ticker skipping a beat before lurching into action at the pulsing orb.

"Is that what I think it is?" Luciana Jane asked, voicing his same question from the co-pilot's chair.

Jin nodded. "By every indication, it's an Enforcer Stingray."

The cranky alarm caught the attention of the rest of the hydrocraft now, the slow gait of interested boots clomping his way.

"Kill that, would ya?" Ford commanded. "Kill our headlights, too, and the engines."

Jin complied, the fish's lights and hums winding down to zero, as well as that blasted alarm that meant nothing good.

"Was I hearing Stingray?" Nia said from behind.

Ford followed the cherry still roaming out there somewhere, about a klick ahead. "Yeah, that's right."

"Between us and Blake Ridge?"

Didn't answer her; didn't need to. Was more a stark observation than a question, one that didn't bode well for them or Blake Ridge, or Phoenix One or whatever.

Alexander came up to his side, joined by Rebekah Kony. He asked, "What's a Stingray doing in these parts?"

She hummed in agreement. "Cannot be jolly well good, that's for certain."

Ford shook his head. Good question; and no it wasn't.

He answered, "Don't know, homefry, but I aim to find out. Hold on tight."

"What are you going to do?" Alexander asked.

Ford asked Lucy for her seat; she gladly complied and scooted behind Jin. He plopped down and grabbed hold of a dual-control stick that was divided in halves, both ends operating independently, and eying the radar for the right moment to act.

"Track down his ass, that's what I'm going to do. Then fry it with bacon grease. Alright, punch it, Jin."

"But—"

Ford waved a dismissive hand, punching the display board to switch the controls to his station just as Jin cranked the engines to full. Rebekah started praying in her Alkebulanan tongue from the former African continent. Good idea.

He sent up his own prayer.

Then banked right, aiming straight for the Republic fish, head-on.

"Huh, now this is odd…" Jin trailed off, leaning toward his dashboard with a furrowed brow.

Ford frowned, swiping at a line of sweat beading at his forehead. "Huh and odd are not two words I'm interested in hearing right now, Jin."

He cleared his throat. "Sorry, sir."

"And stop with the sir nonsense. You make me feel old."

"You *are* old, cowboy," Nia said from behind. "Now what are you saying is odd?"

Old? Who's talking!

That's what he wanted to retort, but didn't. "What she said."

Jin answered, "A preliminary scan shows no lifeforms on board."

"That is not being odd," Nia dismissed. "Surely an AI humanoid is operating the hydrocraft."

"That's the thing. I show neither living nor non-living entities. Nothing but the craft."

"What, like a decoy?" Alexander asked.

The thought grabbed Ford by the scruff of the neck and didn't let go. Supposed that was possible, something set on auto.

He glanced at the dashboard again, the cherry weaving back and forth in a consistent pattern.

Too consistent for his liking.

But they were reaching the Stingray's operating zone in...

Three. Two. One—

A pair of red eyes suddenly sliced through the darkened abyss, spaced apart with charcoal skin and a pair of fins and a tail rising from the backside that took aim with menacing purpose.

Right before the dang thing jerked to a halt, stopping its course and pivoting a new way in the water.

Their way!

The water suddenly glowed a hot orange—which meant only one thing.

The hydrocraft was getting ready for its ultimate weapon of PSV destruction. The stinging Raycannon that was as potent as the Destroyer variety on land. Would right vaporize them into shattered pieces littering the ocean floor in no time flat!

Ford grinned, his heart pounding a mean beat and head blooming with a mixture of panic and bravado that might get them all killed.

Because he had other plans for the Republic.

Yanking the stick again and throwing the other one forward, he zoomed past the hydrocraft by a hair just as it let loose a bolting arsenal of hot orange light.

A shot of fire blasted past the windshield, the heat of it boiling the water as it streaked past. A few beats and a rocky cliff rumbled with a shattering explosion at their stern.

Which gave Ford the opening he needed to bring their PSV around with a wicked swing—their own personal submergence vehicle turning on a dime at the nose while the backside sliced through the water.

The Stingray didn't see it coming. Or didn't bother, because it just sat there like a dumb duck.

Or smart decoy, as Alexander had said.

The thought niggled the back of his lizard brain, the one that had kept his ancestors from being eaten alive by saber-toothed tigers and rammed up the tailpipe by mastodons.

Couldn't worry about that now. All that mattered was saving their own tailpipes in...

Three. Two. One—

With a *one-two* punch, he let loose his own bolting surprise—a pair of old-school missiles leftover from before the Reckoning he had outfitted on their fish.

It was over, just like that.

One skidded across the surface, an unlucky shot Ford cursed.

The other was a different story, the cannon ball connecting in spades and exploding in a fiery *thwump* that sent the Legion fish to Davy Jones's locker in no time flat.

Ford smacked his hands together and threw up a Noramericana "Yee-haw!" for good measure, then engaged the autopilot again to bring 'er home to their outpost roost.

Alexander sighed and sat down. "Nice one, John Mark."

"Yes, way to be going!" Sasha added, throwing in a whistle for good measure.

Nia complained, "I am not sure that was being a good idea, cowboy."

Ford stretched back in his chair and furrowed his brow. "Why not? Scored one for the team and took out the enemy. What's not to like?"

"You should be asking yourself why a Stingray was swimming in these parts, not gloating over your win."

Reeves added, "And so far from any port or deep sea submergence vehicle? Doesn't sit right."

Ford scoffed and shook his head, but that part of the back of his lizard brain flared up again. Because if he listened to that part, the one that had not only saved his ancestors' backsides but his own a time or twelve, then he'd have to admit the obvious.

And the uncomfortable.

No, it didn't sit right.

Sitting up and leaning on the dashboard, Ford asked, "Jin, scan for DSVs. Anything big enough to hold that downed puppy in its docking bay."

The man did his thing on the display board, the seconds ticking into a pair of minutes.

"Nothing, command—erm, I mean, nothing, Ford."

Ford leaned back. "See. You're worrying about nothing."

"No, I am not," Nia said. "Because the question is still remaining: Why was a lone Stingray roaming these parts within shooting distance of Phoenix One?"

The question hit him between the eyeballs. Hadn't considered that.

An indicator light announced their arrival, the autopilot winding down as they crested a ridge leading to home sweet home.

Except...

Something wasn't right.

Ford caught his breath at what his peepers peeped through the darkened maw of ocean blackness outside, barely illuminated by their headlights—which should have been joined by dozens more.

A no-go on that front, which wasn't all of what his peepers peeped.

Not only were there no headlamps from multiple other hydrocrafts, the normal glow of windows lit from inside the outpost was zilcho-rama. Should have been two rings of white lights indicating a large circular structure, with another thicker set at the center looking like windows peering out into the ocean depths.

A no-go on that front either. Just an all-consuming darkness that didn't bode well.

"I am not understanding," Sasha said. "Where is the outpost being?"

"Jin, flip on the high-beams, would you?" Ford asked.

He did, the PSVs headlights casting a stronger white glow into the darkness and flashing against the massive steel structure the size of a Noramericana sports stadium. But again, another set of orbs ringed by lights on the outer edges should be coming into focus. Smaller pods than the main hub connected by corridors.

And actually...

"Shucky ducky!" Ford said, leaping from his seat.

"I am seeing it too," Nia gasped. "*Bozhe moy...*"

A slick fluid trailed the bottom of the outpost, joined by bubbles flooding from a gaping wound in the side of the Resistance deep sea submergence station. Acrid black smoke bloomed from the midst of those bubbles too, which Ford didn't even think possible that far down in the ocean.

What was clear as the nose on his face was clear to the rest.

The worm had turned something fierce. Phoenix One had been attacked.

Which left one question: Were there any survivors?

CHAPTER 10

Alexander paced the cabin as Jin Sung and John Mark Ford navigated their hydrocraft to port—which was quite the undertaking, because all the normal trappings of the deep sea submergence station were completely inoperable.

No string of blinking red lights to guide them into the belly of the beast. No illuminated walls to guide them forward, though they did press in against their hydrocraft. No robotic arms to guide them to safe harbor. They were all on their own.

He shuffled back to one of the seats, sinking down and closing his eyes. Worry wormed through him as the seconds ticked by. Not only that they would bang into the side and it would be all over, a quick trip to the bottom of the ocean. More that something had gone horribly wrong inside Phoenix One—with deadly consequences for those he cared about.

The thought sent his stomach sinking with anxious dread for one in particular: Father Jim.

So he sent up a prayer for help: *Heavenly Father, you have promised that if anybody lacks wisdom, we should ask you, and you will give us that wisdom. I ask you for wisdom and guid-*

ance during our hour of need. O God, make haste to help us, make speed to save us!

Crossing himself—two fingers from forehead to middle chest, then from left to right shoulders—he added for good measure: *Lord Jesus Christ, Son of God, Father Jim better be alright...*

They finally emerged into a larger docking bay, a massive circular pool with a smattering of parked personal submergence vehicles, larger and smaller hydrocrafts than their own, docked with mysterious purpose. All still, all quiet, with no signs of life.

An apt description that may be closer to the mark than Alexander feared.

Ford eased their yellow personal submergence vehicle toward an open bay, which was about as ominous as the ride inside. No blinking green to indicate safe passage, and no mechanical arm to draw them into position. At least there was a pulsing orange glow at the surface, a beacon offering a modicum of hope, so there was that.

A series of thuds and clangs resounded inside, throwing up not a small amount of anxiety. Soon the docking sequence was complete between a pair of hydrocrafts—

Alexander gasped. Were they leaking fuel? And those orange lights were clearer now as they undulated through the waving water just above the surface, mercilessly close to the PSVs they were sandwiched between.

"Are those being flames?" Sasha squeaked, voicing what he feared.

A dark, inky blackness above the water obscured any sense of things. But they had made it. Though, into what manner of hell, it wasn't clear.

Ford was the first to shove out into the docking bay. Nia went to join him then Alexander shoved third, shuffling up the ladder with a clomping clang—instant recognition at just what manner of hell awaited them.

It was fire, alright, coming from the hatch of one of the adjacent hydrocrafts, fingering flames riding high, the inside smoldering with a clinging, cloying acrid smoke billowing high into the massive bay and hovering in a cloud high above.

Ford called down for their own onboard emergency extinguisher. Reeves handed it off to Nia, and she handed it up and out to Ford who hopped onto the craft. Coughing and gagging, he aimed the emergency measure down into the flames and fired away. Reeves hustled up top and leaped to help him while Alexander ushered the others to safe harbor down the steel boardwalk to the far end of the dock.

"Can you manage?" he said to their rescued Unfit, offering him an arm.

The man took it with a smiling nod, and the pair limped along after the others to a steel wall matching the smokey color, more from aged wear than anything but probably from the collecting soot cast about the massive room. Which was oddly abandoned, silent and still. No trace of anyone in the massive circular docking bay, neither coming nor going.

Ford and Reeves managed to get the fire under control, emptying the extinguisher down inside before closing the top hatch tight. Ford returned to their own personal submergence vehicle and disappeared down inside for a spell, while Reeves went to join the others.

A silence settled where the hissing of emergent propellant had been, the lapping of water the only soundtrack to fill the void. Even the expected HVAC hum was nowhere to be found. The smoky haze darkened and obscured the massive space, compounded by the stench of burning chemicals and compounds joined by the steely, oily scent of the deeps sea submergence station. A lone emergency light cast an eerie yellow hue about, but it made barely any purchase.

But they were together, safe and accounted for. What they would discover deeper inside...

The thought sent a panic racing through Alexander. He wanted to get to it—needed to get to it, to make sure Father Jim was safe, along with the others entrusted to his care at the Order of Thaddeus's forward outpost.

"*Oo-wee,*" cried Reeves, sauntering over. "That was crazier than a one armed midget."

"I think the word you're going for," Ford corrected from behind, a Neutralizer and large bags slung around each shoulder, "is little person, but you're right. Quite the welcome back to home sweet home."

"My question is being," Sasha said, eyes darting about, "why was there nobody putting the fire out?"

"*Da.* Why was it left smoldering?" Nia nodded, the purply head of her Scythe casting an eerie glow across the docking bay and water now.

"Quite dangerous I should think," Lucy added in her Valley Girl drawl from the former American West Coast.

"I was thinking the same," added Rebekah with a cough. She brought her arms around her chest and rubbed them. "There's a chill to the air. And not just from the lowered temperature. It feels....crazy."

C-r-r-razy. Loved those rolling Rs of hers. It brought a smile to Alexander's face in an otherwise crazy—*c-r-r-razy*—situation. The lone Stingray patrolling the waters outside the deep sea submergence station; the on-fire personal submergence vehicle; the feeling of abandonment permeating the air, the lapping water making it all the worse accenting the otherwise silent station.

"Think fast," Ford said, tossing him a Neutralizer.

Alexander grabbed it with one hand, his stomach flipping at the thought he'd need it. But with the flaming PSV and darkened station, who knew what they'd find.

Ford had another two Neutralizers in his bag left from their flight from the reprogramming camp. Reeves took one and he gave the other to Sasha, along with passing out enough flashlights for everyone but their rescue.

Alexander clicked his on, other white LED beams slicing through the smoggy haze like lighted sabers and casting the domed space in an eeriness that sent a chill skittering down his spine.

A door stood closed tight at the end of the long steel boardwalk, guarding a corridor that led from the docking bay pod into the main station. Alexander made for it, hunching and holding his breath in the hazy smog as he followed the curved perimeter of the massive bay. Time for answers. The others followed in silence, their boots clanging with the same hustling intent.

Reaching the entrance to the main station, the door stood closed, normally opening on approach but failing to deliver. Alexander looked to Ford for help.

He approached a security panel mounted next to it, the digital controls darkened. He tapped its face.

Nothing.

Hitting it with his fist offered the same response.

Nia snorted a smirking chuckle. "Why don't you offer it that thick skull of yours. Perhaps it will be working this time."

He flashed her not-now eyes and slid a blade from his boot. Jamming it at the bottom of the panel, he wrenched it up and popped its face. Wires and a circuit board with tiny transistors greeted them, digital organs for the door.

Ford fiddled a bit, cursing under his breath like the sailor he'd just been, until there was a faint click inside the wall, and the door unlatched for them.

Shoving his knife back in his boot, he grinned widely and tapped his head. "Offered it that thick skull of mine."

Nia laughed. "*Otlichno,* cowboy. Very good, indeed."

Her enthusiasm was short-lived.

Ford opened the door, and in came a rushing hot breath of stale, staid station air—with a stench that nearly bowled her and the others over.

Alexander threw his arm across his face, groaning as others did the same. His stomach clenched and bile rose high with a tangy tickle at the back of his throat.

It was the stench of battle, of death.

The thought of both sent him shoving past Ford and into the breach chasing for confirmation. It didn't take long to find his answers.

Dim yellow emergency lights pulsed above—with damage, with warning—and frayed wires sparked from the ceiling, with flickering flames smoldering along the wall and farther on. The corridors of cold, dark steel bore humid, stale air smelling of oil and over-ripened bodies, along with the stench of wickedness that had washed over them upon entering. Casting his light down the corridor, Alexander glimpsed mangled metal and piles of debris strewn along the narrow stretch.

"What was happening here?" Nia asked from behind, voice betraying worry.

"It don't look good," Reeves said, "whatever happened."

"Like the Reckoning all over again," Ford said lowly, referencing the great war that had roiled the globe for decades, brother and sister pitted against one another, the death and destruction far-reaching.

A sudden panic seized Alexander, recognition blooming

that whatever happened had threatened the occupants of the deep sea submergence station. That Father Jim and Mama Mara and the rest had been under assault—that their very lives had been threatened.

Or worse...

Alexander took off, Ford calling after him, when—

Something snagged his foot, and he stumbled to the floor.

Landing in a heaping pile of something, firm yet cushioned but reeking of charred beef and vinegar.

"*Bozhe moy,*" Sasha squeaked from behind.

It wasn't clear why, his attention paid to a lancing pain in his ankle from the stumble and the effort climbing off the pile he'd stumbled upon.

Until it was clear!

A young man's face stared back at him with pleading surrender, bruised and bloodied, its brown eyes open with terror but vacant of any life, a swollen gray tongue protruding and lolling lazily to the side. Thick, dried blood matted his hair, and someone else lay slumped next to him, though their face was mercilessly shielded by a curtain of blond hair similarly colored crimson with injury.

It was only then that it dawned on Alexander: The pile he'd stumbled into was a pile of corpses!

Those smells of charred beef and vinegar took on new meaning...

Crying out, he scrambled from the pile, throat growing thick with terror and breaths hard to come by. He slid to the floor and skittered back, scrambling to stand while heaving a desperate, stabilizing breath, but finding it difficult to do either.

Strong hands grabbed him under his arms and drew him to his feet.

"Calm down, homefry," Ford shouted in his face. "You're alright! You're alright!"

Alexander gawped for breath, eyes darting around and the implications of that corridor spinning out all sorts of scenarios while his mouth opened and closed uselessly.

"Breathe, son. Breathe..." Ford said again, less shouty and more brotherly.

They locked eyes, and he managed one good lungful of air. The out-breath stumbled over his thick throat, along with a declaration he didn't want to voice but had to: "He's gone!"

Ford said nothing, eyes darting to the left and right before locking back into Alexander's.

"Listen to me, homefry. We'll find him. We'll get him."

"But—" He heaved a breath for another round of panicked protest when a voice cut through the hellish corridor.

"*'Whoever dwells in the shelter of the Most High will rest in the shadow of the Almighty. I will say of the Lord, 'He is my refuge and my fortress, my God, in whom I trust.'*'"

It was Rebekah, those Rs of hers rolling off her tongue with a groundedness that brought his head soaring with fleeing fright straight back to earth, back to reality.

"*'Surely he will save you from the fowler's snare and from the deadly pestilence. He will cover you with his feathers, and under his wings you will find refuge; his faithfulness will be your shield and rampart.'*'"

She was reciting Psalm 91, with eyes closed and the faintest of smiles playing across her face.

"*'You will not fear the terror of night,'*" Rebekah went on, her voice celestial, angelic, "*'nor the arrow that flies by day, nor the pestilence that stalks in the darkness, nor the plague that destroys at midday.'*'"

"*'A thousand may fall at your side,'*" Lucy joined in, smiling and squeezing her teammate's arm, "*'ten thousand at your right hand, but it will not come near you. You will only observe with your eyes and see the punishment of the wicked.'"*

And now Ford, which was surprising: *"'If you say, 'The Lord is my refuge,' and you make the Most High your dwelling, no harm will overtake you, no disaster will come near your tent.'"*

The man threw an arm around Alexander's shoulder and gave it a squeeze, an appreciative act of solidarity.

Reeves added his own voice, joined by Ford again with the other women. By the final refrain, Alexander's eyes were spilling over with emotion. Both from the balm offered in the psalm's reading as well as the gift of solidarity in his loss.

Swallowing back his emotion, he joined the group in the final stanza:

> *"Because he loves me," says the Lord, "I will*
> *rescue him;*
> *I will protect him, for he acknowledges my*
> *name.*
> *He will call on me, and I will answer him;*
> *I will be with him in trouble,*
> *I will deliver him and honor him.*
> *With long life I will satisfy him*
> *and show him my salvation."*

"Thank you, Rebekah," Lucy said softly, voicing the collective thanksgiving for her solemn declaration.

Alexander wanted to voice the same thanksgiving, grateful for the theological reminder of the Lord's sovereign, saving protection to reorient his heart around his hope. But he couldn't. Throat was too constricted with emotion knowing something had happened to Father Jim—perhaps snatched and stuffed away in the same godforsaken structure they had just escaped from, enduring Lord only knew what.

Or worse...

The next hour felt like a lifetime had passed, the group scattering to scope out the entirety of the outpost in search of survivors. They didn't find any, the destruction and death totalizing, finalizing. Perhaps the modicum of grace and mercy came in the body count: a third of the station was missing, around thirty personnel. Near as they could tell, most of those entrusted to Alexander, the Remnant of the Order of Thaddeus, and support staff—along with one other dear soul.

Father James Ferraro.

He was missing, which meant both that he wasn't dead, but it also meant he had probably been captured. A few escape hatches had been jettisoned, with a few more remaining elsewhere. So, there was the slim hope he had escaped. But with most of the station taken out of commission, their resources were limited in tracking him and the others.

After combing the steely corridors of Phoenix One, and the outer residential pods, the group convened at the main bridge. It was a sad affair, the dark steel matching the outer corridor made all the worse by lack of lighting aside from Junia's Scythe and a dim yellow emergency light at the corner. A raised platform stood at the center of the chamber, a sort of command dais for the outpost's operations. Arrayed along the outer circular walls, broadcaster displays and control panels patiently awaited instructions. All dead and dark, echoing the station itself.

The minutes ticked by, the room not knowing what to do next.

Sighing, Alexander batted away emotion at his eyes and stared off to catch his breath—when he noticed something underneath Sasha's arm.

A workstation laptop.

"Where'd you get that?"

Sasha followed his mate's trembling finger, his gaze landing at his armpit.

"*Kakiye*, this?"

Alexander rushed to his side and slid it out, Sasha grunting a "Hey!" complaint and holding on tight. Then: "Finders keepers!"

"Where?" he demanded, letting go.

Sasha shrugged, shoving it back under his arm. "It was the one from reprogramming camp. I was taking it from the torture—"

"Open. Now."

"Are you being crazy in the head? The Republic will surely be tracking—"

Alexander cut him off: "Then work your DiviNet magic and shield or cloak or—"

"Mask, that is what you are meaning," Sasha interrupted.

He waved a dismissive hand. "Mask, whatever. Just hide our location and our search."

"Our search, homefry?" Ford asked with furrowed brow.

Alexander replied, "You think there's a good chance they've got a database of all the Unfits locked away in all of the Republic's reprogramming camps in that device?"

His eyes suddenly went wide, joined by an equally wide grin.

"I like the way you think!" Ford shook an approving finger before turning to Sasha. "What are you waiting for, doc, you heard the man. Get our location cloaked—"

"*Masked,*" Sasha said with a sigh, already engaging the workstation device and giving his head a shake while muttering something in his homeland tongue.

His fingers raced across the display board, the device a

newer model with two displays sandwiched together. Didn't take long before Sasha whistled and folded his arms. "*Khorosho*. Piece of pie."

"I think you mean piece of cake," Ford corrected.

"*Nyet*. Pie. I am hating cake."

"So you're in?" Alexander said, peering over his shoulder at the display lined with rows of names and numbers, maybe serials given to the prisoners, along with what looked like camp names and cell block numbers.

"*Da*. We are being—"

The screen suddenly shuddered to a light grey background.

"What just happened?"

"I am not knowing!"

Ford said, "Don't you dare tell me your cloak didn't work!"

"Mask, I am saying. *Mask!* And no, it is not being that."

Sasha pointed at the display as a familiar logo appeared against the light gray background. A spinning globe of the Pangea supercontinent from Earth's ancient past, surrounded by olive branches.

The logo of Solterra Republic, followed by the words OneWorld News.

The room settled into an expectant silence. When the Republic had an announcement, there was no getting around paying attention.

What they announced wasn't possible.

Flat wasn't possible.

CHAPTER 11

Were Ford's peepers peeping the bulletin announcement right?

"It is being a shelter-in-place order," Nia said from over his shoulder.

Yup, it was. But it was more than that.

"Why?" Alexander asked, coming in for his own viewing.

Ford knew exactly why. It was something the Republic did when there was an emergency of worldwide significance. Sort of like those tales he'd heard told back home on that family peanut farm of his, the ones passed along through a few generations of Fords who talked about flattening the curve when some respiratory virus escaped some lab in Asiatica. Apparently, some yahoos thought you could stop the spread with a fifteen-day pause on life, not at all understanding the cat had gotten out of the bag something like eight to nine months prior, the novel virus already circulating as later studies had shown. And even when some nations failed miserably at containing the windblown virus, they doubled down on containment lockdown strategies that did bo diddly.

Like before, when those governments had locked down with all seriousness, same for Solterra Republic. Couldn't recall the last time the Regis, Lucius Severus, ordered such a thing. But every single member of the polis knew that when that time came, the Patron was dead serious. And deadly serious, employing all manner of means to ensure compliance. With Tracker drones patrolling the skies and Destroyers roaming the streets, joined by a platoon of Enforcers with each patrol, combined with DiviNet itself keeping tabs on people's roaming about, with a social credit system thrown into the mix to encourage snitching on your neighbors—*'For Humanity!'* of course, as the polis was prone to parrot the regime's slogan of solidarity.

But, as Alexander had asked, why? Must be serious for the Patron to—

"That's why," Sasha said with interruption, another bulletin coming across the wire that announced the craziest thing Ford had heard in ages, perhaps his entire life.

Had to back himself up completely, because it wasn't the Patron instituting anything. Neither the bulletins nor the lockdown.

For the simple fact the Patron was dead.

Lucius Severus, Regis of Solterra Republic had bit the dust.

"*Bozhe moy...*" Nia said on a disbelieving breath. "The Patron, *mertvykh?*"

Which Ford took as exactly what he himself had read from the bulletin. The Patron had kicked the bucket.

Reeves said, "How is that even possible?"

"More importantly," Alexander said, voice low and grave, "what does that mean?"

Ford glanced over his shoulder, throwing him eyes that told him he was picking up what he was putting down.

What did it mean? Not only for the Republic but for Ichthus. For them.

And the folks who'd been captured and hauled away by the Legion in a raid he still couldn't believe had gone down.

The room fell silent, no HVAC hum filling the void. A bead of sweat at his forehead gave way to a trickle of perspiration from his temple down past his ear from the stifling, suffocating heat of the joint. A memory surfaced in the quietness of the moment, of him and the Patron.

He had been hand selected from his unit of Purifiers when the Patron visited the reprogramming camp he'd been assigned to while still working for the Legion. Never planned on becoming a Legion rockstar, just sort of happened. Maybe it was when Pops had passed at the borderland between Noramericana and Americana during the Second Civil War, his love for the man who had never lived up to his natural calling transferring to the Republic, to the Patron who had become the benefactor of Solterra—gifting the world peace, prosperity and progress. Didn't have a lickin' clue.

All Ford knew was that the higher he rose up the Legion ranks, and the deeper he went in his devotion to the Patron, the more success he got. And by success, he meant not only rounding Unfits up like cattle, snatching the Republic's detritus from the highways and byways of life. But also reprogramming them to submit to all the Republic stood for—*For Humanity!*

So, when Lucius Severus came visiting that one April afternoon, and a brilliant rainbow spread across a just-cleared sky after a morning shower in Cascadia, it was like he'd been ushered into the presence of the Messiah himself!

Remembered him as a slight man with soft features who commanded the world with an iron fist. Chosen as the first ruler of Solterra by the delegates of the Republic's regional representatives, he quickly consolidated power. From what the rumor mill churned out, he'd used the leverage he had amassed against a majority of the world's delegates through his network of enterprises spanning the globe. Everything from rare minerals to household goods, social media platforms to casinos and hotels, the man had built for himself an empire to rival ancient Rome itself.

An aspiration that was probably baked into his DNA from generations past, his last name one of the former Roman emperors from yore, Septimius Severus. Boy, would his grand-pappy however-many-times-removed be proud. The Patron ruled Rome's ultramodern incarnation as its titular head—which was a bit odd, because this was Solterra's original vision.

In the aftermath of the Reckoning—the great day of judgment after a century of environmental upheaval brought on by the created order groaning under the weight of climate change, triggering rising seas and extreme drought, bringing coastal cities to their knees; of economic collapse and conflict from the extreme disparities thanks to the ruling 1% that rivaled Israel's cows of Bashan condemned by the prophet Amos; of political chaos brought on by migration patterns and changing demographics across the Western world, spikes in regional conflicts from religious and ideological differences across the Eastern world, and civil wars erupting worldwide from social alienation and nationalism stoked by racial preju-dice on top of the collapse of major centers of power from the seas drowning coastal capitals—all of what the Reckoning sought to reconcile was supposed to usher in the triumphant age of peace, prosperity, and progress the world had been waiting for centuries. With the head honcho Severus riding in on a white horse to hand deliver the goods.

That was the plan, anyway. Except...

It didn't quite turn out that way. Yes, for the first few years, there was the sort of worldwide reigning democracy that American political dynasties had tried to forge through misadventures from North Korea to Vietnam, Afghanistan to Iraq, and on to virtually every nation-state on the former African continent. The citizens of the world had truly united through fair and free elections, through the rule of law dispensed by duly elected officials representing the reconstituted nation-states that formed Solterra, assembling in the Azores to commence the fiction that is government. The Capitolium on that utopian island had witnessed a level of cooperation not seen from the world, all under the careful guidance of their Dear Leader, the Republic's Regis, Lucius Severus. Peace, prosperity, and progress truly had taken hold of the world.

For a time.

Ford snorted a laugh at the notion, given all that had unfolded the past few decades since the turn of the 22nd century.

Droughts continued to persist, resulting in regional food shortages. Water became scarce, so that it was being traded like a commodity with prices rivaling precious metals. Both had the inevitable effect of sparking localized conflicts that burst into flames that raged across sections of sub-Saharan Alkebulana, Noramericana and central Europa, and even across much of the more economically stable Asiatica.

Although the Republic had worked wonders in the early years stamping out radical ideologies and associations across the world, all while preaching the doctrines of freedom of speech and assembly trumpeted by ultramodern liberal democracy, some of the militant nationalism and religious fanaticism began cropping back up through terror attacks targeting the government. So the promised peace, prosperity, and progress was threatened.

Which the Patron could not tolerate. And neither could

the citizens of the one-world government. They had paid the price for too long, going generations deep, to tolerate any hint of the poverty and conflict and regression that had consumed the world.

So the Regis took action, cajoling the Republic Senate to authorize a seizure of private enterprises, exerting control over the media and internet, and curtailing personal liberties—the Patron proclaiming with straight-face insistence that it was all done *'For Humanity!'* of course. Which Ford found just laughable. Nothing was ever done for the polis, but for the Senators and their cronies sitting fat and happy and pretty in their secluded Capitolium up in the Azores—that dollop of island dirt in the middle of the Atlantic Ocean off the coast of Portugal.

Anyhoo, surprisingly (or perhaps not, depending on your view of human nature) a supermajority of the polis agreed that a strong, iron grip was needed to set the world to rights, willingly acquiescing to the demand to hand over their rights in the interest of security. Openhandedly, in fact, offering liberty in exchange for the safety of knowing their peace and prosperity and progress would be secured by the technocrats stuffed away in that island compound.

Yet Benny Franklin, one of the famous founders of the former United States of America, got it right: *'Those who would give up essential Liberty, to purchase a little temporary Safety, deserve neither Liberty nor Safety.'* Not a bad aphorism, even if he was an Americana Yank!

Either way, the entire ultramodern world had been orchestrated by Lucius Severus, affectionately known as the Patron—their voice, their Regis. Their Prime Leader.

And now he was dead?

How that happened—to a guy in his prime of life, barely fifty—none of it computed, not in the slightest.

More importantly, as Alexander had wondered: What did it mean?

"Apollos..."

The voice jolted him from his contemplation. It was Alex. He spun around to inquire.

"Come again, homefry?"

The man was staring off into one of the steel walls of the station's bridge, stroking his stubbled chin.

"Uh, Alex?" he tried again. "Whatcha going on about?"

Alexander startled, taking a breath and folding his arms. "Just recalling something he said a year ago, from the moonlit sky."

The memory of that cray-cray Europan from Germania ran hot and searing in Ford's noggin. Never did catch how he pulled it off, his mug projected across the sky like that for all to see—whether from some ultramodern Solterra ingenuity or some creepy-ass demonic magic, he flat didn't have a clue.

Either way, he remembered exactly what the man had said.

The Scarlet One, Apollos had said he was, hellbent on destroying the Church and feasting upon the blood of the martyrs. Then the kicker: *'The saints of Ichthus shall tremble before my might and bow before my glory!'*

Reminded Ford of the B movie horror flicks he'd watch on WeFlix growing up, the streaming service on WeNet before it was gobbled up by the Republic and assumed into the Solterra-wide network known as DiviNet. Sounded like a laughable campy exorcism movie—except it was anything but fun and games.

A shiver skated down his spine at the recollection. Alex had explained that an evil had risen upon Earth. Definitely made sense for what Comrade Crazy Pants said next: *'I have now risen upon the earth in the fullness of humanity,'* Apollos went on, that cray-cray Voice growing in strength and menacing purpose, *'and I will not be denied my right to rule! I am the Almighty Cosmic Force, and thou shalt deny me naught! I will no longer lie below, but will ascend on high!'*

Wait, wait, there was more!

That cray-cray Voice of Apollos, guttural and growly, boomed with more clarity and conviction about the blessings of Ha-Satan falling upon Solterra. And how, *'in the full authority and enlightenment of the Angel of Light'* Apollos meant to *'topple the Church's idol and dance upon their rubble!'* Even encouraged the polis to take matters into their own hands. Because, according to Comrade Crazy Pants, they'd been *'freed from the Most High. And whom the Beast has set free, is free indeed!'*

Ford's gut felt like rhinos were doing the conga line, his stomach churning with wicked dread at what this turn of things meant. Because without the Regis, without Solterra's Patron, who was going to lead the Republic?

"Apollos promised," Alexander said, shaking him from his memories, "to have more to say in the coming days, and then signed off his message with the triple Republic promise, *'in the Name of the Dragon, the Beast, and the Prophet,'* the Satanic Trinity of the Book of Revelation."

His face grew both pale and dark at the same time—skin went ashen some, shadows grew under narrowing eyes and a down-turned brow.

He continued, "The man was clearly possessed by some unholy power. The Two Witnesses, sent by Christ himself to evangelize the world and call Solterra to repentance, had confirmed the truth of what I instinctively knew: the Antichrist was rising."

"I recall that conversation," Rebekah said on a shaky breath. "It was most unnerving."

"As do I," Lucy agreed. "But that was over a year ago, and Apollos hasn't been heard from since."

"Until now..." Ford said.

The comment settled in the room with a hushing thud, the streaming bulletins from the Republic the only thing stirring.

"What are you saying?" Nia said. "That Apollos Nicolai is being the Antichrist?"

Now that was crazier than a one-legged mule! He stood and made for a mini bar across the bridge in search of a stiff one.

"It makes sense, doesn't it?" Alexander replied. "Apollos was used as an instrument to dismantle Ichthus—the very teachings of the Church, for goodness sake! Look at the lengths he went last year, time traveling to the Council of Nicaea in an attempt to literally blow up its proceedings."

"Time travel?" It was the new guy, the man of mystery stirring from the corner, words accented by a strong lilt. Who was this guy, anyway?

Ford finished pouring his drink, a nice whiskey from Britannia, and sauntered back to his chair.

"Don't worry about it, partner," he replied, patting the man's shoulders. "That'll take a whole bottle of stronger stuff than I've got to explain."

He settled down and threw back a swig, the warm, smokey caramel liquid burning his throat and hitting his stomach hard. Just what the doc ordered.

"I'm with Junia, doesn't make sense."

"But don't you see?" Alexander said, waving his arms around. "He's been at the center of the entire plot to dismantle and destroy Ichthus from the start! Forming Panligo as a direct assault against the Church."

"So has your father," Ford said, taking another swig.

He flinched, the mention of his old man clearly smarting.

Ford quickly followed up with: "Didn't mean nothing by that other than the truth of the matter. Besides, Apollos is a religious wackadoodle with a messiah complex. Not a politician."

"But I am knowing who is," Mystery Man piped up from the shadows again. "And who is being tapped for the job."

Ford glanced at their seventh wheel.

"I don't know about you," he muttered lowly, "but I think it's high time we have a chit-chat with our stowaway."

Alexander nodded. "I agree."

"Hey, partner," Ford said. "Pull up a chair, wouldya? About time we got to know one another."

The old man sauntered over to one of the chairs at the center table, slumping back like a tired sack of bones.

Dude looked bone weary, thin and wiry with sagging skin. And yet it was clear he'd had some heft to him, some major muscle that would've put up a major fight. Maybe he had, and that's what landed him in the Republic clink.

The room waited for him to speak, everyone's mouths closed and peepers trained on their newcomer mystery man.

He took a breath, then a beat.

Then he went to spill the tea.

CHAPTER 12

GERMANIA, EUROPA.

APOLLOS NICOLAI CLOSED HIS EYES, tipped his head back, and sighed with pleasure, his head swirling with delight from the ritual, his heart thudding expectantly in his chest while his pulse raced into the gilded ceremonial vial. Opening his eyes, he eyed it resting on the white marble table, the reed protruding from his arm carefully channeling his life force out of his body and into a rising pool of crimson at the bottom.

A pleasurable sigh escaped him, both from the exhumation of his life force and at the anticipation rising inside at what it was meant to be—at the *gift* it was meant to be.

For the Voice, the Authority who had declared him to be his Chosen One, used in a ceremony stretching back millennia from an ancient entity working in the shadows of the Church's history.

He settled into the plush, gilded chair at the glass table and heaved another pleasurable sigh, the vast, bright room of white marble veined with faint gray lining the floor and walls agreeing with another echoing reply. One end of his mouth curled upward at the view of a ceiling vaulted by soaring Corinthian columns edged by gilt lines circling the white pillars like candy canes. High above, crystals clung to the corners and seams of the ceiling like clusters of grapes, a sort of celestial crown molding that refracted the light from the day with rainbow brilliance, although dimming now from recent astrological and apocalyptic shifts.

Reveling in the view, he sighed. "Like Heaven…"

He smiled knowingly at the tongue slip.

No, like the Republic of Heaven. The one that would replace that Kingdom he had known growing up, the one representative of the Nameless One whose fate had been sealed since the day he was butchered on that cross, along with all his followers.

And Apollos Nicolai would be the Prophet, the *Haruspexi* chosen by the Unseen Realm, to make it come to pass.

He smiled at the notion, his head swimming now with starry delirium from the self-exsanguination. How fitting this task had fallen in his lap, upon his shoulders, given the origin of his name.

The meaning of Apollos was clear: *Destruction*, from the ancient Greek. The origin was all-together different. Given his rearing in the Church, his two fathers having chosen it from the Bible, hoping their son would follow in the men's footsteps.

The original Apollos was found in the Book of Acts, a Jew from the ancient city of Alexandria. He closed his eyes again, recalling how the Scriptures explained the story he had memorized in his youth from just thirty years ago:

> *He was a learned man, with a thorough knowl-*
> *edge of the Scriptures. He had been*
> *instructed in the way of the Lord, and he*
> *spoke with great fervor and taught about*
> *Jesus accurately, though he knew only the*
> *baptism of John. He began to speak boldly*

in the synagogue. When Priscilla and
Aquila heard him, they invited him to their
home and explained to him the way of God
more adequately.
When Apollos wanted to go to Achaia, the
brothers and sisters encouraged him and
wrote to the disciples there to welcome
him. When he arrived, he was a great help
to those who by grace had believed. For he
vigorously refuted his Jewish opponents in
public debate, proving from the Scriptures
that Jesus was the Messiah.

A knowing laugh simmered in his chest. For while this Jewish Apollos had found his messiah in the Nameless One, *this* Apollos, the Christian one, had found his messiah in the Authority—in the Shining One, the one revealing himself in greater measure from the Unseen Realm!

Ahh, the ironies of it all, his namesake having been a reliable evangelist in the ancient city of Corinth, the Apostle Paul's first letter to that ancient Ichthus community testifying to the man's bountiful fruit of conversions.

Apollos Nicolai aimed for something far higher.

The conversion of Solterra to the Shining One and his coming reign!

The vial was nearly full now, its purity glinting in the sunlight streaming into the hall from massive open windows letting in a surprisingly warm breeze for this time of year. The air was laced with the acrid smell of woodsmoke and dead leaves, his favorite of smells.

The room itself had been apparently patterned after another that had been destroyed by an ancient enemy over a century ago, the Order of Thaddeus. His predecessor, Martin

Zarruq, had sourced the best materials the Universe had to offer, ones that had unfortunately gone by the wayside in Solterra Republic. He agreed with the old man that ancient, alchemic metals and stones were far better than the sleek, ultramodern ones of gleaming glass and polished chrome. They bespoke the original state of nature, the noble savage who was connected to the Universe in all its glory, reveling in the Force that permeated it from ages past—extending its hand in invitation to taste and see the goodness it offered.

This was a proper temple, built as a proper testament to the Universe's invitation, along with its original inhabitants— the brilliance of the gilded columns and refracting crystals only outmatched by the real center of attention: a mural of celestial beings locked in arms with recognizable figures peering down at him, witnessing his moment of self-pleasure.

The full range of scenery from across Solterra's religious landscape was depicted, beginning with the Bible: From the Garden of Eden to Abraham sacrificing Isaac on Mount Moriah, Moses parting the Red Sea to the birth of Jesus, his feeding of the five thousand miracle to his crucifixion. But then it continued on in a way the in-the-know observer would have found confusing, depicting neither Christ's resurrection nor ascension. Of course Martin had it designed that way, adding still other familiar religious depictions that would have seemed out of place in what one might have assumed was a place of Christian worship. There was Muhammad's First Revelation, the event described in Islam where the prophet was visited by the angel Jibrīl and revealed to him the beginnings of what would later become the Qur'an. And then another: a familiar depiction of Siddhartha Gautama, Buddha, sitting cross-legged in a crimson sash, one hand raised with enlightenment.

It was a magisterial depiction of the coming movement to

consolidate spiritual power, one he had been part of building years ago that culminated with Panligo—the one-world religious entity corralling Solterra's religious affections and uniting them under the singular, ancient one that had existed long before his chosen one.

Something primal, something seated at the heart of mankind, at the heart of the Universe itself that rose to challenge the Nameless One from the days of old.

Perhaps he shouldn't be too surprised of his recent ascent to his position of power, given his fascination with the alternative.

The thought brought the trace signature of a memory rushing to the fore, jolting his heart rate and sending a tingling sensation across his tongue.

It was his final year of secondary school, and he was out frolicking with his mates on Halloween. A bonfire with a case of beer thrown into the mix. It was his dark phase, when his shadow side began piquing his interest more than the light of Christ—culminating in his exaltation to his current position in life, in the Universe itself.

He smirked, the grooming so innocent, so pedestrian and provincial. A Ouija board, of all things. A perfectly coined cliché straight out of some pre-Reckoning WeFlix limited series, but that's the truth of it.

It was his girlfriend at the time who had introduced it to him. Which was ironic on so many levels.

Apollos took in a measured breath, clenching his hand into a fist, giving aid and comfort to the coiling tube channeling his life force into that vial.

It had all started innocently enough at Dalia's house. Could still see the vintage board of the Unseen Realm in his mind's eye, made of honey wood with black lettering and numbers branded into it, smelling of moth balls and a musty basement.

Apollos had been skeptical of it all, teasing her for her superstitious beliefs. The thing about that cliché was that it had worked, spelling out short answers to questions only he could have known. Had never seen anything like it, and initially chalked up the experience to the pair of joints Dalia had swiped from her brother's stash. But the more they toyed with the device over the coming months, the more Apollos wanted to plumb the depths of its secrets.

Culminating in that fateful Halloween the fall before university.

At the time, he didn't understand it all, believing it to be some sort of board game or trick of the eye. It was only later that he had understood it to be a doorway, a portal into the Unseen Realm.

Which he stepped through, willingly and with abandon.

Yes, he had grown up in Ichthus. However, he hadn't grown up in the Church. Or, at least *a* church—both fathers preferring their Christianity to be personal and freelance more than religious and institutional. He hadn't been very grounded in his faith, even though he had gone on to university to train to be a priest. More than that, he had been curious with what had occurred that evening at his girlfriend's house, which led to a sleepover.

And other things...

The pagan mixing with the primal in an unholy union that cracked a door and sparked a thirst for more.

That door was more a window into still wider and more thorough experiences. Healing crystals, books on magic at a local High Street store. He grinned at the innocence of it all.

Of course, that wasn't the entirety of it...

Apollos shook away his past and focused himself upon the

tapestry of all he was building for the Republic to unify the polis into a singular religious affection.

With him as the head, the Dark Prophet.

The Haruspexi, Great Seer to the Authority. Equal in power to the one yet coming and joined by the Shining One in a cosmic trinity rivaling the bastardized one Ichthus had trumpeted for ages.

The Antichrist was nigh, now that the Regis had been eliminated, with Apollos Nicolai at his right hand and empowered by the Shining One himself. They would be unstoppable.

The air seemed to hum with agreement as his blood continued pouring out, readying him for his offering to the Universe, the rise and fall of his chest in sync with his heart pumping his blood into the sacred vessel. Even the furniture pieces, edged in gold leafing and adding to the sense of brightness, seemed to glow especially bright in the presence of his act of letting.

His tongue began tingling now with anticipation as the ceremonial vial filled, desire welling with a climactic groan within his belly for what would come next, down below in the bowels of Panligo's sanctum, the climax to his anointing by the Authority as his emissary to Solterra Republic.

The one who would aid in the Nameless One's undoing.

There he was, sitting in the Sacradi's seat of power, readying himself for one of the most important acts he would undergo. A simple boy from a small Deutschland town no one had ever heard of.

Things have a way of working themselves out; the Universe has a way of course correcting, for which he was eternally grateful. Or at least presently so, given what he was up against.

Apollos snapped open his eyes, his head feeling suddenly faint. He eyed the gilded vial and startled. The thing was nearly filled to the brim! No wonder he was feeling it, a goodly amount of the crimson liquid having been let from his arm during his absentminded contemplation.

Grasping the slender stem with his thumb and forefinger, he pulled the long end from his arm, the centimeter worth stuck inside his vein sliding out easily. Blood seeped from the hole in his arm, but he left it. It also collected at the end of the reed, that quickening stirring again.

He eased it carefully into his mouth even as it salivated with lustful hunger, pressing the bloodied end against his tongue. The coppery sensation of old-world pennies sent an instant jolt of orgasmic delight through every nerve ending. He sucked at the reed, his life force slowly sapping into his mouth like a straw. His skin rippled with goose pimples at the amplified coppery taste compounded by the salty scent, his head growing dizzy again.

Then he set the slender stem on his desk. Mustn't get too greedy. Soon he would have his fill, and so would the others.

A rapping against the door of polished chrome at the far end of the vast room of white marble stole his attention, cutting off his moment of secret pleasure.

Apollos carefully sealed the gilded vial with a cork and set it aside, then stood and called out for the intruder to enter. The door slid open. In strode Dominic Weiss, skin white and hair silver, and the Sacradi himself, Martin Zarruq. His silver handlebar mustache seemed to sag at the sight of Apollos at his former desk.

Excellent. Even he would succumb to his designs. After all, they were from a power more potent than one could possibly imagine from on high—or from down below, however you might view such things, such sources of power.

"Come along," he said, gesturing toward the far end and trotting off.

His charcoal silk robe swished, and bare feet slapped against the cold, hard marble with each step. He met the men at the same cluster of couches at one end that he and Lucius Severus had sat at days ago. The man had demanded to know the next phase of Conversion, the plan dealing a finalizing blow to Ichthus, which the newly arrived Authority, the Shining One himself, had outlined before the Senate, along with his retinue of celestial advisors.

Apollos smirked at the memory, the Patron having referred to them as aliens, as if mere space invaders rather than the powerful divine Beings they were.

The Authority quickly lost confidence in the man, resulting in his untimely death. The turn had rankled the Senate, but they quickly jumped on board, awaiting the coming unveiling—the next phase of Conversion that would raise up both the Chosen One and reveal his right-hand confidant.

Him.

"Care for a drink?" Apollos asked, stopping at a long mahogany table, bottles of wine and liquor arrayed on top.

"Yes, Bishop—"

He snapped his head toward the sound of his previous title. The one he'd held before his exaltation to the right hand of the Authority.

It was Martin Zarruq, eyes wide and searching for help from Dominic, with those pathetic handlebars curling tighter with worry.

The man gave a curt smile and offered a short bow toward Apollos. Weiss said, "Yes, *Haruspexi*, the Authority's great seer, that would be splendid. Whatever you are imbibing should suit us, isn't that right?"

"Ye—yes, Haruspexi," that pitiful Sacradi stammered. "Whatever you are imbibing should suit us."

Apollos stamped down a satisfied grin. It seemed like only yesterday he himself was stammering in the same manner. My my my, how the tables had turned.

He opened a bottle of Brunello bottled from the Tuscany region in Roma, 2105. A good year. The year he had been ordained into ministry with the Church. Seemed like an apropos offering, considering what would soon take place. Pouring three glasses, he joined the men who were seated on a cream couch rimed in gilt.

Passing out the two glasses, he raised his own. *"Laus sit auctoritas!"*

"Praise be the Authority, indeed," Dominic said, raising his glass before taking a sip.

Martin quickly agreed: "Yes, praise be..." Then he filled his mouth with something other than words.

A chime rang out on the other side of the hall from near his glass desk, its echo clear as the bell inside that vintage wooden Howard Miller grandfather clock from pre-Reckoning. The dreadful piece was a hold-over from when Martin Zarruq, the so-called Sacradi, titular head over Panligo, had occupied that very space. Apparently, he cherished such antique treasures, which was a bit ironic given his fondness for progressing his ancient faith forward into ultramodern realms.

Apollos did not share his partiality to the past. He had meant to replace it with an ultramodern digital device, but his hands had been busy with more important matters.

Like crushing Ichthus and establishing the Republic of Heaven, the Authority's reign on Earth as it is in the Unseen Realm.

The doors suddenly shuddered before throwing open. A retinue of Purifiers stormed inside, arrayed in all their crimson glory, with Neutralizers gleaming black and polished, their boots clattering across the tiled floor to intercept them.

He smiled, understanding what was happening.

And what would happen next...

Two Purifiers suddenly seized the Sacradi by the arms, his wine taking a tumble and spilling down his white robes.

"What's this about?" he demanded, voice strained and shrilly, clearly of fright as much as indignation.

Apollos leaned forward, spotting Weiss shrink from the corner of his eye, and grinned with narrowed eyes.

"Progress..." was all he offered.

The Sacradi recoiled with wide eyes, then was dragged from his seat.

That ridiculous clock continued its doleful chimes, Martin Zarruq's screams joining the tone that spelled the next phase of Conversion.

Time to make history.

Or rather: Destroy it.

CHAPTER 13

ALEXANDER STARTLED at the suggestion their rescue had any insight into what had transpired in the Capitolium. The seat of republican power had always carried a shroud over it, the island capital removed and distant from the rest of Solterra—by design.

It was the perfect paradise island planted in the near-middle of the Atlantic Ocean off Europa's western coast, a far-off distant compound from Portus Calia, the former nation of Portugal. It was inaccessible except by boat, planes having been outlawed by the Republic as a response to the cataclysmic climate change wrought by fossil fuels—leading to their current lot in life twenty thousand leagues under the sea. The polis knew better, however. They understood the technorati were enthralled by not only their own version of the apocalypse but also the power to save humanity, and control it. Same for the Republic, the Patron and his Senate lackeys clamping down on free-travel access points through limited magnarail lines and deep submergence vehicles.

Either way, it ensured the seat of governmental power was well-protected from would-be terrorists and rebellions, as well as unsullied by the lingering problems of the far-flung corners of the Republic. Its tropical climate, regulated temperature, and insular community had created the perfect paradise for the ruling elite. It was a slice of Heaven on Earth, an Elysian field for the reconstituted Roman Empire, planted in the center of Solterra as a gleaming, sanitized beacon of hope modeling the triple promises of peace, prosperity, and progress.

For Humanity!

Except Ichthus had never gotten close to the Capitolium, and the Resistance had no connections to the seat of power. As far as Alexander knew, anyway. So to hear from this brother in Christ, to hear this mystery Christian had knowledge of the political goings on and machinations of the Republic—the very replacement of the now-dead Patron...it was most unnerving.

And intriguing.

Alexander had wondered who their rescue had been. He'd carried himself like he had been someone important in his former life—even in his weakened, tortured state. A man of means perhaps, or someone who had been a leader, whether in business or in Ichthus, perhaps in the Republic itself.

The man had piercing silver eyes that almost glowed against his tanned, ruddy skin. Perhaps from Roma or España, or in the Solterra south across the Atlantic. He held his age well, his hair matching his eyes though full and wavy, falling to his shoulders. Looked about the same age as Father, the observation seizing something in his chest. His heart, tugging at his emotions at losing the man—to what he thought was at first his suicidal death, only to realize it had been staged for an even greater wickedness: the revelation he had sought to bring about the Church's demise.

The man winced shifting in his chair, but his eyes were bright and full of life, and he used them to address each and every person, looking them squarely in the eyes before sitting straight and heaving a breath. He threw back his shoulders and straightened, readying to confess.

Whoever he was, Alexander prayed the man proved useful to Ichthus's cause during these dark, apocalyptic times.

"My name is Thomás Polanco. Well, Polanco-Kolocovich, but that is another story. *My* story, I suppose you could say."

He flinched at their rescue's revelation, the name familiar, though he couldn't place it.

"Kolocovich?" Sasha said. "Are you being from Vostokana?"

"*Da*, originally from Polandia."

Junia and Sasha gave one another smirking glances—one of *those* glances. The same one's his teenage mates had given one another when they came across someone from Sub-Saharan Alkebulana. He was ashamed at how the discrimination of Tripolitania culture had led him to view his fellow Alkebulana brothers and sisters with darker skin in such a manner. Such was the way of humanity, he supposed, dividing along tribal lines. Wondered if that was the same attitude exchanged between his best mate and his fellow Ukrainski, but he left it alone.

"But you speak Muscovia," Lucy said.

The man nodded. "We all do in that part of Solterra, thanks to the spinelessness of Europa a century ago and the Great Bear steamrolling across Eastern Europa." Polanco spat to the side, a rather impressive glob of spittle for an old guy.

Alexander said, "If I recall, they decimated your language, your histories, a century ago."

"Such is the way of all totalitarian regimes, which is why I much prefer *mi madre's* native Latino tongue. The first thing to go is the past to make way for the future."

"Just like the Great Reckoning, when Solterra Republic rose to power."

Ford snorted a laugh. "Peace, prosperity, and progress is the way of ultramodern man."

Polanco put up a finger. "It is the way of man."

He held Ford's eye, the man shifting uneasily under his gaze.

Clearing his throat, he took another swig of his drink. "You said you knew what was about to go down." Ford gestured toward Sasha's workstation device. "At the Capitolium."

"*Sí*, but first some background."

"Background?"

"It gets to why I am knowing what I am knowing."

Ford nodded, saying nothing more.

Alexander leaned back and folded his arms, intrigued by the man and his story. His accent was thick, and his dual nationality, Vostokana and some roots in España, which sounded rooted in his parents' mixed-race marriage, was evident in his two last names. He favored one while seeming to disavow the other. Again, intrigued...

Polanco leaned forward. "Before I was in reprogramming camp, I was simple priest who had stumbled upon a plot."

Ford threw back some more of his drink. "What plot? What were you in for?"

"I was in for what much of Ichthus is now in for," the priest replied cryptically.

"Meaning..." Nia asked.

"Meaning, I refused to say men have periods and women have penises."

Ford sputtered on his drink, choking and coughing, the whiskey dribbling down his chin.

Alexander was taken aback by his frankness, as was the

rest of the group. He had heard rumors of Solterran sectors beginning to demand verbal allegiance to the shifting definitions of reality—mostly targeting Ichthus and its members, believing they were prime candidates for pestering and jackbooting. But he had never met someone so open in his refusal to pay lip service to the Republic's demands.

"Simple truths, really. Like 2 plus 2 is four. And humanoids aren't humans. And ignorance is not strength. But the Republic demands what it demands. And it has begun to require you to deny what is plainly true. After all, truth is the first thing to go in the interest of the Narrative."

Recovering, adding another cough for good measure, Ford asked, "Come again, partner?"

"I refused to live by lies," Polanco sneered, spitting to the side again. "Refused to confess my allegiance to the Patron and his demented values."

Alexander asked, "You said originally from Polandia. Where are you from now?"

"Americana."

Now Ford smirked. "What part of Yank country?"

"A small town called Mill Creek Junction, in the province of Michindihio."

"Ahh, yes, those former Midwest states of America all scrunched together. What's a fella like you doing in them parts?"

"Something is happening again," Sasha said with interruption, pointing at the display.

"It's just OneWorld News again," Ford said, swatting at the air. "Probably just a commercial for one of their sleazy bachelor shows with humanoids chasing a horny fella—not that I would know anything about that or anything," he quickly added, throwing back more of his drink.

"It's the Republic alright," Alexander said, getting out of his chair and moving to the display.

"I wouldn't worry about it. Probably the Senate doing their senating thing to nominate us a new Patron."

"*Oo-oo*," Sasha said, shrinking back in his seat. "It is being that, but more. And worse."

Lucy and Rebekah gasped, and Alexander quickly realized things had taken a massive turn for Ichthus.

For him, for the one he most cared about.

With devastating consequences.

Ford scoffed, never trusting OneWorld for anything as far as you could shake a stick at it. Or was it than you could throw it? Either way, he figured he should check out what the hubbub was all about.

He threw back the rest of his whiskey, the burn strong with this one outmatched only by the strong oakiness. Both of which he liked, which called for a refill! Standing, and bracing a hand on the back of Sasha's chair for support—that whiskey was strong in more ways than just the burn and oak!—he took a gander at what had them all hot and bothered.

Then sucked in a breath at what he saw, the quick intake sending that oakiness rushing back across his taste buds and through his head.

Shucky ducky...

They were both right. That and worse.

For Ichthus.

Because emerging into view was Max Bacchus himself, in all of his chipper glory, and on location, by the look of it. Somewhere made of stone, which was an odd sight for his peepers to behold in a land of glass and chrome and titanium.

But that wasn't what sent his lungs searching for breath.

He was joined by someone seated, a black sack cinched tight over his head.

The Shroud...

Whoever it was looked old, long silver hair stringing out from underneath the black hood; with trembling, bony hands, veins popping through onion-thin skin; his shoulders broad and bony but sinking; figured it was a him, on account of his height.

Without even the sound on, they all knew what the Republic's propaganda mouthpiece was reporting on.

And it was not good. The chyron said it all.

Radical Ichthusan Assassins Captured!

Ford's mouth went dryer than the Yazoo-Mississippi Delta, and his bowels went weak. "The worm has turned, folks."

Ever the showman that man was, Max Bacchus, tracing the outline of the poor soul with a long finger, joined by a long nail painted black, as he pranced around him in—wherever the hot Hades he was! Which was old, ancient old; definitely pre-Reckoning old. Was lit by flickering torches mounted on a curved outer wall of cut stone, oversized stone chairs up on a platform behind and glowing orange in the light, the chair itself with the Republic's victim planted down inside some center stone well.

Was about to ask who the hot Hades the gang thought had been captured—the supposed assassin—when the room gasped and moaned at the sight that said it all.

And who.

Max Bacchus had whipped the Shroud off the victim's noggin. And there was Father James Ferraro, the Master of the Ministerium and chief cardinal of Ichthus. If there was a pope in these ultramodern times, Padre Ferraro was it.

A fire burned inside Ford against the man he knew of as Charles Carson, and boy did the man pluck Ford's ever-living nerves! Not only because of the spectacle on display, but also because the two had a history—in the Legion, of all places.

He knew Max Bacchus as Charles Carson. Or Chucky the Flunky, as he was known around his Legion unit. And flunk out he did, right until he was plucked by the Patron himself to be the Republic's propaganda maestro. The son of a Senator, Chucky had been given a special position with Ford's unit even though the cat could barely lift a fork and pissed himself at shooting practice. A wet scaredy-cat, really, when the Legion needed bulldogs who were built to enforce the will of Solterra. But he'd survived boot camp, then the first year of basic training the Legion put all new recruits through. Ford and everyone around him knew the kid wouldn't cut it, but his pops pulled strings to keep him in—until he wasn't.

One morning, Chucky was gone. Bed stripped clean and locker cleared. No clue what had happened, but rumors tended to go in the OD-dark direction after kicking back too much speed and nose candy. Never could take the pressure of both the Legion and his pops's expectations. Except the guy's mug appeared on OneWorld News as the new mouthpiece of the Republic. Ford near well shat himself, along with the other fellas in the unit, completely disbelieving what his peepers were seeing.

Chucky had always been a bit of a dandy, with a healthy dollop of the dramatic flair to the fella. Was always messing with his hair and worrying about his appearance in a world where bad BO and unshaven chins was a definite thing. Traipsing the backwater and backwoods towns of the Sahara and muddy Amazon and Canadian tundra to spread Solterra peace, prosperity, and progress—who the heck cared what they smelled like or how their hair was falling? Chucky did, and some of the guys had pestered him about it too. Some even wondered at first if he'd offed himself because of the pestering.

Until he was being broadcasted into every home and business and pocket device around Solterra, with that big hair and bright clothes and those gleaming teeth. Part carnival barker, part ringmaster, the man attracted the attention of the masses around the world to breaking news throughout the Republic while moderating that news. Since Solterra operated the only source of news—'*For Humanity!*' of course—he was more a propaganda maestro than anything resembling a news anchor.

And there he was, Max Bacchus, in all of his chipper glory, the stage name for the face of OneWorld News a throwback to the Roman god of entertainment. He was chatting away, face drawn and serious. Teeth bleached and gleaming. Hair airbrushed a macabre bloody crimson, eyelids accented a similar shade, and wearing a black coat sequenced with complementary bloody crimson accenting.

Continuing to babble away with that face drawn into an emotive, dramatic pose, he clutched his chest as he gestured toward Padre Ferraro, then leaned forward and shook his finger at the screen while holding his hallmark ivory walking cane tipped in gold and capped with an onyx knob.

"*NOOO!!!*" Alexander screamed, collapsing to his knees and throwing his hands on his head.

The sound was unlike anything Ford had heard. Actually, no, that's not right. It was exactly like something he'd heard before. Back in Noramericana, on his family farm. The bleating of a slaughtered goat just as Pops grabbed it by the scruff of the neck and slit his throat.

Strangled, freaked-out, agonizing.

Ford understood the feeling.

Padre meant just as much to Ford as he did to Alexander.

Probably more, given the lifeline Father Jim had thrown him, the second chance. The redemption.

It was why he was in that bucket of deep-sea bolts to begin with. So, actually, Ford had the old man to blame for his lot in life resisting the Republic and running from no uncertain doom!

Was kidding, of course. Ford's redemption and second chance at life was in no small measure thanks to the gracious hand of mercy extended to him by Padre. After he'd converted to the Church, then met back up with Brother Benedict after escaping the reprogramming camp, the man had connected him with Father Jim, recommending him as chief of operations to the Ministerium. Apparently the pair had gone way back, and the cardinal agreed to take him in. Had he not looked past his past, not let him live and lean into his new-creation birth as a child of God, a rescued sinner—well, Ford didn't even want to think about where he'd be!

And now that man was threatened, by the Republic—and no thanks to who Ford had been way back when, his techniques now threatening the closest thing he'd had to a padre of his own.

Things had just gotten real...

"*Este es sólo el comienzo,*" someone said from behind, low and gravelly—and gravely. "*El principio del fin.*"

Ford spun around, Alexander now crouched, head between his legs with the three women consoling one another in their tears, Sasha silent and stoic and whiter than his tighty-whities.

It was that Thomás Polanco or Kowalski character or whoever the hey-ho day he was. Didn't speak no Latino, let alone the Muscovia of his Ukrainski compadres.

"What was that, hombre?" Ford asked, about the extent of his Latino.

"I was saying, this is only the beginning. The beginning of the end, really—the precursor before the Lawless One rises upon Solterra's stage. Or Shining One, however you look at it."

Lawless One, Shining One? Who the hot Hades was he talking about—and *what* the hot Hades was he going on about, all this talk of this being only the beginning? And the beginning of the end?

More important and germane to the moment at hand: Who the hot Hades was *he*?

Time to find out.

Brushing his long, greasy hair out from his face, he stomped up to Polanco and crouched low, throwing his hands on the man's knees and getting a few inches from his face. Regretted his maneuver, the chap in desperate need of a shower, but it was time for answers. And he was fixin' to get 'em.

He growled, "I think it's about time you come clean with us, son. Who are you, what do you know?"

Polanco looked him in the eyes, those silver orbs watery and holding an endless corridor of secrets.

Then he nodded. "*Sí*. Pull up a chair."

Ford wasn't sure he was ready for the sit-down.

CHAPTER 14

"WHAT WAS THAT, HOMBRE?" Ford asked, his voice echoey and distant in Alexander's head. Was thoroughly confused why the man was speaking Latino, but it didn't really matter anyhow, because it was the last thing that was on his mind.

The only thing that did matter was the picture staring him in the face on the workstation display.

And the person on it.

Alexander's mind swam with the implications of it all, his chest constricting and clawing for breath, his heart pounding and pulsing in his head growing dizzy and faint with dread.

There he was, Father Jim. Padre.

Until that dreadful hood had been yanked off his head by that carnival barker propaganda-meister, Alexander had held out hope. Though not confirmed, he figured he had been captured from Phoenix One by the Republic in a terrifying raid. Had hoped the man was merely brought to some off-site facility to be used as a bargaining chip to get at the rest of Ichthus. Perhaps interrogated, but nothing torturous. After all, the man was the Master of the Ministerium, the functional head of Ichthus as senior cardinal over Christ's undershep-herds. A dignitary of sorts over hundreds of millions of Christians, surely the Patron would treat such a man with the respect he deserved.

But once that chyron displayed the Republic's dreadful declaration—*Radical Ichthusan Assassins Captured!*—that hope began to sieve right through his fingers. And when the image shifted to the dimly lit chamber, with those ghastly flickering flames casting ghostly shadows about a lone figure who was clearly an elder—well, then his stomach sank with horrifying terror, along with all remaining hope.

Father Jim's hair was long and flowing all around him in a disheveled nest of silver. Much longer than Alexander last recalled, having left Phoenix One with Ford months ago in pursuit of intelligence on Kareema Salam before their fated operation.

His throat grew tight seeing it like that, his hair, along with the memories surrounding it. He had liked to keep it long from back when he knew Padre at university, skirting Oxford's rules against such unkempt looks. But as with all things with Father Jim, he liked what he liked and that was that, and he would bend the rules to his will at times. He liked that about his mentor, his friend, pushing the boundaries when life called for it.

Whether it was his hair or smoking his pipe—

That tightness grew into a sandpapery constriction now, and his eyes began to spill over.

Pipe...

Could still smell his vanilla-laced tobacco, a Britannia blend of some coarsely cut mixture of bright and dark leaves that carried a delicious musty, earthy, and spicy aroma. Had even introduced Alexander to the practice, gifting him his very own pipe for his twenty-first birthday, telling him it was high time he had himself a proper bowl, with a curved black stem and a sack of his favorite blend to go along with it. What was it called? Prohibition, paddy wagon—some sort of P-word Father Jim found mildly scandalous.

That's right. Presbyterian. Thought it ironic he puffed about on a blend named after a former major denomination of the Church.

Hadn't recalled those times in ages. But seeing him like that—bound and seated in a chair in the middle of Lord only knew where; something foreign to ultramodern Solterra, something ancient that stretched back centuries—the sight surfaced a flood of memories tied to the dear soul.

"I was saying," another voice announced, deep and growly from behind, laced in a Latin lilt, "this is only the beginning. The precursor before the Lawless One rises upon Solterra's stage. Or Shining One, however you look at it."

Alexander's mind was momentarily yanked from the screen by the sound of two men chatting, and those words. Lawless One, Shining One?

They registered, but barely, his head still grappling with the improbable sight of Father Jim bound to a chair like a common criminal. Understood both of those names from his life as a priest—a life Father Jim had nurtured, hammered, and honed through years of university seminars on the New Testament and ancient Koine Greek, on eschatology and narrower topics concerning the end times. Through years of friendship and mentoring, of care and love.

That mentorship—that *friendship*—was the reason he was a priest to begin with, his father roping him into the profession but Father Jim carrying him through. Not only through graduate school but also through years struggling as a small-town parish pastor, counseling him through tough decisions and caring for his soul through rancorous seasons of self-doubt and parish strain.

In fact, he was the entire reason Alexander was standing

inside that bridge on the smoldering station hundreds of kilometers at the bottom of the ocean, having sent that blasted telegram along with that traitorous woman, Tara Rodriguez, beckoning him to that conclave addressing the rising apostasy plaguing Ichthus.

Tears spilled over down his cheeks now, warm and wet and winding past his stubbled face.

Father Jim had called on him—*him!*—to lead the charge to save Ichthus, which had led to experiencing so much heartache and suffering, so many trials and tribulations, not to mention witnessing so much death and destruction.

And he wouldn't change it for anything.

There was a stomping of feet plodding behind Alexander, his mind still swimming, his heart exploding in his chest, his lungs clawing for oxygen at the personal turn of things—

Then: "I think it's about time you come clean with us, son. Who are you, what do you know?"

—until Alexander couldn't take any more.

"*NOOOO!!!*" he cried out for a second time before launching at the workstation display, yanking it from the table and smashing it against the cold, hard steel floor.

"*Nyet!*" Sasha yelled, echoing his own cry of negation before scrambling to the floor.

Alexander suddenly realized what he had done. He'd just smashed their lifeline to the Republic. Probably to Father Jim himself.

"What the..." Ford said, spinning around and casting his eyes from him to the floor and back again. He huffed a sigh but didn't lay into him. Instead, he planted a hand on his shoulder. "You alright, homefry?"

Alexander went rigid, closing his eyes and heaving desperate breaths, the air hot and humid and cloying, face burning with rage and sweat beading on his forehead.

"*Pochemu,*" Sasha said from the floor. "Why were you doing that, Alex?"

"I-I-I..." He swallowed, his parched tongue stumbling over his sandpapery throat. He croaked, "I couldn't take it any more, seeing him like that."

Sasha stood cradling the workstation. The screen was black, blank of any visual, any further view of Father Jim's suffering, and a wicked spiderweb crack spread from the center. What had he done?

"*On mertv?*" Nia asked as Sasha raced to one of the other workstations arrayed along the bridge's edge. She asked again, "Is it being dead?"

"Hold your ponies, alright?" he replied, the man bringing the station device online and fiddling with the one Alexander had broken. "Let me work magic."

"I'm sorry," Alexander whispered, hanging his head.

Lucy and Rebekah edged to either side now, their arms wrapped around his waist and heads lolled against his shoulders, whimpering cries echoing softly.

"I'm sorry..." he repeated, closing his eyes in shame now.

"No," Ford said, voice commanding, insistent. "There is no shame in this rodeo, son."

Alexander raised his head, looking Ford dead in the eyes through a blurry, watery spectrum.

"Don't you worry a lick about it. You did what any one of us would've done. Hell, I wanted to take a fist and sock that bozo Bacchus from here to Sunday!"

"Bu-Bu-But I destroyed the only lifeline we have to the Republic!" He gestured Sasha's way, toward the ruined workstation. "To Father Jim..."

"We'll think of something. Besides, we've been in this rodeo before and lived to tell about it."

Alexander took in a measured breath and nodded. "On a buck and a prayer, right?"

Ford smiled. "You know it."

"*Otlichnyy!*" Sasha exclaimed from across the room, adding a *clap-clap-clap* and a giggle. "Sometimes I am surprising even myself..."

Before Alexander could ask what he'd done, one of the large broadcaster displays flickered to life—

And there was Max Bacchus, standing like a field general —arms behind his back, legs spread apart, dressed the part— next to Father Jim.

"How'd you manage that?" Reeves asked.

Sasha spun toward him and clasped his hands together. "You see, even with the ruined display I was able to assign a mirroring algorithm to the workstation kernel and extract—"

"It don't matter," Ford said with interruption, batting at the air. "All that does is we're back in business. You got sound on that thing, doc?"

His face fell and he went back to the revived workstation, muttering something in Muscovia under his breath, drowned out by an ear-piercing scream from the speakers before—

"...in a daring undertaking by the Classis, our navy boys executing a flawless operation to avenge the dastardly assassination of our Patron!"

Alexander winced, both from the screaming speakers but more from what Bacchus was saying. Sasha apologized and turned them down to a comfortable volume.

"*And this is the perpetrator of the violence against the Republic!*" Max Bacchus roared, face darkening crimson beneath a darkly silver makeup foundation, eyes going wide with rage, spittle flying from his mouth.

The carnival barker slapped a hand on Father Jim's head, grinning from ear to ear before stepping to the side, hand still planted on his head, and flashing him those white teeth. Petting his hair with a single white-gloved hand, he cooed, "But no worries, fearless polis. Justice will be served."

Father Jim looked pathetic sitting in that chair, enduring such disrespect, such belittlement, such—

He sucked in a startled breath, the camera zooming in closer. It was only then that Alexander saw the full measure of that disrespect!

One eye was swelled shut, bulbous and puffy, rimmed by a winey raccoon stain that signaled blunt force and broken blood vessels and bruised tissue. There was more of it, too, blotting his cheeks and nose. Looked like blood had crusted at his nostrils, and a brown gash shone through the bed of long silver hair on the left side of his head. He was shivering, a tremor working through his long limbs from either a subterranean chill or the shock of torture.

Either way, a rage welled within Alexander at the sight, neck burning hot and chest tightening. He worried he would destroy a second crucial device this go around, one that might not be as easily replaced or circumvented by Sasha. He clenched his fists instead, barely noticing the pain pricking his palms from his nails digging into his skin. He matched Father Jim's shaking, his entire body a taut, live wire ready to unleash a holy fury against the Republic in a snap!

What had they done to him? What had he endured?

"Where is this being broadcast from?" Nia asked, shaking him loose.

"That is a good question," Rebekah said. "It's something ancient, wherever it is."

"Pre-Reckoning, that's for darn tootin'," Reeves added.

"Hey, doc," Ford called to Sasha, "can you use your techno-magic to run some sort of algorithm doohickey and find out where this OneWorld signal is coming from?"

"*Khorosho,*" he said, spinning back to the device. "That is being a good idea. I will be seeing what I can find."

The hard tapping of Sasha's fingers racing across the display board rose above the broadcaster's din, Bacchus pausing for a breath and the picture dissolving into a familiar sight.

Phoenix One.

First the outside, video murky and dark but brightening at the launch of a plasma cannon that raced hot through the water until blooming in the side of the deep sea submergence station—exploding in a ball of fire and fury.

"*Wahoo!*" Bacchus shouted in a voiceover as the picture transitioned to the inside of the DS3. "Our valiant Legion stormed the gates of hell itself to seek the perpetrators of the injustice against our Patron!"

Vessels surfaced inside the docking bay—quite possibly the one they themselves had just docked inside—and figures dressed in charcoal and navy, wielding menacing Neutralizers, stormed across the boardwalk. More footage saw them shooting (and no doubt killing civilians stationed in the outpost, though that part wasn't shown) before apprehending a long train of detainees. A backdrop of patriotic music—horns and flutes and crashing cymbals, with a choir of voices chanting the global anthem—joined by an overlay of the black-red-and-white Republic flag gave the distinct feel of a victory celebration over some conquered enemy.

Alexander swallowed hard. Supposed that was the truth of it, wasn't it? The Republic and Ichthus, locked in a battle.

To the death.

"I am pleased to report," Bacchus returned in that chipper voice as painful as munching on glass, "that the Republic lost not a single soul in our quest for justice."

"Bulldookie!" Ford exclaimed. "I know I saw smoldering Enforcer remains—"

Nia shushed him and threw up a palm. "*Tikho*, cowboy! This is being important."

"It is because of their bravery," Bacchus went on, "that Solterra can find justice. No, *demand* justice from the religious terrorists who murdered our Dear Patron."

The carnival barker retrieved the black hood and pulled it back over Padre's head, the room reacting with a moaning wince at the wickedness. For his part, Father Jim just sat there, silent and unmoving.

Like a lamb before the slaughter...

Alexander shook away the thought, vowing with every fiber of his being to not let that happen. Not to the man who'd cared for him and made him who he was, not to Father Jim.

Not under his watch!

Cinching the hood around Padre's neck, Bacchus flashed that wicked smile at the camera, gooseflesh sweeping across his skin at the sight as the Republic anthem returned in the backdrop.

"Justice will be served, Solterra Republic. In twenty-four hours, we will have ourselves a little trial. Yes yes, we will! This miscreant, along with the others who plotted and planned the demise of the Republic—which is to say nothing of their assassination of the Patron—they will be brought to justice."

He paused, clenching his teeth together in that Cheshire grin of his and looked at Father Jim. He crouched, craning his head an inch from the cardinal and tracing that nasty nail painted black down his head's profile.

"And suffer the consequences..."

Then Bacchus sprang back to his feet, straight and stiff,

and shuddered to a rigid standstill, clapping his feet together and jutting his arm out with a clenched fist.

"For Humanity!"

He imagined the rest of Solterra doing the same, a legal requirement, actually, those broadcasters coming in handy with eyes to see and ears to hear to make sure the polis complied. Alexander just turned his head and lobbed a wad of spittle to the side. He couldn't bear to watch any further, and saluting the Republic was the last thing on his life he would ever do—no way, no how.

The broadcaster faded to black before Solterra Republic's logo returned, the white spinning globe of the Pangea supercontinent surrounded by olive branches set against light gray.

The room hummed with the revelation, even though the room itself had wound down to zero. No sound, no movement, no coughs or breaths.

Just the sickening revelation that Father Jim would be tried, found guilty, then—

Then?

The ellipses to the end of that question sent Alexander's pulse soaring and lungs searching for air again.

But he knew the answer.

Then it was off to a reprogramming camp for him.

Unless they did something about it.

Unless *he* did something about it.

CHAPTER 15

Ford was numb. All over, from head to toe.

Couldn't think, couldn't feel, couldn't see or hear straight. Something had snapped in his head from the turn of things. Supposed it made sense the Republic turned on Ichthus like this, blaming the Dear Leader's death on the Church—on Father Jim, even. All of which was cray-to-the-Z.

For one, the fact Lucius Severus had been assassinated—by whoever it was, and hopefully not one of their own. One of *his* own, the ones still under his command as chief of operations for the Ministerium, as shattered as it was. Either way, the fact the Patron had kicked the bucket, however he'd bit the dirt and whatever cliché euphemism for death was apropos, was not only crazy—it meant nothing good. No telling who came to fill Severus's shoes. And he'd been more accommodating to the Church than most the past century! No telling what the Republic had in store for his replacement.

The other side to the cray-cray coin was that the Republic had launched such a brazenly hostile incursion into their parts, storming one of the Church's outposts and rounding up its leaders. The Purge had certainly kept Ichthus on its toes the past few years, scattering Christians underground as it swept across Solterra. But that operation was more about destroying infrastructure and seizing assets to disrupt the Church, rounding up believers as Unfits when they could, taking them off the streets and out of circulation. Not this, parading them around on stage—especially not fingering them for an assassination they didn't have anything to do with!

With Chucky the Flunky as the ringleader...

The most paralyzing part of it was the fact the Republic had launched a ticking-clock countdown to Father Jim's demise—whatever that was. Given what they'd just witnessed at the reprogramming camp in Canadia, had a hunch it was a mixture between torture and coerced allegiance to the Republic, like Kareema Salam had endured.

With death on the table.

A loud smack yanked Ford back to the land of the living.

Alexander, pulling his hand back from the solid steel bridge walls, face set as flint with narrowed eyes and set jaw.

"We've got to get him!" he growled.

"Get him?" Ford said.

"Rescue him, we've got to!"

Ford put up a staying hand. "Hold on, homefry. We don't even know where he is. We've got no manpower, no plan."

Alexander waved an arm around the room. "We got all the manpower we need, right here. Got into the Canadian reprogramming camp just fine."

"And look where that got us!"

"I suppose," Nia offered, "we would have rescued Kareema had we been getting to her in time."

"There you go!" Alexander said, gesturing to the Ukrainski chickadee.

Ford raced a frustrated hand through his shaggy hair. Understood where he was coming from, even agreed. Heck, he'd lead the charge with bells on if he thought it would do any good. But he knew better. Father Jim was a goner. That much was true given what they'd just seen in Canadia. And whatever the Republic had planned would be even worse for Ichthus.

"What do you suggest we do, huh?" he asked. "We're stuck down inside this tin can, and we've got no intel on his whereabouts!"

Alexander turned to the doc. "How are you faring on that front, Sasha? Making any progress?"

He just shrugged. "*Boleye meneye*. It is being more or less. But it will be taking some more time."

Lucy offered, "There is some wisdom to what John Mark is saying. We don't even know the bigger picture."

Ford gestured to her. "There you go! Thank you, Luciana Jane."

She threw him a smile; his heart picked up pace, and he threw her a wink.

"What bigger picture is there?" Alexander said. "Father Jim is in trouble. He needs rescuing. We've got to rescue him. End of story."

"What I mean is," she went on, "we don't know why the Republic is wagging a finger in his direction to begin with, why they're accusing Ichthus of assassinating the Patron. Why he's even dead in the first place, how it happened!"

She voiced everything that was rumbling around in Ford's own noggin. Was why he liked her so much. Lucy was a thinker, that one.

The room fell silent, her questions settling hard.

"What about the Resistance," Ford offered, "what about Joshie? Maybe it was them that offed the Patron."

"*Moy syn?*" Nia exclaimed, eyes going wide.

"*Da*, sister ma-gister. Your...S-O-N, I take as your meaning."

"*Nyet.* No way." Now she crossed her arms and threw him narrowed eyes.

Tread lightly, Johnny Mark.

"Have you been in contact with him?" Lucy asked, intervening.

Nia shook her head.

"Then you don't know for sure, do you?"

She heaved a breath and shook her head, eyes casting down.

Reeves said, "Certainly sounds like something the Resistance might try their hand at."

Ford nodded. "Agree."

"I suppose," Rebekah added, "this is what you were talking about, Lucy. The bigger picture."

"Exactly," Lucy answered. "None of this makes any sense. Not only is Father Jim and the others taken captive, after a pretty sophisticated raid. He's paraded in front of the polis as a treasonous *assassin*! That's not even touching on the remarkable fact the Regis, our Dear Patron, is dead—no, killed! Clearly by factions within the Republic. Has to be. Unless, like you were alluding to, John Mark, the Resistance had something to do with it."

"*Nyet nyet nyet!*" Nia exclaimed. "There is no way—"

"All I'm saying," she went on, putting up a staying hand, "is that all of this is bonkers."

Ford nodded. "I was thinking the same thing. The worm has turned something fierce."

"Cray-to-the-Z fierce."

His eyes brightened and heart leaped at the sound of her using his own phrase. A kindred spirit, that one was. Glad she was on their side. On his side...

"This is only the beginning, you know."

There was that grave, gravelly voice again, interrupting

and throwing Ford off his interrogatory game. Polanco's or Kolocovich's or whomever.

Ford turned to him. "Yeah yeah yeah, you said as much earlier without further elucidatin' on the specifics. What's coming?"

The priest shrugged. "What has come before. Exactly what Alexander Solzhenitsyn described."

"Soldier-nazi-who?"

Polanco gasped and clutched his chest. "*Solzhenitsyn*, you dolt. Solzhenitsyn! *Aye yai yai...*"

"Who is that?" Alexander asked, joining the party now. "Why is he important?"

"A Russian dissident, from the ancient empire before it was being Muscovia. When it still ruled the world. He detailed what prisoners of the totalitarian regime had suffered in his historical overview of the Gulag forced labor camps from the 20th century. And we will suffer what *they* suffered, mark my words."

Ford's stomach sank at the mention of them parts of history, the ones he'd leveraged to rise through the Legion ranks. He also didn't care for the man's warning.

Sasha gulped back a squeak. "What sort of suffering?"

"For one, prisoners would have their skulls squeezed inside iron rings. Others would be lowered into acid baths. Still more would get hung up by their wrists, naked, and then covered with ants and bed bugs, only to be bitten and gnawed and nibbled. Those were the fortunate ones."

Memories flashed hot and heavy in Ford of the same kinds of suffering he himself had doled out. Now he was gulping back his own squeaking wince at what he knew went on behind closed Purifier doors.

The doc brought a hand to his mouth. "Why were they being the fortunate ones?"

Polanco shrugged. "Because the other naked kind would get a ramrod heated in the hell-fires of a primus stove shoved up their bottoms. The 'secret brand' it was called. If you were a particularly unruly person, or more valuable of an asset who needed encouragement to talk, your genitals would be slowly crushed beneath the toe of a goose stepper's jackboot while his helpers would hold back your arms. Even then, by that time you were too weak to fight back from the stress and strain on the body anyhow."

The room fell silent at the historical revelation. Ford thought he would puke. His hands went to the family jewels on instinct, cupping them as a shield.

"The luckiest prisoners were merely tortured by being kept from sleeping for a week, or denied water for days on end and driven to a wicked thirst, or just beaten to a bloody pulp until their skulls caved in. Or their fingers were snipped one at a time until they either passed out, they bled out, or they recanted."

Ford shuddered, not at all wanting to hear about what was all too familiar. Both professionally, having doled out such torturous pain, and having experienced it personally.

"It's all part of the plan," the geezer went on.

"What plan?" Alexander asked.

"Why, to bring Solterra under the thumb of the Antichrist and force Ichthus to choose."

Ford swallowed. Didn't want to ask, but: "Choose?"

He snapped his head toward him, those silver eyes drilling into him something fierce.

"*Así es.* Choose. Between the Kingdom of Heaven and the Republic of Heaven. Between the Second Adam and the Dragon, between Christ's Kingdom or Satan's."

Satan? As in the horned dude from nightmares? It was worse than he feared possible...

A *bring-brong* chime sounded from Sasha's workstation, interrupting any further discussion on that cray-cray matter. The doc glanced at it, squatting and leaning forward, then smiled and slapped his hands together.

"*Pobeda!*" he exclaimed with a giggle, bouncing up and down, his nest of tight curly hair bouncing in sync. "It worked!"

"What worked, doc?" Ford asked.

"That trace you were asking me to put on the OneWorld News broadcast."

"You actually found where it was coming from?"

"*Da.* I was able to trace it using a reverse algorithmic—"

"Skip the travelogue," Ford interrupted, "and cut to the chase, would ya, doc?"

Sasha huffed a sigh and muttered something in Muscovia beneath his breath.

"A small town in Germania," he answered.

"Germania?" Polanco said.

"Germania."

Ford smirked. "Is there an echo in here?"

Nia approached the priest. "What is there being in Germania?"

"Apparently our Padre."

Rebekah added, "And whoever knows how many more of our brethren and sistren."

The thought quieted the room. And that.

Polanco laughed, then asked, "What part of Germania?"

Sasha answered, "The town of Bruen."

"Bruen?" he startled. "Do you mean Büren?"

He returned to the workstation and shrugged. "*Da.* I suppose that is being correct."

"Büren..." Another laugh, the curious man giving his head a shake. "Of course! This is all making perfect sense."

Ford threw Alexander narrowed searching eyes. Who was this rescue dude they'd picked up?

Alex just shook his head and shrugged, then asked, "What is making perfect sense, Thomás?"

Ford nodded. "Yeah, you've yet to give us the 411 on what you know. Spill the beans, hombre."

There was a breath, then a flinch, then a beat. Then: "I was working inside Solterra government for a spell."

That was sure unexpected! But something inside those eyes told Ford it wasn't the full story. Years as a Purifier, interrogating Unfits had hammered and honed his spidey senses enough to know when there was more simmering beneath the surface.

"Wait, for the Republic?" Alexander asked.

"*Sí*. For a spell."

"*Bozhe moy...*" Nia gripped her Scythe tighter and shifted. Good girl.

"How long?" Lucy asked, crossing her arms with the same guarded look.

"For a spell."

"You said that already, Zeke," Ford responded, catching a whiff of evasion. "What I want to know is, what the hot Hades was your role?"

Polanco waved a dismissive hand. "*No importa.*"

"It is *importa* to me, hombre! Because if you left the service of the Republic, that would make you a Defector. Like me."

Another thought hit Ford, from the back of his lizard brain, sending the hairs on the back of his neck rising at attention with a warning that burned bright and strong.

He stepped closer to the man. Getting in his face, he said lowly, "Or maybe you're still in cahoots with the Patron, or whoever's in charge now. Maybe this was all a ruse, and you were meant to be rescued to infiltrate our ranks…"

The man's face darkened, his eyes narrowing and shadows growing thick at his brow and cheeks. Thought he might recoil back on his heels, or punch him square in the kisser. Didn't do either. Just stood his ground and stared Ford down.

"I am *not* an infiltrator," he said with conviction. "But you are right that I am a Defector. And if it is true that you are as well, then we are both under the same judgment of Solterra Republic, and *Jesucristo* is the only one who can save us."

Ford took a breath, searching that face, those eyes, for a lie. He found none. Still knew there was more to the story, which he didn't like. But he might need to bide his time.

"Let's remember we're all friends here," Alexander said with intervention. "Brothers in Christ."

That we know of, because so says our rescue dog!

Ford didn't say that, instead throwing him a frown but moving it along.

"Give it to us, hombre. You said earlier you knew who was coming down the pike. So, who's this new Patron, Lucius Severus's replacement?"

Polanco cast his eyes to the floor, whispering softly, "Someone who I was loving very much."

CHAPTER 16

"How do you know him?" Alexander asked.

The priest sucked in a measured breath, then sighed, as if reliving a painful memory.

"*Es simple.* I rescued him."

"When?"

"And from what?" Ford asked.

"From what I thought was an exposure pile in an abandoned village where I had been living in Vostokana, during those convulsive years of the Great Reckoning, a decade or so before the Realignment when the Republic was formed."

"Exposure piles are officially illegal."

"Officially. But we know how that works, don't we?"

Alexander nodded, knowing the ancient practice of exposure had received a renaissance in the ultramodern world, though the Republic had not taken kindly to former abortive practices after the world had progressed beyond its barbarism. Yet perhaps its continuation was an inevitable, logical extension of what the 20th century had normalized. And even when others began to recognize the full monstrosity of it in the 21st, it never really passed from modern civilization.

More likely, with overpopulation a perennial, worldwide

concern, some regions of the Republic increasingly employed more extreme measures to limit the human race. A practice Solterra had turned a blind eye to with disinterest.

Polanco continued, "I had been part of a movement against the barbaric practice while serving as a regional governor, my late wife and myself."

Alexander offered, "Just as Christians had before during the time of Rome, caring for infants abandoned to the unforgiving elements and wild beasts of the wilderness, dying from exposure to the bite of the bitter cold or roaming wolves."

"*Sí*. One morning, I saw what can only be considered a sign from heaven itself."

"A sign?" Nia asked.

"A meteor streaking through the dawn sky. Hot and bright. A starry host falling from heaven and crashing into a field nearby."

Alexander flashed Ford a curious glance, wondering the man's meaning.

He continued, "I followed the omen, wondering what had happened, when I heard the frantic cries of a baby. I had originally assumed the child had been abandoned because of the fallout during those bitter times—left to die to the elements or from ravenous wolves. However, coming to the site, I saw the expected pile of refuse, but there was no child. Hearing his cries of dereliction farther on, I went to investigate and stumbled upon the crashed meteor—or rather a fiery hole in the ground."

Pausing, he took a breath, then: "And there he was."

"There who was, hombre?" Ford asked.

Instead of answering, Polanco explained, "I saw his milky white skin and those piercing red eyes and a tuft of silver straw hair."

Milky skin, piercing eyes, silver hair? That's a shocker! Meant only one thing.

Ford voiced it: "You mean an albino boy?"

Polanco nodded, a ripple of surprise echoing softly in the room. "Obviously, albinism had been virtually eliminated from Solterra through genetic breeding and engineering techniques. So, seeing the boy, healthy with a strong set of lungs, I took it as a sign from God himself. A Chosen One meant to do extraordinary things for the Kingdom of Heaven. I named him Mateo, a gift from God."

"Why do I sense a *but* coming?" Nia said, shifting and switching that Scythe of hers to another hand.

Polanco swallowed. "But...upon further reflection, it is also known in the ancient world that the starry hosts signal darker Beings, from the Unseen Realm."

"And you are believing," Nia said, "this boy was brought to Earth by such Beings?"

He nodded slowly. "Especially because one day, a few years into the Realignment at the turn of the century, some men came for him."

"Who?" Alexander said.

"One was another, with white hair and fair skin, with flaming eyes like a rabid bat."

Something in the back of Alexander's mind prickled at the mention of that one, something familiar. An unusual and rare genetic anomaly of the human condition, especially nowadays. The Republic didn't look too kindly on such folks, usually designating them as Unfits—*For Humanity!* of course.

"A man with albinism?" Alexander said, flashing Ford wide eyes.

The priest nodded. "And another, with a tattoo in the shape of a bird."

"A bird?" Ford said, returning the same wide eyes.

Alexander's gut went watery with recognition, the memory of a similar tattoo surfacing the past few years—first returning to his parish church before it blew to high heaven and then with one of their former Ministerium agents, Tara Rodriguez.

He swallowed. "Did this tattoo bear intersecting lines that were bent at either end—the vertical down and the horizontal inward? Almost like a cross, except...a bird, as you said?"

Polanco's face darkened, his eyes narrowing and lips growing thin. "It sounds like you are familiar with this tattoo, and the entity behind it."

Alexander didn't answer, eyes casting down with contemplation at the implication that that *entity*, as Polanco put it, had been involved in the lads capture. That Nous, the archenemy of the Church had been involved.

This did not bode well...

"At any rate," the priest went on, "Mateo was twelve when he was taken, a demand of the Republic. Because of what I was involved with at the time, I relented." He paused, taking a breath and casting his eyes to the floor. "To my shame..."

He took another beat, another breath, before clenching his jaw and recovering.

"It was a decade later," Polanco went on, "and I was working for Ichthus, as a simple parish priest, when I saw him."

"The boy?" Alexander wondered.

"*Sí*. But he was now a man, maybe twenty-one or twenty-two."

Ford asked, "And who was he with?"

"I saw him with the same white-haired man in a market. I could hardly believe my eyes! I took it as a sign, and so I followed him, Mateo and the man, to the town of Büren. But I lost him. I asked around, but no one knew who I was speaking about. So I stayed, I watched, I hid. Until a week later I spotted him again, him and the man, and followed them to a castle."

"A castle?" Alexander asked, curious and confused.

"A castle."

"What castle?"

"Perhaps I should say a former castle, for it isn't a castle anymore."

"What is it?" Ford asked.

"What *was* it, more like it."

He rolled his eyes with impatience. "Alright. What *was* it then?"

Polanco answered, "Castle Wewelsburg was its name, with a long sordid history connected to the fascist regime of the 20th century that ravaged Europa."

"I recall reading about them during primary school," Alexander said.

Lucy offered, "The Third Reich, isn't that right?"

Polanco nodded. "*Sí*. They put the Republic to shame. And actually, the Republic learned much of their own totalitarian tactics from them, along with the others of that era. But that is beside the point."

Clearing his throat, Ford asked, "What is the point, hombre?"

"That there is more to Castle Wewelsburg's story."

"What more?"

He spat to the side, then spat out the name. "Nous. The ancient enemy of Ichthus. Which I suspect you had already suspected, given your familiarity with the bird insignia."

"An enemy of not only the Church," Alexander added, "but of the Order of Thaddeus."

"That is right!" Polanco exclaimed. "How do you know?"

"Because, well, I'm its Master."

Took him a beat, then Polanco's eyes widened with recognition. "Zarruq, that is your surname? The Sacradi's son?"

Alexander's face fell. "That's right."

"Then you know of Dominic Weiss."

"Unfortunately."

"He is the one who took Mateo into his care, aided by Nous."

"For the Republic?" Ford said.

"That is right. Now, I am told he goes by a different name."

"What name?" Nia asked.

He hesitated, heaving a breath as if gathering his wits and strength to voice the unvoicable. Like one of those he-who-shall-not-be-named types.

Then: "Neron Kaisar."

Ford snorted a laugh. "Sounds like a comic book character."

Sasha said, "I am not understanding the significance of the name. Who is—"

"'*Then I saw a second beast,*'" Polanco interrupted, "'*coming out of the earth.*'"

"What are you going on about?" Nia asked.

Closing his eyes, he continued, "'*It had two horns like a lamb, but it spoke like a dragon. It exercised all the authority of the first beast on its behalf, and made the earth and its inhabitants worship the first beast, whose fatal wound had been healed.*'"

Alexander said, "From the Book of Revelation, chapter 13."

The priest quoted the rest of the chapter before taking a breath, snapping his eyes open and drilling them into each person as he finished: "'*Let the person who has insight calcu-*

late the number of the beast, for it is the number of a man. That number is 666.'"

"666?" Sasha asked, clearly unfamiliar with the end-times passage.

"The Mark of the Beast," Ford said, nodding. "Meemaw drilled that cray-cray nonsense into my noggin as a teenager with her left-behind theology. Never did understand what it means."

Polanco explained, "The number is a gematria in the original Hebrew."

"A gem-a-whatchamacallit?"

"Gematria," Alexander explained. "The practice of assigning a numerical value to a name, word, or phrase according to an alphanumerical cipher."

"A code, you are saying," Sasha said.

"That's right."

"What is its meaning?"

Before Polanco could answer, an alarm sounded. Sudden and slicing and cranky as all get out, as if the station was thrown off balance at the revelation, or something far worse.

Alexander's stomach lurched. Panic pinged his brain.

He looked to Ford. "What's going on?"

▭

Ford understood exactly what was going on, straight away.

"The worm has turned, that's what." He looked to Alexander and frowned. "Twice over now."

Was somewhat relieved for the interruption after all that talk about those 20th century authoritarians. Heat had raced up Ford's neck something fierce, feeling exposed at the connection between those horrific torture practices and the ones going on under the Republic's nose, at their request.

Because it was him who'd learned of those tactics from those Third Reich bozos and put them to work for the Republic.

Then with all the talk about the Book of Revelation and the rising Beast, the Mark of the Beast and 666—Ford was about to beeline it for that mini bar again before being saved by the bell.

Except there was no salvation found in that cranky alarm. Could only mean one thing.

Emergency.

The Republic kind.

Didn't waste any time sidling up to Doc Pavlovich and leaning in for a gander in search of answers. No time like the present to suss out the source of a screaming alarm!

"Talk to me, doc. What's the dealio?"

"I am not knowing!" he exclaimed, planting both hands on that nest of curls of his before *tap-tap-tapping* away on the display board.

All the while that cranky alarm kept at it something fierce, signaling nothing good.

"I know!" It was Reeves, shouting from the other side of the bridge planted at another workstation. Ford hustled to join him.

And immediately saw the cause for alarm.

And emergency.

He swallowed, racing a hand through his shaggy hair. "Are those what I think they are?"

Reeves nodded. "'Fraid so. Eight Classis bogeys coming in hot and heavy for our position."

Shucky ducky...

"Stingrays, if I had to venture a guess."

"A few look bigger than Stingrays," Lucy said, pointing over Ford's shoulder. "Are those Destroyers?"

Double shucky ducky!

The alarm continued blaring as the group huddled in wait —wondering, intuiting, praying against what came next.

"I don't understand," Alexander said, glancing around. "Why aren't they firing on the station?"

Sasha shushed him. "Don't be giving the Republic any ideas!"

"Alex has got a good point," Rebekah said. "If they cleared the station of personnel, only to return a second time with more firepower, you would think their aim was to destroy what was left of the Resistance."

Polanco leaned forward for a look, and grunted. "Because those aren't Destroyers. At least the only larger ships moving our way."

Ford looked from him to the display, the pulsing cherries kicking his heart rate into a full-on gallop now. Wasn't as familiar with the echo traces of Classis hydrocrafts, the Legion's navy brethren. Only thing he knew was that the smaller red orbs were joined by bigger red orbs.

Spelling nothing good.

"What are they then?" he asked.

"Transporters..." Reeves said on a shaky breath.

Polanco said nothing, only nodding gravely.

Sasha threw up a startled squeak from Ford's other side. "What are they needing Transporters for?"

Reeves turned to him. "What do you think?"

Sasha gestured to himself; Reeves nodded.

Lucy added, "Bet they've got a platoon of Enforcers, too."

Alexander said, "Also makes more sense why we encountered the lone Stingray on our way in. It wasn't just an AI guard, it was a tripwire."

Ford's stomach sank to the steel floor, recognition slicing into his brain: They'd tripped the wire.

No, *he'd* tripped the wire when he blew up the dang thing!

Alerting the Republic to their arrival.

Alexander turned to him. "What do we do?"

"We fight!" Nia said, clenching her Scythe and slamming it down with a thud. "That's what we are going to be doing."

"Against a platoon, maybe two or three, of Legion Enforcers? Are you mad?"

"I'm with Alexander," Rebekah said. "I say we return to our hydrocraft and escape before it's too late."

"How?" Nia said. "Do you think we are going to be making it back once they dock? And even if we manage it, they are quickly closing in on our position. No way are we getting past them with our hydrocraft."

Good points. All of them.

They also gave Ford an idea.

He turned to Sasha: "Doc, you think you can see if there's an escape pod left?"

"Escape pod?" Nia asked, brow furrowed.

"They're more like a souped up hydrocraft. Made to withstand minor blasts and reach peak speeds—"

"To flee from blasting Stingrays or exploding deep sea submergence stations?"

He frowned. "Something like that. On our jaunt through Dante's Inferno upon arrival, I saw the south bay cleared of them suckers. At least some of the station personnel must've jettisoned before Comrade Crazy Pants rained the funk down on the station. Thought the cardinal might have escaped until..."

Didn't want to finish that thought; didn't need to.

He shook it away, and the regret.

Heaving a breath, he raced a hand through his hair. "You think you can find one, doc—if there's one left to find?"

"*Da.* I will go look." Sasha raced back to his workstation and started clattering away on the display board.

Ford prayed for a bone from the good Lord above. Because without it, they were screwed.

Sideways.

A light suddenly bloomed dim from his left. Curious, Ford turned toward it.

What was left of his bowels sank with a mixture of confusion and dread.

A man with a bald, bulbous head, all neck and wearing the dark navy colors of a Classis commander, had suddenly appeared on the broadcaster display. Looked like a wide-mouthed bass, with funny yellow teeth grinning from ear to ear, and large beady eyes set wide apart. Hit with the ugly pan, this guy was.

"Greetings," the voice announced, as oily and slobbery as his fishy mug.

Which startled the rest of the group, sending it spinning toward the broadcaster.

"You are surrounded by Stingrays and Destroyers, with two Transporters of Enforcers ready to apprehend—" Fish Face squinted before brightening. "Ahh, Senator Kolocovich, it is you. Jolly good to see you are alive and well, though it is unfortunate you've taken up with the Resistance scum."

Senator Kolocovich?

Ice skated through Ford's veins, cold and dreadful, followed quickly by an irritated heat that raced up his neck at being kept out of the know.

Narrowing his eyes, he snapped his head toward the man. "What the hot Hades is he talking about?"

Fish Face intercepted any reply: "Capturing two birds with one stone will make High Command most relieved.

Wouldn't want your knowledge falling into the hands of Ichthus rebels, now would we?"

Ford's head spun with the cray-cray revelation.

"That's right..." Alexander whispered from behind. "I knew he looked familiar."

Ford threw him a glance but couldn't go deeper on that one.

Polanco or Kolocovich or whoever-the-hell-he-was didn't move, didn't flinch. And he damn well didn't answer Ford.

Which irritated the snot out of him.

Instead, face set as flint, the Senator—simple priest my ass!—faced the broadcaster and addressed Fish Face: "I will never return to the clutches of the Republic. *También*, the Asset will be thwarted, and I assure you—"

A jarring, bassy rumble shuddered through the floors with a faint bluish glow spreading outside one of the windows.

That bass-like grin disappeared and those off-side eyes narrowed with fury. "That was a warning shot, a plasma blast at the base of the outpost. Don't worry, the station will remain steadfast, for now. Surrender upon our boarding, or face the—"

"What the..."

Ford spun around, seeing the problem. The broadcaster had zapped to nothing but nothing!

Polanco had killed it from a control panel.

And Nia was on him like a rabid dog, slinging that Scythe of hers around and planting it at his throat. Go Junia!

"What were you doing that for?"

Polanco clenched his jaw and craned his neck away from the weapon.

"We need to go, not talk to Commander Reicher."

Ford couldn't believe his ears. "What, you know Fish Face?"

"Who are you?" Nia pressed—both her questioning and her Scythe into the hombre.

Polanco edged backward, his backside bonking into a bay of controls. He swallowed, putting up his hands.

"I told you. A simple parish—"

Nia pressed the Scythe into his neck, drawing a line of blood. "No lies!"

"*No estoy mintiendo!*" he cried out. "I not lie. I am a priest. Before that I was a Senator. That's why I know of the plot."

Alexander put a hand on Nia's weapon, gently pulling it back. She gave him the stink eye but relented in a huff.

He turned to Polanco. "What plot?"

Another bassy rumble, followed by *clangity-clang* noises that meant nothing good, cut off any response and put an exclamation point on the urgency of the matter.

Nia went back to the man, but Ford grabbed her arm. "Leave it be." Then drilled Polanco with narrowed eyes. "For now. We need to get out of Dodge right quick unless you're fixin' to make a second appearance at that Canadian reprogramming camp."

"*Nyet spasibo!*" Sasha exclaimed. "No thank you."

"What's the plan?" Alexander asked, retrieving his Neutralizer from the center table.

Ford did the same, pulling the Blastgun from his back and checking it over, then stuffing it at his waist for backup before slinging his weapon of choice around his shoulder.

Locked and loaded and ready for a good time.

He shouted to Sasha, "How we coming on that escape pod, doc?"

The door swung open to the bridge with a wicked thudding clang, cutting off any reply—

And all weapons trained with a shudder toward the newcomers.

Or newcomer, as was the case.

"Whoa whoa whoa!" the man said, throwing his arms above his head.

"Jin! You were supposed to stay with the fish." Ford lowered his weapon. "What the hot Hades are you do—"

"We've got company!" Jin Sung said out of breath, swallowing hard before doubling over.

"Don't you know it. They're about ready to blow this thing to kingdom come if we don't—"

"No, I mean a platoon of Enforcers just docked—in our bay at our six several yards away. Saw them before they surfaced, so I scrambled out just in time to warn you all."

Reeves cursed. "There goes our ticket out of this joint."

Ford turned to Sasha: "Any luck on that escape pod?"

"*Da!* There is being one left. Made for seven people according to schematics."

"Seven?"

He eyed the mystery Senator who was becoming more mysterious by the second. Supposed they could leave the sorry sack of bones for the Republic as a consolation prize.

Shaking away the thought, he nodded. "It'll be a tight squeeze with us eight, but we'll make it work. Where's our ride?"

"The north side of the station, down a ways from the bridge but reachable."

He huffed a sigh. Had to be a mile away, given the size of the station.

"We best hop to it then."

What they would encounter...

To be determined.

CHAPTER 17

SWALLOWING HARD, Ford shoved past Jin, ready for anything.

Nothing yet, but an echoey clang and another shuddering bassy rumble told him all he needed to know.

The Republic was nigh.

Not only had they laid a trap for any returning Resisters to the deep sea submergence station they'd raided. They'd also come for one of their own—one of their former own. A Senator—of all things!—who had intel the Republic didn't want leaked. Two reasons right there for a platoon of Enforcers to risk life and limb to drag them all back to that Canadian reprogramming camp.

No way in hot Hades would he let that happen.

Heart was rapping a mean beat now and lungs were clawing for relief. All they found was a thick mess of hot and humid air still burdened by the acrid stench of motor oil and charred beef. Clothes were soaked through with sweat, too, a line of it beading down into his mouth and throwing up all kinds of saltiness made all the worse by the coppery tang of adrenaline coursing through his body and the chalkiness of his bone-dry tongue.

Not the way to jump into the fray of things, but he had no choice. The Grip was right around the corner if he thought about it too much, and that would do nobody no good.

Had to get his head in the game, so head in the game he would get.

Gripping his neutralizer, Ford pressed out into the hallway a few paces, taking careful steps with his weapon trained forward down the bending corridor. Waiting, intuiting, discerning incoming Republic whack jobs.

Nada. Zip, zero, zilch.

For now.

Had to be just a few minutes behind Jin if he tore through the station to find them while the Republic fishies docked. Which meant they needed to hop to it.

Double time.

The corridor was a dim mess of sparking wires and pulsing emergency lights still hanging on by a tapped-out Duracell. Hoped there was enough juice to carry them onward.

Nia was at his heels along with Alexander and Jin, who had come packing. Good lad. The men were ready with their own Neutralizers while Nia held her Scythe aloft, ready to lop off as many heads as she needed.

There were the faintest echoes of activity now from back where they'd arrived, the winding corridors of the massive circular structure of steel and titanium masking the true nature of the sounds—and their threats. Another corridor jutted off to the right, toward the north. Toward freedom.

Or so Ford hoped.

Nia was quick on the draw to usher the other two ladies and Sasha out from the bridge, leading them with her Scythe down the yellow-lighted corridor. The doc had three black cases slung around his shoulders, and he did all he could to keep from toppling. Ford didn't have a clue what all he carried. Figured stuffed inside were at least the pair of time-travel doohickeys the Ministerium had used to rally Christians the past few years with the Church's memory. Smart man. Imagined they'd come in real handy real soon.

For Father Polanco's part, or suppose it was Senator Kolocovich, he'd found himself a Blastgun in some bridge cupboard. Looked much more chipper now than when they'd found him at the reprogramming camp, following Nia all on his own. A skip tends to infuse your step when you're—

Smacking blue plasma exploded on the wall above Ford's head, sending him crouching to the floor as it spread its electric tendrils across the wall, with two more sailing inside the bridge deep from the hallway.

—running for your life!

Alexander and Jin backed up around a bend in the corridor, the two offering a *chew-chew-chew* rejoinder that opened up a window for Ford to turn tail and take his own advice.

"How'd they get up on us so quick?" He stood and sent a volley of plasma down into the void himself.

Which opened up a relentless spray of suppression fire from the platoon of Enforcers down the way.

"Here, this should help." Jin withdrew a silver ball from a pocket and squeezed it—once, then again.

Arming what Ford knew would buy them enough time to scram.

"Where'd you get that Disruptor grenade?"

"I stocked up before we left for the original operation."

"And you didn't think to hand off the goods to the rest of us?"

He shrugged. "You didn't ask."

Ford frowned but knew it was neither the time nor the place.

"Now's your chance to kiss and make up, son. Get rid of that thing, would ya?"

He grinned. "Your wish is my command..."

Jin sent the Disruptor sailing down the corridor. The round ball clanged and clattered across the metal floor on toward destiny.

Ford took off the other way, Jin close behind. Then—

A furious explosion of fire engulfed the dust they'd left behind, and those Enforcer goons. Screams and cries of agony could be heard through the shuddering blast.

Ford just smirked. That'll teach 'em to mess with the Church.

They followed the arching corridor, the dim emergency lighting barely allowing for visual purchase. Large doors jutted off toward other parts of the station—residential pods and galleys serving up plant-based meat products and hydroponically grown veggies. They were cracked open and splintered with damage, showing signs of the previous invasion.

That wasn't all.

More bodies lay along the way. Some wedged in those doors, flopped face down with crimson gashes at the back of the head and more darkened pools spread underneath. Some charred beyond recognition, others flopped over one another with injury and death.

Ford heaved a breath and swallowed. Couldn't worry about that now. All that mattered was getting to the escape pod and getting the hot Hades off this—

A figure suddenly sprang into view from stage left.

Hulking and bulky. Wearing the classic Enforcer charcoal getup and wielding the classic Enforcer Neutralizer.

Happened so fast the pair collided with a smacking thud, somersaulting over one another in a tangled mess of limbs that wrenched Ford's ankle something fierce.

Just as two more Enforcer goons emerged from the same hallway.

Didn't have time to pay them any mind. Had to trust his teammates to enter the fray.

While he kicked some major Legion ass.

Thankfully, Ford had had enough sense to sling his Neutralizer strap around his neck and shoulder, so it had held fast but was lying all cattywampus above his head. Had that going for him at least.

Using those abdominal muscles he'd taken pride in maintaining (two-hundo sit-ups a day, baby!), Ford sat up and slung his weapon around for the kill—

Just as Enforcer Goon planted a solid hoof in its barrel.

Sending his Neutralizer sailing from his head and skittering across the floor.

So much for that strap!

Should get his money back, but complaints could wait.

What mattered was round two coming at his head.

He slammed back down against the steel floor (again: abs!), the foot narrowly missing his face.

Which gave him an idea of his own.

The corridor exploded in blue light from an explosion of Neutralizer fire. Not his, not Enforcer Goon's. From behind.

Hope his side, not theirs. But couldn't tell and couldn't worry about that. Alex and Jin were on point to save their own backsides!

Speaking of which...

Enforcer Goon had lost his own Neutralizer in the collision, so he was scrambling for a fight, using his legs to do all the talking.

Until he leaped to his feet—a real Goliath of a dude, head nearly touching the ceiling!

Ford was still on the floor, ankle screaming with lancing pain from the tumble. So he did the only thing he could do.

Reached back with his good leg and sent a horse kick into the dude's gonads.

Low blow, sure, and for the second time. So sue him!

Threw the dude off his game, the goon stumbling forward on weak knees.

Took a swipe at Ford as he skittered back, then another, but he batted them away easily enough with one hand.

Just as his second reached behind for his trusty Blastgun to finish the job.

Yanking it out, he pushed off with his good leg to stand and took aim—

While the goon huffed and puffed and went barreling at him, head down.

Like a bull in a china shop! Or a Resistance outpost.

Either way, maintained abs or not, he'd be no match for Enforcer Goon's thick-skull sledge hammer.

Putting those twinkle toes to good use, Ford managed to step aside just right, at just the right moment—giving the Enforcer's backside a good kick and sending him plowing into the station wall.

Enforcer Goon thudded off from it, more Neutralizer fire erupting from behind.

A quick glance saw two figures lying on the ground, electric blue tendrils winding down with two heroes standing over them. The former were clad in charcoal, the latter were not, wearing relief and a small amount of pride.

Score two for the good guys!

Thank the good Lord above...

Time to finish the job.

Enforcer Goon bounced from the wall and Ford used the

reverse-motion force to his advantage. Newtonian physics does wonders during a brawl.

Yanked him back just at the right stage of motion and sent him stumbling to the floor again. Then took aim and sent three *pew-pew-pew* Blastgun shots into his kisser.

The peashooter did the trick.

The red particle beams shattered the face shield and drilled into the Legion goon's face.

Sizzling his backside in no time flat.

Ford sighed a breath he didn't know he was holding, wincing as he hobbled off from the fight.

"That was a close one," Jin said, out of breath.

Alexander nodded. "On a buck and a prayer, isn't that right, John Mark?"

"'Tis the Ichthus way." Retrieving his Neutralizer, Ford swiped at a line of sweat and swallowed hard, lusting after a thimble of water to take away his thirst. "Don't got time to tarry. Come on!"

Out of breath and out of time, Ford limped as daggers of pain sliced through his ankle. He was getting too old for—

Neutralizer fire erupted from behind, a volley of *chew-chew-chews* reminding him they were far from out of the woods.

Ford spun back and unloaded his Blastgun, the weapon offering a weak *pew-pew-pew* before winding down to zero.

Never did like those peashooters. Held way less charge than the beefier Neutralizers, so he tossed it to the floor.

Alex and Jin covered his limp-wristed reply, opening up a *one-two-three* punch volley while the trio skittered backward.

Rounding a bend and picking up the pace, Ford heard a familiar voice.

"*Idti!*" Nia called from behind, waving her arms. "Move it or lose it, cowboy!"

Ford gripped his Neutralizer and shouted for Jin and Alexander to join her while he laid down suppressive fire. They ran and rejoined the team.

Kept at it until he offered a final *chew-chew-chew*, receiving no more response—for a beat, then another.

Counted that as a sign he'd gotten the last of them or they'd turned tail.

Just the window they needed.

Ford hiked it to Nia, where three Enforcers were lying a few yards away. Deader than doornails.

"Whoa. Looks like you've had action. What happened?"

She shrugged, holding up her Scythe. "A few Enforcers got the raw end of the stick."

He laughed. "Glad you're on our side."

"The others are already being inside the hatch. Come on!"

"After you." He waved toward the entrance big enough to crouch inside.

She threw him a smile and nodded, stepping inside.

He quickly followed, turning back for a look-see but satisfied they were good to go.

The escape hydrocraft was much more like the pod Sasha had described—long, cramped, narrow, cramped, low-ceilinged, and very cramped. Definitely made for seven people, max, with a row of seats down the center walkway leading to the controls at the front.

Sasha was there, black cases stuffed in the corner, along with Alexander. Ford joined them, finding the release valve that would send them sailing.

Rubbing his hands together, he punched it, thankful for the good Lord's graces.

Nothing.

He frowned, then pressed it harder, longer, with more oomph.

More nothing.

Nia said, "Now would be a good time to engage the controls to get us, you know—*escaping!*"

He clenched back a retort that wasn't needed. "I did! It's not working."

Ford punched it again, then another time, the rear end throwing up a very uncouth sound, a barking cough that meant nothing good.

"Sounds like it's stuck," Alexander noted. "Like it hasn't been used in ages."

Sasha smirked. "That's because it hasn't. It's an escape pod!"

"Why do things always get worse..." Ford complained.

"What do we do?" Alexander asked.

"There's a manual override," Jin said, making his way to the entrance. "Saw it on the way in."

"Manual override," Ford muttered, fiddling with the switch again before giving it a hard smack—yielding the same atrophied results.

Sasha smirked. "Sure, I am sure that will be working. Why don't you try hitting it again..."

"Manual override?" he questioned again, ignoring the doc before giving up. Getting no reply from Jin, he turned toward the stern and started off. "What does that me—"

The sight stopped him cold.

Jin had crawled back out and was standing on the other side of the crawl entrance—face set as flint and eyes locking onto Ford's, over Alexander's shoulder and straight back down the long narrow gangway.

Time stood still, confusion and misunderstanding swirling in the split-second silence between him wondering about Jin's meaning and him catching sight of him outside the escape hydrocraft.

Outside. Not inside.

Until time cycled down to a singular, narrow point of revelation.

Manual override.

Outside. Not inside.

Ford sucked in a breath. "Jin..."

"Give the Republic hell, Ford," Jin shouted back.

"Jin!" he yelled back before shoving past Alexander and running to intercept the man.

Was a few paces back when the door slammed in his face, with a clangy turning of gears locking it into place and shutting it for good.

And Jin outside.

Not inside!

Ford grabbed the handle, but it wouldn't budge, grunting as he wrestled to make it turn. Tried again, putting his back into it and giving it another grunting heave-ho. All he got was the same sad story.

Nothing but nothing.

With Jin outside.

Not inside!

Ford pressed against the small glass window, cupping his hands for a viewing of things. Could see Jin fiddling with something on the other side, so he pounded on it, then again.

"Jin! Open up this door. That's an order!"

"Ford, what's going on?" Alexander said from behind.

He ignored him, catching sight of Jin closing his eyes and taking a breath, then reaching for the wall—

As two Enforcers emerged from the shadows. Tall and wide and clad in charcoal armor.

Raising their Neutralizers and taking aim. Then—

A fiery, furious blast of electric blue plasma shots exploded from the weapons and slammed into Jin.

His body lurched forward, and he stumbled on uncertain feet, eyes going wide and mouth opening as if in a question.

But not before punching the wall.

"No no no! Jin, don't you even—"

He was cut off by a sudden rushing of engines, the water churning something fierce.

Then he was gone—Jin's face obscured in a boiling cauldron of bubbles that faded to darkness.

Going, going, and *G-O-N-E!*

With Jin left behind in their wake at the mercy of the Republic.

The man had done it. He'd saved their lives.

Sacrificing his own.

Ford stumbled into the wall, banging his noggin on a bulkhead as the hydrocraft gained speed. He shuffled down the narrow walkway and dove for a seat, strapping himself down inside.

Didn't take long before the escape pod shot out of the station in a blaze of bubbly glory and into the darkened ocean void—no beady red eyes from Stingrays, no hulking bulky Destroyers to be found. Wouldn't matter anyway with the initial speed topping eighty knots—double the fastest Stingray and well beyond any Destroyer. Would wind down to half that in a mile, but by then they'd be well outside the range of any Republic danger.

Ford leaned back and closed his eyes, heaving a sigh of relief.

They were free as a bird.

For now.

But the relief of escape was overshadowed by Jin's sacrifice—supercharged by the knowledge they'd been hounded and nearly captured because of their rescue dude.

Which sent Ford sloughing off his restraints and spinning

to his feet, then storming after their newcomer seated at the end of the line. Time for answers.

"That seat was meant for Jin, you lily-liver, chicken-hearted lickspittle!" Was planted in front of the apparent Senator, arms crossed and face hard—jaw locked and lips thin, with eyes narrowed under a deep-ridged brow.

Polanco put up both hands, averting his stare. "I am sorry for your friend, and I understand your frustration—"

"*Frustration?*" Ford threw back his head and laughed. "That ain't half of what I am!"

"John Mark..." Alexander said seated next to the newcomer. "Let's not—"

"No, let's! I want answers."

"And I have them," Polanco said.

"Then talk!"

His voice resounded in the cramped space, a low hum from the engines zooming them toward safety the only sound to be heard. All heads had spun toward the former senator-turned-priest, looking like they were interested in the same thing as Ford.

He backed up to give the man some space, then gestured for him to get to it.

Polanco heaved a breath then huffed a sigh, his age showing now, as well as the exhaustion from the last twenty hours. Supposed he'd been through the wringer too, giving Ford a bit more compassion for the man.

A bit.

"Where was I?" the priest asked.

"The silver-haired teenager with milky skin," Ford answered. "Snatched by the Republic and later spotted in some Germanian castle."

"Former castle..."

"Whatev. Then there was the bit about who he was, who

you learned he'd become."

"And the code from the Apocalypse," Sasha added.

"Right. And that."

Alexander said, "You mentioned the name Neron Kaisar."

As if anticipating the question, the priest said, "666 translates into Neron Kaisar."

Took a beat until everyone recognized what he was saying.

"The name..." Alexander whispered.

That was crazier than a one armed mermaid. But Ford knew it was more than that.

"He's the revelation Fish Face was talking about. What he didn't want you blabbin' about."

"Fish Man." Polanco chuckled. "*Si.* Through some backchannels still open to me at the Capitolium, I learned the Authority intended to dispose of Severus and install Neron as the next Patron."

Alexander said, "The one raised in that Germanian castle."

"Which means," Ford replied, "all roads lead to that Bruen town."

Polanco nodded. "Büren, but yes. It appears so."

"Well, homefry—" He smacked Alex's knee, "looks like you've got your wish."

Alexander turned to him, sighing a breath. "Germania or bust?"

"Not sure *bust* is the word I'd use in this moment after the Republic nearly shattered our backsides—but, yeah. What else do we got to lose?"

He glanced behind, his face falling. "Lots, I'm afraid..."

The truth was more painful than Ford wanted to contemplate.

Instead, he settled back for the ride.

From one danger and into the next.

CHAPTER 18

GERMANIA, EUROPA.

Rain slapped against the window with a rage Apollos hadn't recalled in some time. He wondered whether it was truly rain water, or the wicked mixture of blood that had destroyed many of the rivers and seas across Solterra.

Apollos shivered at the thought, a ping of excitement ratcheting up his spine until the tingle of impending thrill sparked a wide grin across his face and kindled climactic desire in his belly.

The moment was drawing closer by the hour, he could feel it in his bones.

With him at the center of it all.

He stood from his desk and moved to the window, the stone floor beneath his feet cold, an ache he welcomed. He parted drawn emerald curtains at a large picture window, revealing all.

A curtain of watery crimson joined by ash slapped the panes, the town below nothing but a swirl of mud and dead grass, joined by the charred remains of old houses and shops, the husks of scraggly trees groping at the air for a second chance at life.

The image of decay and rot, of apocalyptic judgment,

made him hunger for what was to come—for what the portents beyond the glass announced loud and clear more than a year ago, confirming and affirming those cryptic teachings of old his fathers had always wondered about from the Scriptures.

Staring through the blood-streaked panes of glass into the darkened world, Apollos drew in a pleasurable breath, the taste of pennies dancing upon his tongue. Wished it was the after burn of sanguiphilia, whether his own fluids or those letting from Nature's own bosom, but he knew it was adrenaline, those ancient words coming to him from the Book of Revelation he had memorized chronicling the unfolding of the beginning of the end.

There was the first angel with the first trumpet bringing hail and fire mixed with blood, torching a third of Solterra.

Then the second, large portions of the sea turning bloody.

And finally the third angel, his trumpet calling forth a great star, blazing like a torch from the sky, turning many of the rivers bitter.

"Yes..." he whispered, stroking his hair now, the blond locks silver in the faint light.

There were more apocalyptic events the past year, of course, all driving toward the finalizing, totalizing conclusion he and his kind had been anticipating for generations. The climactic clash was nigh. With him the handmaid to the soon-arriving midwife, the pair of them vessels for the Authority to have his way in the world—with them and through them—before the climactic clash of powers.

Good versus evil.

The Kingdom of Heaven versus the Republic of Heaven.

The Nameless One versus the Shining One.

Desire churned in his belly again, a rise at his waist beneath his dark robes warm and firm, triggered by the anticipation of all that was to come—born by the memory of how it had all come about.

He was a Chosenborn. A child of the Authority—whether birthed for this moment or rescued, it wasn't clear. He barely recalled his childhood, those memories purged from him, along with his faith the moment he'd opened himself up to the Shining One, nearly half a lifetime ago now.

One Halloween, his final year of university, while he was neck deep in his studies with Father Ferraro and on the cusp of being granted his post in Ichthus, he and his mates had attended a Black Mass service put on by a local Wiccan outfit.

A sudden wind from behind joined the memory, gushing and rushing, as if sparked by the recollection, the atmosphere running chillier and smelling of sulfur and ash.

Probably just his imagination, but a layer of gooseflesh confirmed at least the temperature drop, and he could swear there was an acrid smell to the air.

At any rate, it was only years later that he had understood he'd participated in such an extremely occult service currying the favor of Satan. The Black Mass was the heart of the satanic. A direct assault against the person and work of Jesus Christ himself, making a mockery of his broken Body and shed Blood that anchors the Christian faith.

Although at the time, Apollos had convinced himself he didn't know what it was he was participating in, he knew better. Going into it, he understood he was stepping onto unholy, wicked ground. That it might even rend a rift in his soul.

He didn't care.

Because that early rift as a teenager had led him to his singular purpose in life.

A double agent.

A member of the cloth with the only motivation to position himself within Ichthus to bring about its destruction.

He smiled, continuing to stroke his hair, an apropos quotation surfacing from a century and a half ago: *"I am become Death, Destroyer of worlds."*

"Destroyer, yes..." His namesake. But not of the world.

Of Ichthus!

It was only later, at the end of his university tenure, when he attended the Black Mass, that the Presence had been activated, a sort of demon or Force or whatever lying dormant until the unholy ceremony awakened it.

While seemingly preposterous—after all, how can a believer be filled with the Devil and his minions?—the New Testament is filled with such occurrences.

Prime amongst them being Judas Iscariot, one of Jesus' own Twelve Disciples. The Evangelist Luke makes plain that *'Satan entered Judas'* before he carried out his wicked deeds. And even Peter, the rock upon which the Church was founded, Jesus warned him that *'Satan has asked to sift all of you as wheat.'* The Devil obtained permission to try and drag them into his dastardly designs. And he did, Peter thrice denying his Lord!

Then Ananias, another disciple of Christ, whom Luke quotes Peter asking, *'How is it that Satan has so filled your heart that you have lied to the Holy Spirit?'* Suggesting a contrast between two possible 'fillings'—between Satan and the Spirit of God, even within believers.

Most Christians would consign the Devil and his minions to the realm of *oppressing* the people of God, not possessing them. Job seems to make that case pretty clear. They would even acknowledge that believers are *tempted* by the Evil One. Jesus Christ said as much in the prayer he gave his people, and even he himself was tempted by the Devil.

But *possession*, someone who had joined the Church, experiencing the same power being exerted from the inside? They would hear nothing of the sort! Yet thousands, even millions, of Christians have lived to tell about it. So does the Bible, with Judas and Ananias.

Rumbling thunder in the distance brought Apollos back to the moment, desire churning in his belly again from the weight and pleasure of what was to come. He went to a panel on a blank wall that disguised what was below. Pressing his hand against the device, it pulsed blue before flashing green. The wall shuddered before revealing a stairwell that stretched downward.

On toward destiny.

The floor felt cold under Apollos's bare feet as he slowly descended the stone stairway of his sanctum, earth and stone, mold and must mixing with delight. He had always had a certain fascination with the elemental, the earthen, believing as his Indo-Europan ancestors did. That there was a life force that permeated all things, binding them together in divinity.

That One is all, and all is One.

And unlike Ichthus, who insisted we all move and have our being in the Most High One—the Nameless One—he knew otherwise, the Presence revealing all to him, possessing him until the time was ripe for the full unveiling and confrontation.

Those portents, the trumpets unfolding the Nameless One's pathetic attempts at controlling Solterra were all the signal he and the Authority needed to trigger the next phase of Purity.

The absolute destruction of Ichthus—beginning with its head. At least its *earthly* head. The spiritual one would come later.

Thunder rumbled as Apollos continued his descent, LED

lights along the base of the stairwell wall lighting his way to the chamber below. The wind howled now as a mixture of rain and heavy, wet ash continued its beating assault against the thick, interlocking stones of the ancient castle, a violent reflection of the nature of what was about to take place below the legendary, rebuilt heart of all he was planning, something begun centuries ago from a fabled entity that had waged war against the Church from this very locale.

Nous...

Originally built in the seventeenth century, it later became the central headquarters of the German SS and central command for Heinrich Himmler. Though it had become a sort of museum and youth hostel post-WWII, the estate had been acquired by a former Grand Master of Nous over a century ago—before his unfortunate demise, and much of the headquarters were destroyed by a rival that eventually became an ally.

Apollos had studied the legends with great interest, finding a kindred spirit in the former Grand Master, Rudolph Borg. He had been the one to reactivate the enemy of the Church stretching back to its founding, transforming the castle and the alt-spiritual Nous organization into his own needs: a nerve center of spiritual enlightenment and war. Bless the Universe he had the foresight to train his successor in the ways of Nous, ironically a twin to a Master of the Order of Thaddeus. What they preserved for decades through the past century paved the way for a new rising, finalizing force that would finally eliminate the Christians, the Church.

The Christ, even!

Apollos continued his descent, the black silk robe swishing with every step. Reaching the bottom, he kept on toward the chamber, but he stopped when he reached a statue.

Bird-Man Thoth, the ancient Egyptian god of wisdom. Of

revelation. Of *gnostikos*, the divine knowledge. It was a perfect replica of the colossal statue artifact discovered near the mortuary temple of Amenhotep III in Luxor, surviving the original destruction of the Nous compound. Universe only knows how, but it stood as a testament to the enduring legacy of the entity that had made the future possible, beginning with Panligo and carrying toward the end. Measuring eleven-and-half feet tall and made of pure, red granite culled from ancient quarries in Egypt, the statue towered over Apollos, reminding him of his ancient calling and setting his face like flint against Ichthus.

He focused his attention on the ancient face, the ibis head peering down at him with a mask of pure gold, with a black onyx beak, flanked by indigo ribbons, and the Atef crown of white and red feathers stretching upward. It was truly a testimony to the enduring legacy of the ancient Nous cult.

Thoth served as a mediating power between good and evil, as a scribe of the gods, and was regarded as self-begotten and self-produced—like the Übermensch of his own ancient Germanic ancestors, the ultramodern superior man. He was the master of both natural and divine law, directing the motions of the heavenly bodies and affairs of men. His power was unlimited and unrivaled by all other gods, the true author of every work of every branch of knowledge.

Human and divine.

"*'You know all that is hidden under the heavenly vault,'*" Apollos intoned, bowing his head reverently before the stone effigy as he quoted from the mystical sayings surrounding the god. "'*Now, that which has been hidden shall be revealed.*' And it shall be mine," he finished, clenching his fist with resolve.

Lightning flashed behind him through the windows up the stairwell, illuminating the god of knowledge in flickering white light. A few seconds later, thunder rumbled in the distance, bringing Apollos out of his trance. He stiffened with purpose and continued down the darkly lit hallway, striding forth to meet his gathered brothers.

A glowing light up ahead pulled him onward, orange and warm. Voices, low and incoherent, were chanting the ancient mantra he knew by heart. A bleating screech sliced through the noise, and he quickened his pace. He reached the heavy golden door standing ajar and pushed it open. The voices stopped as he entered. Facing him were seventeen Bird-Men, all wearing the face of Thoth.

The god of divine knowledge.

"Brothers," Apollos said, striding toward them. The Bird-Men nodded in silent unison, welcoming their new Grand Master, crowned after Martin Zarruq had been...disposed of.

He stepped into the circular cavern, high and domed. Made out of quarried stone, the room was illuminated by eight windows that flickered every so often with the storm's light. Thirteen torches displayed around the room offered a soft glow to provide the remaining light. They hung above thirteen small, stone seats upon which bare-chested Bird-Men sat with ornamented shoulder drapes of gold and indigo beadwork, all wearing masks of pure gold, flanked by ribbons of indigo, with beaks of black onyx.

Apollos scanned the room, then lifted his head toward the high dome, smiling reverently at the symbol adorning its center: a swastika, made infamous by the radicals of the 20th century. Far from a modern symbol of fascist oppression, it was an ancient religious one, taking the form of the familiar equilateral cross with its four legs bent at ninety degrees. Considered to be a sacred symbol of ancient spiritualities, it held all the divine promises of these pre-modern cultures for such a time as this.

Directly beneath the dome, in the middle of the room, was

the crown jewel of the crypt: the ceremonial basin. It acted as a baptismal pool for the rite of passage into the upper echelon of the ancient order of divine knowledge and power.

Tonight, it would be used for a very different purpose, a sacred purpose.

He strode farther into the chamber, the cool, dank air making the blond hairs on the back of his neck stand upright in delight. Seats were arrayed around the outer rim of the room for the Thirteen, the coterie of high-ranking associates representing the Wheel of the Year and the perfection of the earthly and heavenly alignment of seasons. Five more lined the front of the chamber, holding the Council of Five. The seats of the Pentagram.

Of the God-Man...

Apollos breathed deeply and moved toward a throne-like chair in the middle of the Pentagram seats. His chair. He took his place among the Council at the center reserved for the Grand Master. To his right was the ceremonial ibis dress. It mirrored the statue of Thoth he had just passed, white and red plumes, gold mask and all. He smiled and placed the head-dress upon his head, then affixed the gold mask to his face, along with an intricately beaded gold and indigo sash hanging at his shoulders.

A small, muffled goat's bleat was heard from the center of the ceremonial basin. He spun toward it and peered through his gold mask, over the onyx beak, to the four-legged victim tied and muzzled in the center of the floor. It strained violently against its restraints, nibbling at the muzzle keeping his mouth tightly closed, as if it anticipated what was impending.

The snapping of the torch flames provided the only sound in the chamber as Apollos strolled toward the center, his black garment swishing in sync. He untied the animal and undid the muzzle. A bleating, mournful cry instantly escaped its lips.

Out from under his robe, Apollos removed a jewel-encrusted athame knife passed down from Grand Master to Grand Master from each successive generation to use in ceremonies such as this one. In one swift swipe, he sliced the blade across the goat's throat. The bleating stopped as blood spilled from its neck onto the cold, hard stone floor. The animal twitched in his tight grip, then went limp, its life force draining into the baptismal pool.

He withdrew the golden vial of his blood from his robe and uncorked it, pouring the contents of his life force into the pool, his blood mixing with that of the goat. The animal was a symbol of purity and preciousness, and the regenerative nature of the Universe, ancient civilizations lionizing the goat as a god of nature—Pan.

Joining him was another. Someone bound and gagged, his long, silvery hair flowing around his prone body.

Apollos grinned through the ibis mask, looming over the figure.

"Hello, James Ferraro. It's been too long."

The door slammed shut from behind; the cardinal gave a pitiful, muffled yelp.

Excellent. Time to get the party started.

CHAPTER 19

BÜREN, GERMANIA.

Alexander flipped his jacket collar up and pulled it tight around his neck, an electric charge skittering up his spine and spreading gooseflesh across his body. He steeled himself for the hour ahead, for the path ahead that led him into the heart of darkness down below.

He didn't want to be here; didn't want to go there, the monstrosity of glass and chrome and stone that loomed in the darkness. The world around seemed to crackle with an unholy energy from the place, wind still gusting around after a thunderstorm had blown through the area the night before. Now all that remained was a bite to the air, a clawing and cloying wickedness that echoed what had befallen Solterra Republic a year ago.

Upon arriving on the north shores of Germania, they rode out the wicked onslaught of blood and ash in an abandoned suburban house that looked like a seaside cottage, the seas having overtaken large swaths of what had been the outskirts of an industrialized urban center. Had no interest navigating through hostile territory during such a storm, though it probably would have been sensible, taking advantage of the cover of darkness and sheeting rain. Eventually they managed to traipse across the barren countryside, landing on that overlook and readying to execute their rescue operation—for the second time.

Wet ground and charred foliage clung to the air around, along with the stench of spoiled beef and rotting blood. It was the opposite of fecund, the opposite of a lush, fertile land eager to spring forth new life or waiting for harvesters to reap its bounty.

Shivering and steeling himself, he pushed back his sleeve. It was almost time. Still had a few hours before the ticking-clock countdown wound down to zero, but they were cutting it mercilessly close. For Father Jim's sake. He just hoped they reached him in time.

They *had* to reach him in time. No hope about it.

He was perched on a bluff overlooking a massive triangular structure with three round towers—one made of ancient stone, the other two of chrome and titanium—connected by massive walls of the same ultramodern material nestled in the valley below. A rolling shallow river tinged crimson snaked through the small Germanian town past the Renaissance castle that promised to hold the terminus for their operation.

Rescuing Father Jim.

Thunder rumbled in the distance, a stiff, frigid breeze picking up and sending dried, dead foliage dancing in a whirling dervish that seemed to beckon the Devil himself. Ash and soot blew along with it, a stark reminder they were still in the midst of the apocalypse.

The static charge of a thunderstorm tinged by woodsmoke and those dancing dead leaves filled Alexander's head with a dizzying sense of fall, except it was springtime. The risen apocalypse had made a mess of things, and made a mess of his sense of things, making him second guess his intuition.

Perhaps that's all it was. Lightning in the stratosphere, the electrostatic discharge from two electrically charged regions in the atmosphere disturbing the peace—*his* peace—rather than an unholy wickedness permeating their target.

Except—

There it was again.

He brought his collar higher against his neck, forcing his attention at the ancient building renovated in the ghastly ultramodern architecture of the Republic. An energy seemed to pulse from the castle down below, sending an electric dread ratcheting up his spine again and sending all of his hairs standing at attention. He brought his arms close around his chest now, wondering what lay below—what resided below.

Something sinister, something familiar.

Something not of this world.

The bitter wind picked up its pace from behind, more dried grass and plant stalks joined by ash and soot blowing past again. It was the scent of decay, of death, of a world quickly unraveling. Acrid ash and rotting leaves, bloodied and soiled garments.

Perhaps that salty-sweet tang from the electrical charge wasn't so bad after all, whatever and whoever it was connected to.

Alexander turned away and sauntered back down the narrow pathway to his teammates—Ford and Reeves, joined by Nia and Sasha. The original crew from the original operation that had gone to hell. He just hoped this one turned out far differently.

Father Thomás Polanco had stayed behind in the escape hydrocraft with Lucy and Rebekah. They had wanted to join but everyone agreed they couldn't risk losing another hydrocraft and that five Unfits traipsing across Solterra was enough

of a risk. They would meet up with them after the fact, hopefully with the package.

*Lord Jesus Christ, Son of God, surely with the package,
with Father Jim...*

Ford's head emerged from the trunk of an older-model
magnacar sedan. They had found it parked at a supermarket
and managed to hijack its central computer terminal to bring
it under their control. Wasn't proud of stealing it, not in the
slightest. Hadn't been proud of many choices he'd made the
past few years since leaving the quiet comforts of his former
life as a simple parish priest. But such was life now—such was
his life now, after a rising apostasy had overtaken Ichthus and
after the apocalypse had overtaken Solterra.

After the storm died down, they'd driven from the abandoned suburban home to the outskirts of the tiny Germanian
town of Büren, where they motored to their lookout point
staking out the old German structure that had once been
home to the Schutzstaffel. The Nazi paramilitary organization
headed by Heinrich Himmler, known simply as the SS.

There was nothing available on DiviNet, its history
having been wiped. Found one reference to it in the Order
Archives, a passing mention of its demise during a similar
operation with the Order of Thaddeus. Polanco said it had
been the lair of Nous, the ancient enemy of Ichthus stretching
back to the Church's founding.

Whatever it was, the dimmed sun was setting fast,
shrouded by a thick canopy of rain clouds that portended
doom whilst his teammates were rummaging around for
equipment to storm the ancient building.

There was that energy again, coming from behind up the
trail, coming from all around—an electrified pulse that meant
nothing good.

"Think fast, homefry." Ford tossed Alexander a Neutralizer and slammed the trunk shut.

He caught it and slung it around his shoulder, his gut twisting with anticipation and regret. Never could get used to wielding one of these things. Hated guns and had sworn off violence as a priest. But desperate times required one's scruples be set aside, at least some of them.

Alexander checked his watch again. Time was running out, with less than a few hours remaining.

"Everything in order? Because we've got to move."

"It is, but hold your horses." Ford turned to Sasha. "You find out anything more about this building, some schematic or floor plan?"

He frowned, stuffing a slate device in a backpack. "*Nyet.* It is like this building is never existing."

"Shucky ducky..."

"I am not liking this," Nia said, turning toward another narrow path winding down to the shallow river that butted up against the castle. "The bad energy, the blind assault."

"What choice do we have?" Alexander said, growing impatient.

Ford nodded. "Alex is right. No other choice. So let's get to it."

The others agreed, and soon they were hustling toward their target.

The evening had quickly turned to night now, the sun already darkened from both the fourth trumpet from last year and clouds, and the celestial orb having sunk farther beneath the horizon. The cover of darkness was welcomed.

Didn't take long before they crossed the river, the thickened sludge a shallow mixture of slow-moving water and mud with tendrils of crimson winding through the liquid. Like an oil slick blooming from a wounded ocean tanker. Was grateful for the thick military boots to guard his feet.

Reaching the building, the flash of a purplish electric charge flared against it from the canopy above. Thunder rumbled on cue, as did a letting of a frigid rain from above slapping against Alexander's face. Had hoped to avoid getting caught in a storm, but he was banking his prayers for the success of the operation.

The water was cold and tingly against his skin, a light pink and gray hue signaling a toxicity to it that perhaps explained the tingle.

"*Mne ne nravitsya...*" Sasha complained, glancing around with wide eyes.

"I don't like it either, *bratishka*," Nia said, "but what choice do we have?"

"Best hop to it," Ford agreed, glancing around and craning up the shearing stone wall, the only part still intact from the original castle structure, joined by one of three turrets. "That window, the one right there with the balcony, should do the trick."

"*Khorosho.* Step aside," Nia instructed.

He did, along with Alexander and Sasha. She wielded a large weapon of sorts, with a spike and rope attached to the end.

Taking aim straight above, she fired. A loud *chu-cu* sounded from the utensil, its echo riding above the din of the stream winding behind.

Alexander worried they would be heard rummaging around the base of the castle. But as the rope sailed high into the sky, and then wrapped securely around the railing, no one came.

"*Uspekh!*" Nia said, making a fist of success. "All set."

"Bravo, sister ma-gister," Ford said. "No time like the

present to make like a jackrabbit and hop to it. I imagine you'll want first dibs."

"*Da.* I'm going first." And she did.

Without waiting for confirmation, Nia secured the rope to a belt wrapped around her waist, then wrapped one end around her arm and gripped it before starting her ascent.

Ford pointed at Sasha, then Alexander. "You follow your fellow Ukrainski chickadee, doc, with Alexander close behind. Reeves and I will take up the rear."

Sasha swallowed hard but offered no complaint.

Nia made quick work climbing up the wall, the military-grade boots not slipping once. Before long, she was resting on the balcony whilst Sasha was following her lead and Alexander was coaching from behind.

Took longer, Sasha not as adept at wall climbing, but they made it, soon joining Nia and tossing the rope down to Ford and Reeves. The pair reached them without issue and without much effort, the special-ops men trained for such a thing.

The balcony barely held the quintet, made of titanium and glass. The window was a solid door of the same, with a chrome handle that was locked.

Ford cupped his hands at the window. "Looks clear, and quite homey. And boujee to beat the band."

"What is this boogie business?" Nia asked.

"Boujee. Boujee. Slang in my parts of Solterra for the luxurious lifestyle of the super luxe. You know, named after those bourgeoisie characters who control the means of production in a capitalist society from Karl Marx's fever dream."

She twisted up her face. "You are referencing the foundational ideology of a totalitarian regime on the threshold of infiltrating a military compound of another totalitarian regime?"

He frowned. "Good point. Hey, doc, you said you could hack your way into this military compound."

Sasha held up his slate device and smiled. "*Da.* I am having my locking picking kit right here."

"Have at it partner before this storm melts us quicker than Gulch sizzled to nothing but nothing."

Sasha tapped away and Alexander turned to Ford. "Another Karl Marx reference?"

"Naw. *The Wizard of Oz.*"

"*Khorosho.* I am finished," Sasha announced.

There was a soft click, and the door released a crack.

Ford clapped him on the shoulder. "Remind me to put you in for a promotion."

Without waiting, he brought his Neutralizer around, reached out an arm, and grabbed the glass, nodding at Alexander.

He returned the nod, bringing his own weapon around at the ready with a clatter and edging to the entrance—holding his breath and steeling himself.

Moment of truth...

In one motion, Ford opened the door and Alexander pushed through white sheer curtains.

Ready for anything.

The room was cold, the air stale. It echoed with his footfalls as he darted inside to sweep for hostiles, joined now by Ford and Nia, her Scythe's head casting an eerie purple glow around the vast space.

There was no one. No Enforcers, no Purifiers, no casual civilians.

And no Father Jim.

To be expected, knowing he had been held in an ancient vault, but still. It was a reminder they had a long way to go, with time quickly ticking down to zero.

The space itself was vast and vaulted, the ceiling high but plain and void of any ornate decorations. No gilt whorls or large, fancy chandcliers of small crystal balls anchored at the center. The walls were gray, and furniture angular and boring as all get out, a few couches, armchairs, end tables. No surprise, given the Republic's panache for whittling the beauty of traditional forms down to their functional ultra-modern expression. A thin layer of dust blanketed the pieces and black marble floors, indicating disuse for some time.

Alexander brought his rifle against his chest and exhaled a breath he didn't know he was holding. Relief washed over him upon entering without incident.

But they were far from out of the woods.

He led the way to a closed door, the others following close behind. Coming up to it, he turned the knob.

It gave without issue.

Easing it open—

Neglected hinges threw up a hideous cry.

Ford winced and put up a staying hand—wedging his foot in the open doorway to keep their position but not going any further.

Waiting a beat, then another, Alexander was satisfied no one had paid the sound any mind.

Gesturing to Ford, who grabbed the knob, Alexander nudged his Neutralizer into the darkened hallway.

Ford flung the door open to mitigate the hinges' complaint.

They squealed, but that was the end of it.

The five quickly emerged into a vacant hallway painted a ghastly bloody pinkish hue from a floor-to-ceiling window at the end.

"Why are we not yet seeing resistance?" Nia whispered at Alexander's side.

"Agree," Reeves said from his other.

"Perhaps they are busy elsewhere," Ford answered.

Perhaps they are busy...

Alexander recoiled inside at the thought. The memory of Father Jim tied to that chair, bloody and beaten, sent him moving faster.

Swallowing, he padded down the hallway, the marble tiles throwing up squeaking protests from his boots.

"*Da*, but where are they being busy?" Sasha asked.

He glanced behind, the question settling hard in his already churning gut.

Another hallway appeared, the other side of the triangle.

The group padded to the edge, pressing against the cool wall.

Alexander held his breath at the line's head. Waiting, intuiting, discerning any movement beyond the threshold.

Because Nia was right. It was odd they hadn't met any resistance, either outside or inside. Given this was a secure Republic compound, housing one of their most valuable assets—the figurehead of Ichthus—Alexander had thought they'd have to shoot their way to Padre.

Expected at least a passing show of security. But nothing so far.

Perhaps that was a sign of good things to come.

Feeling safe to proceed, he glanced behind for confirmation.

Ford nodded him to proceed, Nia coming up next to him and shining her Scythe onward.

He nodded back and stepped out to round the bend.

And was met by a hulking, bulky figure sauntering down the hallway on careful steps, Neutralizer raised and ready.

Rising a head above him. All neck with wide shoulders. Arms bulging through his charcoal armored suit and face shielded by the wicked helmet that gave him the appearance of a praying mantis.

Didn't even have time to react, because a sudden purply orb sliced past his field of vision and planted firmly in that bug face.

Nia, taking the Enforcer out in an instant without any eruption of weapons, least of all his.

The body slumped to its knees, held only by Nia's Scythe sticking out of its face. In one motion, she yanked the staff from the helmet, and the body completed its descent.

She said, "No need to alert the Republic just yet."

Voices farther down the hallway startled Alexander. He glanced at Ford, who sprang into action, grabbing the fallen Enforcer's arms and whispering for Alexander's help.

He quickly grabbed the body's legs, and the pair dragged it around the corner, the others edging out of the way.

Holding his breath, Alexander chanced a glance around the corner.

Two figures, clad in crimson this time, stopped halfway down the hallway, followed by the turning of a knob and the opening of a door on far-better oiled hinges than their entrance into this bedlam.

Purifiers...

Only one reason for those kind.

He swallowed hard, his tongue tripping over itself and that seared memory of Padre activating him.

"I think we've discovered our destination." He edged out into the hallway, Neutralizer outstretched and motioning at the entrance. "Two Purifiers went into that door."

"We should get to it, then," Ford said, gripping his Neutralizer with the same activation.

Alexander nodded and carried on, heart pulsing in his

head now and air hard to come by as he padded toward the entrance.

A faint white glow danced in the hallway through a cracked doorway, along with the trace scent of woodsmoke.

He led the way toward the open invitation, slowing his pace as soft voices echoed toward him.

Coming up to the entrance, he padded around the threshold, weapon ready for confrontation.

Then pushed through to the other side.

Empty.

The other four quickly followed.

Sweeping the room, he was struck by its vastness and brilliance. It was nothing like he had seen before in Solterra.

It was bright and made of white marble veined with faint gray lining the floor and walls. The ceiling was vaulted by soaring Corinthian columns edged by gilt lines circling the white pillars like candy canes. High above, crystals clung to the corners and seams of the ceiling like clusters of grapes, a sort of celestial crown molding he imagined would refract the light with a rainbow brilliance from the day through large windows anchored at one end. Anchored at the center of the ceiling, a mural of celestial beings locked in arms with recognizable figures peered down at him, witnessing their intrusion. Plush, gilded chairs were arranged at one end, along with a glass coffee table. A glass desk stood nearby.

"They must have gone down below," Ford said softly, gesturing with his Neutralizer to a hidden open door, stairs spiraling downward. "Which means into the portal of doom we go..."

Alexander swallowed and nodded, padding across the floor and edging to the entrance leading beneath the castle.

He stopped short, took a breath.

Then plunged down inside.

Swinging his Neutralizer around in one quick motion, Alexander confirmed the stairwell was empty. Although the voices filtered up from below the winding case of stone stairs.

He took them, one by one, inching ever downward with the cold, rough-cut blocks at his back.

Thunder rolled with a muffle from beyond the stone walls as they made their descent, LED lights along the base of the stairwell wall lighting each step down into the void. What lay beneath was anyone's clue, which Alexander didn't at all fancy.

The wind howled now as a mixture of rain and heavy, wet ash beat against the thick, interlocking stones of the ancient castle. The voices trailed to nothing as they reached the bottom, finding a subterranean chamber that opened into a vestibule and stretched into a corridor leading toward a glowing chamber.

Greeting them was an unexpected sight.

A statue of a bird-man. Thoth, if Alexander recognized it. The ancient Egyptian god of wisdom. Of revelation. Of divine knowledge.

The sight of it sent a shiver up his spine.

"Look," Ford said.

Alexander followed his pointed finger. Past Thoth, down a corridor, and to a closed set of heavy doors. The stone running through the passageway and underneath looked exactly like the kind they'd glimpsed from the broadcaster.

Where Padre had been sitting.

He ran to it, Ford and Nia throwing up a rushing complaint to halt.

No way, no how. Not with Father Jim in reach.

In one motion, he twisted the handle and barged inside, training his Neutralizer forward for action as he swept the dim space—

And finding it empty.

Empty?

Empty!

Except for a crusted pool of blood at the center of the stone well, there was no one around.

More importantly: No Father Jim around.

Dear Lord...

CHAPTER 20

Ford raced to follow Alex, coming up to a skidding stop behind him and immediately seeing the problem.

What the...

"Where's Father Jim?"

Alexander spun around, eyes wide and frantic. "Not here!"

Before he could answer, there was a flash from the corner of his eyes.

Crimson, hulking and bulky, in the shadows.

The goons they'd spotted, the voices they'd heard!

Wondered where they'd gotten off to. Now he—

A wicked blow struck his head, followed by starlight and dimming darkness.

That'd leave a mark.

But nothing he couldn't handle.

And nothing that really surprised him.

Ducking for a second blow, the hostile reached for a Blastgun strapped to his side.

Dude was way too close to fire his Neutralizer, so Ford did the next best thing. Didn't even need to think about what came next.

Letting go of his own weapon, the strap catching it against his neck, he swung his open, stiff palm at his neck.

Swing and chop.

Hard against a bulging Adam's apple exposed beneath that hideous bulbous black shiny face shield that made him look like a hornet. An unfortunate feature of Republic regulation uniform.

Once and done. Just as the Patron's government had taught him back in the day.

The hand reaching for the Blastgun instantly went to his neck instead, joined by the other, along with a hideous choking sound.

A pasty gurgle searching for desperate breaths.

His quick-on-the-draw fancy handiwork had crushed that bobbing Adam's apple, lodging it in his windpipe.

He was suffocating. Slowly.

Wanted to let the whack job suffocate and suffer a painful death. Pre-Christian Ford would've, too. But the Holy Ghost had softened his heart some since his days with the Legion. So he did the next best thing instead, putting his fancy footwork to, well, work.

Darting around to the Purifier's back, he kicked the back of his legs.

The goon slumped to the floor, and he slung one arm around to join those hands. The other reached around his forehead and grabbed hold of that bulbous helmet of his and wrenched it off.

It came loose, revealing a shaved head and hard face scarred by wicked acne.

In one motion, cinching his one arm tighter against his throat and the other around his forehead, he twisted. Just like the chickens he'd snatch from the coop for dinner time on his family farm—before clenching their necks and spinning them around until their heads popped off.

A soft *crack* sounded from his neck after it was snapped.

Severing his spinal cord and relieving the man of his suffocation.

It was over, just like that.

He huffed a breath he forgot he was holding—but a cry on the other side of the room told him not to revel in his victory too soon.

Goon Two had Nia held by the neck and was backing up, a Blastgun aimed at her temple!

Which instantly activated Ford, followed by Reeves. Didn't even think about it, the pair taking aim with their Neutralizers in no time flat.

"Back off!" the goon commanded, giving the Blastgun a shake for emphasis. "Or the lady's brains are toast."

He gripped his Neutralizer tighter, cursing under his breath before spitting to the side.

Shucky ducky...

"Let her go," Reeves said calmly, taking a subtle step toward the Purifier.

Which he didn't like, not in the slightest.

He shuddered back a step of his own, pressing the Blastgun harder against Nia's head to put an exclamation point on his demand.

For her part, she gave not a squeak nor a peep. Better woman than he was a man, that's for darn tootin'.

But what to do, what to do?

Obviously they couldn't stay down there forever. Someone would have to break. Most likely them, either relenting to save Nia, or some of his buddies coming down to fetch their missing pal.

So, again, what to do, what to do!

A beat ticked by, then another, his brain spinning out all sorts of scenarios.

Until—

He had it.

Hoped his childhood safety ditty from yore translated into Ukrainski alright, otherwise this would be a quick trip around the merry-go-round.

Taking a breath, Ford shouted. "Stop, drop, and roll, sister ma-gister!"

Took her a beat, her eyes locking his so that he thought she thought he was cuckoo for Cocoa-Puffs. Well, he was, but that was beside the point.

Confused the heck out of the Purifier.

Then it clicked, her eyes narrowing into resolve and nodding. She'd picked up what he was putting down.

Nia hiked up her feet real good, sudden and swift.

Which shifted all hundred-forty pounds of her solid muscle into the arms of the Republic's finest.

Totally throwing off the poor lad's equilibrium, and his hold on her.

Nia slipped through his arms before he knew what was what, sliding to a thudding *whomp* on the stone floor and following through with the fire-safety roll out of harm's way.

The sudden turn of things startled the Purifier's reflexes into popping off a *pew-pew* shot.

Not so finest after all.

Which Ford and Reeves followed up with by opening up a duel can of Neutralizer whoop ass on the fella—falling him in no time flat.

He shuddered to a dying stand-still, slumping to join Nia like a used bathrobe.

Recovering, Nia started for her feet. Ford went to her and

gave her a helping hand. She took it and threw him a smile and a nod.

"*Spasibo*, cowboy. Thanks for saving me."

"Thank us both," Ford said, nodding to Reeves. "You alright?"

"I am being fine, but we are having bigger things in our bowl than me."

She gestured to the blood-stained floor missing the goods.

The Father Jim goods.

Alexander shoved back his sleeve and checked his wrist, then cursed before collapsing to his knees.

"It's too late..."

He buried his head in his hands, a soft whimper of remorse, probably regret, coming from the fella.

Felt bad for him, real bad. Knew how much the man meant to Alex. Heck, he'd meant the world to him as well. So the fact he wasn't where he was supposed to be...

Flat didn't make sense. And flat meant nothing good.

Ford checked his own watch. Alex was right. The ticking-clock countdown had wound down to zero several minutes ago.

Dang...

Reeves asked, "Where do you suppose they've taken him?"

"Are you supposing," Sasha wondered, "he is being somewhere in the compound?"

"Good call. Maybe there's another room, some torture chamber they've got him holed up in."

Ford shook his head. Hadn't a clue. More than likely they'd shuttled him off the compound.

"Wait...The study above!" Alexander sprang to his feet, making for the door.

"Huh? Hey, homefry, why don't you—" Ford grabbed his arm, but he sloughed him off, jerking it back and taking off.

"Alex, wait!" he shouted after him, but it was no use.

"What's he talking about?" Nia asked, waving her Scythe toward the exit. "Where's he going?"

"I saw it too," Reeves said. "There was a broadcaster mounted above the fireplace. Must be thinking that's the Republic's next move."

Ford sucked in a measured breath, understanding what that move was.

And dreading it.

Heading for the door, he called back, "We should catch up to Alex before—"

He couldn't voice the end to that sentence. What it would mean for Father Jim, what it might mean for them if there was an army of Enforcers waiting for them up top.

"This way," he commanded, shaking away the thoughts.

Ford darted back out into the corridor, his weapon more than at the ready.

It was empty, but for that cray-cray statue standing guard.

He raced past, the rest following quickly.

Aiming straight up the well of the staircase, he pounded up the stone stairs, taking them by twos, finger firmly at the trigger and ready for anything as he neared the top.

Reached it quickly, along with the other three close behind, encountering no resistance.

Alex had already shoved back into the bright white room that felt like a little slice of Heaven—an odd juxtaposition, given it was like a tenth circle of hell!

No one was waiting for them, no one was around. Supposed they had that going for them. There was one thing awaiting them though.

The broadcaster, planted on a white marble wall above an

old-school fireplace that looked like it had seen recent use. Still smelled sooty and woodsy, taking Ford back a klick to fall childhoods of yore.

The device was on, and the Republic was doing their propaganda thing broadcasting who knew what level of hooey to the polis masses.

Max Bacchus, that wackadoodle clown, was yammering on about something he couldn't hear. He moved closer to join Alex for a better hearing.

Then he did.

Shucky ducky...

⬜

Alexander couldn't move, couldn't think, couldn't breathe.

All for one reason.

"That is not being the same place that Max character was before."

It was Sasha, coming up to his side now.

No, it wasn't...

"It's the Capitolium," Ford confirmed, voice low and grave.

Alexander wondered how he could be so certain, but he had other things to worry about.

Like what was about to happen to Father Jim!

Because dead center, in a room looking very much like their own, sat the cardinal.

James Ferraro.

Alexander's mentor and confidant. His friend.

The closest thing he had to a father.

Before he could process what was happening—what had *happened*, the turn of things with not making it on time, or not making it at all, Padre having been shuttled away to the Solterran capital—another figure joined him.

Tall and lithe, with silver hair and white, almost translucent skin. He wore white robes that dripped from his angular, bony frame. A hooked nose was anchored under a generous forehead between two fiery red eyes.

At first, Alexander thought it was Dominic Weiss, the man looking similar to the cardinal but younger.

It wasn't him. Knew it wasn't him.

He had yet to be introduced to the Republic, but Alexander knew instantly who was standing over Father Jim—looming, really, the figure towering above him.

Neron Kaisar.

If their new companion was to be believed, Thomás Polanco, formerly Senator Kolocovich, then this was the Antichrist.

"Greetings, Solterra Republic. We have yet to be introduced. My name is Neron Kaisar. Your new Patron."

A rushing whisper of Muscovia was exchanged between Nia and Sasha. Reeves started humming lowly and Ford just looked at Alexander with vacant eyes, face whiter than his best dress *thawb*.

The man stood tall, a slight smile playing across his face. It was a beautiful face, if not intriguing. With the red eyes and lily white skin, the curtain of silvery Basset Hound hair parted down the middle and hanging low, framing the angular cheekbones that yielded cutting shadows. And again, tall. Near nine feet as far as he could tell.

"Hours ago, the Senate ratified my ascension to Summum Regis, the Prime Leader, taking the place of our fallen Dear Leader, Lucius Severus. We will become more acquainted in short time, and I promise my polis a coming revolution that will finally bring about the ultimate peace, prosperity, and progress we have longed for ages. For now, you should know—"

Before he knew what had happened, the man turned sharply and Father Jim's head went snapping to the side, a hideous *smack* sounding from the broadcaster.

Neron, or the Patron, or whoever—he'd hit Father Jim!

"Sonofa—" Ford cursed before spitting to the side.

Alexander didn't have time to respond; Neron did it for him.

"He is the one responsible!" he screamed at Padre. "Him and his whole lot. The Christians. *Ichthus.*"

He spat those words out like sour olives. And if Alexander didn't know better, it sounded like there was a hissing behind them.

Neron returned back to his audience, taking a breath and smiling again.

"But, as you will discover, I am a forgiving man. A merciful Patron. And so I shall extend my hand of grace. For one tiny consolation."

Father Jim didn't move, didn't blink. Instead, he faced forward, a curious grin playing across his face, one side blooming a shade of crimson. As if unfazed by his turn of circumstances, as if not at all worried about what was to come.

As if at peace with what was to come...

There was a loud *clap-clap*, Neron rapping his hands together in a final clasp. But wait...were those—

Alexander gasped, counting the fingers. Six on each hand!

"Now, all you must do," Neron went on, "is repeat after me. *I confess that I have sinned against the Patron—in thought, word and deed. By what I have done and what I have left undone.*"

He instantly recognized what was happening.

"That confession again," Reeves said. "From the Anglican *Book of Common Prayer*."

Ford added, "The one Kareema…"

He trailed off. No need to complete that thought.

"*O my Patron,*" the new Patron went on, Father Jim still unmoving, "*with all my heart I am heartily sorry for having offended you, and I detest all my sins.*"

More nothing from Father Jim—

Until his face whipped sideways again, preceded by another loud *smack*. Alexander jumped, along with the others.

"*Confess!*" Neron shouted.

The tears flowed now, Alexander's throat constricting with emotion. Nia whimpered behind, same as Sasha, the two holding one another.

Reeves and Ford stood stoic, faces bearing witness to the atrocity and unable to help, feet planted wide and arms planted behind their backs.

"*In choosing to do wrong and failing to do good,*" Neron went on, "*I have offended you whom I should serve above all things. I firmly intend, with your help, to do penance, to offend you no more, and to avoid whatever leads me in offending the Authority.*"

He slid down next to Father Jim's side, that silvery curtain of hair falling and obscuring his face.

"You will make the necessary confession, or you will die as a terrorist and traitor to the Republic."

Now Padre spoke: "Better die a traitor to mankind than an apostate to Christ."

Then he straightened, sitting stiff and brightening. Then: "I confess that Jesus Christ is King of kings and Lord of lords —" with a slight glance to Neron, and a widened smile, he added "—and Patron of patrons."

The room erupted in hoots and hollers. Go Padre!

"Further, *I believe in God, the Father almighty,*" he went on, voice resounding, "*creator of Heaven and Earth.*"

Recognition instantly hit Alexander. It was the Apostles' Creed. Ichthus's anchor stretching back to the Church's earliest beginnings. The one he and Rebekah had saved from destruction a year ago. So it made sense this would be Father Jim's response.

"*I believe in Jesus Christ, his only Son, our Lord, who was conceived by the Holy Spirit and born of the virgin Mary. He suffered under Pontius Pilate, was crucified, died, and was buried; he descended to Hell. The third day he rose again from the dead. He ascended to Heaven and is seated at the right hand of God the Father almighty. From there he will come to judge the living and the dead.*"

Now the room joined in as one, repeating what Father Jim was confessing: "*I believe in the Holy Spirit, the holy catholic church, the communion of saints, the forgiveness of sins, the resurrection of the body, and the life everlasting.*"

"*Amen!*" Ford and Reeves shouted together.

"*Amin,*" Sasha and Nia echoed in their foreign tongue.

"Amen," whispered Alexander, bracing for what came next.

"*This* is my confession," Father Jim offered. "It shall be no other."

Neron eased upright, putting his hair back in place behind his ears. Rage flashed hot across the man's lily skin, the vessels puckering pink before melting back into the whitish glow.

"Suit yourself," he sneered, turning his back on Padre.

From off-stage, he was handed a long object.

Light glinted from its metal, from its sharpened edge.

A sword!

Panic swept through Alexander, his bowels growing watery and lungs screaming for air but making no purchase.

He reached for the broadcaster, knowing what came next. "No..."

His vision blurred. Not from dimming darkness, but from emotion flooding his eyes. What he could make out was already underway.

Neron Kaisar raised the sword over his shoulder, swinging it toward Padre's neck like a bat toward a Tee-Ball stand.

In the split second, as the sword fell, Father Jim's first words to him rose to the surface, back when all this craziness began: *All things worth fighting for demand sacrifice.*

Sacrifice...

This was Padre's sacrifice. For his Lord and Savior, Jesus Christ.

For the Church, even.

For Alexander.

The sword stopped, Neron easing it within a hair length of Father Jim's brain stem.

Then he pulled back for a second go of it after a trial run.

Alexander heaved a stabilizing breath, refusing to take his eyes from the broadcaster. In many ways, he couldn't, the adrenaline rush and sheer curiosity at what was about to happen gluing his eyes to the display. But it was more than that.

He wouldn't. He refused to look away, bearing witness to Padre's martyrdom in all of its horrifying glory.

Then it happened—

The sword came down a second time, in the blink of an eye. In fact, he did blink and only knew what had happened because of the *shlopping* sound resounding through the quieted space, like slicing a chef's knife through a cantaloupe.

A split second later, when he opened his eyes, he hadn't even had time to prepare for what was registering on his retina.

The weapon was no longer visible, the force of it sending Father Jim's head one way, his body another.

Blood bubbled up in a geyser from the vacancy, then spurted in an unholy spray that spread across the stark white room, painting the floor in crimson specks and streaks before gathering beneath in a spreading pool.

Father Jim's eyes had opened with the look of shock, as if he himself hadn't prepared for the moment, his mouth hanging open as if in a question, with his tongue lolling out like a panting dog.

The sight would stay with Alexander until his last dying breath. So would the implications of what had just gone down.

Father James Ferraro—Father Jim, Padre—was dead. The Ministerium's head, the Church's force of cohesion, Alexander's anchor these past years.

What was he going to do?

"What are we going to be doing?" Sasha whispered, voicing his own confusion.

Except there was no confusion. There was only clarity.

"I know exactly what I'm going to do."

Alexander spun around, seething with a white-hot rage and giving his teammates wide, ready eyes.

"Blow this place to hell!"

CHAPTER 21

Father Jim was dead.

Could hardly believe what his peepers were peeping! Much less the thought that surfaced in Ford's tired, spent mind after several days of cray-to-the-Z. Did not compute, not in the slightest.

But there he was—there it was, the truth of it.

And in the most horrifying way imaginable.

Decapitation.

Wanted to puke just thinking about it. The stuff of night-mares. *His* nightmares, the singular one that had haunted him since childhood. Had yanked him from too many sleeps to count stretching back well past his teens into the single digits. Not sure how or why his subconscious dreamland noggin had latched on to it. Might've been something he'd seen on Divi-Net, some extreme vid he'd seen when he shouldn't have seen it, from a film or whatnot.

Couldn't recall now. Didn't much matter. What did was what the Republic had done—what the new Patron himself had done—employing such a measure on an Unfit.

On Father Jim!

This took the Purge to a whole new level of cray-cray he didn't want no part of.

The Church was in disarray. Common Christians were on the run, hiding for their lives, ostracized and cut off from the rest of the Republic—hunted by the polis, even. And—

Father Jim was dead!

Somehow, through the fog of dumbfounded disbelief, Ford heard tale of some other nonsense that didn't compute at first.

"Blow this place to hell, that's what!"

It was Alexander, mumbling some crazy talk. Before he understood what was what, homefry had pulled something from his jacket.

Something round, something silver.

Something like a Disruptor grenade.

He squeezed it once, then again, and tossed it across the floor.

It all happened so fast, yet in wicked slo-mo.

Shoot, he watched it happen.

His lips opened with a cry of warning, but nothing but nothing came of his vocal chords.

The orb rolled across the floor with a scraping skitter until it reached the threshold to the stairwell—and disappeared into the darkened void, the *plunkety-plunkety* echo of it bouncing down the stairs fading until—

A *whumping* explosion sounded deep in the bowels of the castle.

"*Idti!*" Nia said, the word of warning he'd meant to voice but couldn't snapping him from his confusion.

Had heard that bit of Ukrainski enough to know it meant scram to beat the band!

"Run!" he screamed. "Go. *Go. GO!*"

Just as the floor surrounding the doorway to the stone stairwell began to crack. Then crumble. Then—

Entirely give way!

Shucky ducky...

"We need to scram!"

Looked like he was the odd man out on that directive, because spinning back found him at the tail end of the magnarail getting out of Dodge!

Took cues from his teammates and kicked it into high gear as the world behind crumbled away to nothing but nothing.

They were through the door, but he needed a few more steps before—

His foot slipped from behind.

Sending him stumbling forward on his one solid leg while the other slipped into a void that meant nothing good.

He was weightless, the mawing emptiness pulling him down.

Until two strong hands grabbed his arms. Reeves and Alexander.

They pulled him to the surface, the crumbling floor stalling its advance, and dragged him through the study entrance and out into the hallway.

Catching his breath, he chanced a glance back inside. It was toast. Burnt toast! Blackened rocks and a gaping hole of doom was all that was left, with fingering flames far down casting a wicked orange from the crater's depth.

Reeves helped Ford stand, and he thanked him, then turned to Alexander.

"Get why you did what you did, homefry. But how about throwing up a warning beforehand next time!"

"Sorry," Alexander replied, face falling. Shaking his head, he added, "It was impulsive. It was rash. It was—"

"Exactly what I would've done." Ford planted a hand of

solidarity on his shoulder, giving it a reassuring squeeze. Not only that it was the truth, something he would've done, but also that he was with him in his grief over Father Jim.

He offered a half smile and nodded.

"*Poydem!*" Nia shouted, gesturing with her Scythe glowing a wicked purple in the darkened hallway. "Unless you are wanting an early death, we need to be moving."

An explosion from behind put an exclamation point on that one! Distant and down below, but growing into a roiling boil crescendoing into a growl that meant nothing good.

Ford led the way, Nia and Sasha close behind, with Reeves and Alexander making up the rear.

He hustled down the corridor, coming up fast to the corner that would lead them back to their entry point. Backtracking seemed best, given they didn't know the lay of the land and didn't have time to get to know it. Most of the mayhem seemed to be unfolding down below anyway, but it would catch up to them soon if they didn't hike it.

Edging to the corner, Ford whipped his Neutralizer around then pivoted stage left to face the threat—Nia and Reeves quick on their own draw and backup.

All calm and quiet on the Western Front.

He sighed with relief then kept at it, racing toward the next leg as another echoey explosion was thrown up from behind, emphasizing the urgency of their flight.

So flee they did, pounding across the marble without even worrying about concealing their steps.

In return, they'd gotten no voices, no shouts for help. No doors flinging open along the way, whether in flight or fight. Was almost like the Republic had abandoned—

A face suddenly appeared, then a body, connected to the nose of a Neutralizer.

Didn't have time to fire, so Ford did the next best thing.

He grabbed it and yanked it his way, then jerked it toward the ceiling.

Catching the Enforcer goon totally off guard.

Dude stumbled forward, the strap taking the dude with it, but not before setting off *one-two-three-four* plasma blasts sailing on instinct.

Went high and wide and didn't do any damage, but Enforcer Dude managed to recover his footing, then his grip.

With a powerful heave-ho, the Enforcer yanked back his weapon and went to open up on the hostiles—*them* hostiles!

But Nia was already in motion, leaping from behind with her Scythe and swinging it with an arcing slice into the Enforcer's neck.

Connected in spades.

Head went one way, body went another, a geyser of crimson blooming.

One for one, in his book.

The sudden connection with his brain stem must've either set off a neuro reaction or completed the circuit from his instinctual response to hostiles. Either way, his Neutralizer exploded in a rapid *chew-chew-chew* release, the blasting blue plasma blobs racing toward him and his crew.

Had to skitter to the side himself to miss the blasts!

But they'd sailed past without issue, sinking into the floor and far down the corridor.

Ford sighed with relief—

Until a cry was thrown up.

He spun around to Sasha on the floor holding his foot. He raced to his side, grateful the foot was still there. The appendage must've caught the tail end of the electric tendrils. Looked like it might've been taken out of commission.

Ford offered him his hand. "You alright, doc?"

Took a beat, but the doc caught his breath.

"I am being fine." Sasha clasped his hand and stood—but faltered his step.

"You don't look fine. What happened?"

He winced. "The Neutralizer blast grabbed my foot. I can't feel it. Like my funny bone was hit hard, but in my foot."

Ford nodded. Understood the feeling. Not cool and not fun.

"Can you walk?"

"*Da.* I will do it."

Sasha hobbled forward, wincing again before recovering his breath and straightening. Then he adjusted his grip on his Neutralizer and set his face forward. Good lad.

Ford joined him and led the charge toward destiny.

When two more figures appeared, guns outstretched and ready to—

Menacing *chew-chew-chews* exploded. From behind.

The two bodies slumped to the floor like used bathrobes, in an instant.

"You're welcome," Reeves said, racing past.

"Nice shot." Ford followed, with Nia carrying Sasha along now.

Was mighty sick of Enforcers getting the jump on them—on him! Just glad he had the backup to save his backside.

Took some doing, some racing down the corridor that led to their entry point, but they reached the door. Grabbing it, he wrenched it open—

And only managed to wrench his hand!

Locked.

Shucky ducky...

"Things always get worse," he cursed.

Alexander asked, "What are we going to do?"

"This—"

Without waiting a beat, he took aim and sent a *one-two-*

three-four punch into the door knob. Splintered the wood and sent the chrome doohickey sailing into the room beyond.

"*Kakogo cherta!*" Nia cursed. "Why were you doing that?"

Sasha joined, "Do you want Enforcers to come up on our backsides?"

Ford kicked the door in. "A little late for that."

And took aim again.

It was empty.

"Besides, all that matters is—"

He was cut off by something deep in the castle's belly rumbling again. Grumbly and mumbly and cranky as all get out.

An explosion of fire and fury that was surely making its way their way!

"—getting the hot Hades out of Dodge. Scram cats and kittens!"

Everyone hiked it like there was no tomorrow—because there wouldn't be for them if they didn't make for their exit. Aimed straight for the sheer curtains wet with rain and streaked light crimson and dark gray ash waving like phantoms in the frigid wind. Gave Ford the willies, it did!

Reeves arrived at the railing first, the grappling hook still secured. Slinging his rifle around his back, he started his descent. Nia mounted the rappelling rope next, and Sasha was brought around after her.

Alexander asked, "Can you manage rappelling down the face of the wall?"

Sasha inched toward the railing and peered over the edge. "I think I—"

Another explosion from behind cut him off, sending him skittering over the edge.

Nia took her time, coaching Sasha through the moves. When he was secure, Reeves followed, then Alexander.

Before Ford descended, he crossed himself on instinct, which was odd because his wing of the Ichthus Christian bench didn't do that sort of thing. Seemed apropos for the moment at hand.

Then he took the plunge.

Didn't take long to reach the bottom. The others were gathered beneath.

Just as a wicked explosion above sent glass sailing from a wall farther down. The shards tinkled down to the ground, followed by flowers of fire blooming from its wounded side.

Didn't have to convince him twice to hippity hoppity!

The quintet raced through the forest of barren trees across wet, dead leaves before plunging into the slow-moving stream winding through the valley.

Ice flooded Ford's veins as the water flowed past his calves. Thankfully, the military boots kept them from going numb— and kept him from retching with the coagulating bloody mud reaching inside. The rest of his body took care of keeping him warm, adrenaline and his racing heart doing the heavy lifting.

Halfway now. Made good progress.

"Go, go, go!" Reeves shouted from the middle, waving the rest across.

"Don't have to tell me twice," Nia said, leading the charge.

Sasha said, "Or thrice—"

He faltered a step and fell into the water, throwing up a cry.

Alexander raced to his side. "Up you go..."

He and Nia lifted him back up to his feet.

"I think I was twisting my ankle in the fall." He winced and muttered a curse.

Ford took over for Nia. "Let's go, doc. We'll help you."

Reeves reached the other side first, the man gesturing wildly for them to hurry it along.

"Yeah yeah yeah," he muttered. "Hold your horses..."

"Watch your step, Sasha," Alexander said, the water at their ankles now. "Almost on to the other—"

An explosion thundered from behind, the blooming force tossing the group from the river against the shallow beachhead.

Luckily, Ford's face and chest managed to reach safe ground. But his boots—his ankles!

A coagulated mess of muddy, bloody rain instantly seeped through his boots, reaching down to his feet.

Shucky ducky...

But that wasn't even close to the worst of it.

Heat quickly followed. Not scorching, but hot enough to warn of danger.

Without looking, he scrambled across the shoreline to join his crew. They all beelined it down the narrow path and up the face of the cliff, helping Sasha hobble to the top until they all collapsed where they began the whole dang operation.

After getting Sasha comfy on the ground, Ford spun toward the castle, the world below painted orange and crimson, shrouded in billowing blackness.

Flames rose high into the midnight sky from the centuries-old structure, the downpour doing nothing to stay the fires of hot Hades overtaking the old Nazi headquarters. And apparently a former Nous base of operations—perhaps a current one, in cahoots with the Republic. Which was quite the revelation.

Another explosion told him all he needed to know. The building was a goner. Hopefully for good this time.

They stood there for several beats, catching their breath and unable to peel their eyes from rubbernecking the 5-alarm fire.

Finally, Ford turned away. "We best make like an egg and scramble on out of here!"

"But where?" Alexander asked.

"Where's the nearest Order outpost?"

"Francia, I believe."

"But we've got to get back to Lucy and Rebekah and our newcomer. Not the best of options."

"What else do we have left?"

He looked back at the inflamed structure, huffing a sigh. Was about the truth of it. And was about the best option.

Father Jim was dead. Murdered—no, martyred. For his faith, for the Church.

They were on the run, again, with little options left after the Republic took out one of the only remaining Resistance stations.

Alexander grasped his shoulder and smiled. "I've got an inkling of an idea about what to do next."

"What's that, homefry?"

"The embers of a plot Father Jim himself had set into motion when he'd beckoned me to the original conclave that set it all in motion three years ago now."

Ford nodded. After all that had gone down, he didn't know what was left to do. Didn't have anything left. Was plumb tuckered.

So he was relieved someone else could take charge for a change and have a plan through to the other side of the cray-cray.

And it started in Francia, of all places.

Go fig!

Alexander awoke with a sudden start—his body jolting and lurching through the air before his face smacked against solid wood.

He was upside down, feet suspended above, legs twisted in fabric, his face smarting and head throbbing—

Head.

A sudden intake of air reminded him of his dream.

The chrome blade was glinting and glistering under bright lights, a sharpened wedge of solid metal slicing through the hot and humid air before connecting with his neck!

Could feel its fine edge biting into his skin and muscles before severing his carotid artery and brain stem—snapping his connection to most of his body's automatic functions, his breathing, his heartbeat.

His living.

The realness of the event was hard to grasp in his dreamy state, especially with the pain blooming from his nose!

"Where...what?"

He managed to push off from the floor and twist around, his legs falling to join the rest of his body in a messy pile of white linens. It was then his mind found clarity, his eyes darting about a small modest room painted white and catching the tiny plain-spoken wood cross mounted to the wall above his head, then the simple blue curtains covering a small window.

The smell of fresh-baked bread, frying salted bacon, melting cheese, and strong coffee quickly confirmed the dueling truths: he was still alive, and he was waking up in an Order of Thaddeus safe house.

Alexander heaved stabilizing breaths and swallowed, his throat a desert in need of water. Those heavenly scents of nourishment competed now with the faint scent of old wood and an even older musty building, his olfactory a blessing that grounded him back to present reality.

He was alive, he was safe, he was—

But then the past reality came rushing forth.

The sword, the severing.

The head.

Father Jim...

A coldness spread through Alexander, even though he was soaked through with sweat and the room stifling. The fogginess of dreamland lifted to reveal the fallout from the past few days' events.

Kareema Salam and Padre, their deaths.

The rescuing of the man of mystery, Thomás Polanco-Kolocovich, who turned out to be a former Republic Senator turned parish priest.

The bloody Antichrist rising upon the Solterran stage, this Neron Kaisar fellow whom Polanco had raised, only to be secreted away by Nous and crowned the new Patron after Severus's mysterious assassination.

Closing his eyes, Alexander brought his hands to his face and tried massaging away the memories, tried rubbing away the truth of the turn of things—for Father Jim and Ichthus, for the Republic.

For him.

But the world beyond those tiny walls beckoned for his attention, as did breakfast. He was famished, his stomach rumbling in protest now and clenching in on itself, as much from hunger as from the painful memories reminding him he still had work to do.

Ichthus was in distress, in hiding and on the run thanks to the Purge. The apocalypse was ravaging Solterra, with surely more promised destructive judgment drawing nigh. And the Antichrist had appeared, rising from the shadows to exterminate Christians, extinguish Ichthus.

He was not ready to face it all.

But face it he would. For Father Jim, yes, but also for Christ. What other choice did he have? Not only was he his follower, he was his undershepherd. A Master of the singular religious order tasked with protecting and promoting the faith —even during these last end-times days.

All that could wait. Bacon and eggs were the first order of business, and hopefully a proper pot of tea to soothe the soul.

Standing, Alexander parted the curtains for a glimpse of the day ahead. A clear, still-darkened sky greeted him with a half moon, dimmed of its white-light brilliance, and a sea of stars reduced to a puddle—all the fallout from the apocalypse that had risen upon Solterra.

He groaned and nursed a headache still needling his temple as he slipped into the black jeans he had been wearing since the raid on the reprogramming camp days earlier, only to put them on again for an ill-fated operation saving Father Jim—

A lump sprang to his throat.

Father Jim...

Dead.

How was that possible?

The sun, as dimmed as it was, was still contemplating whether or not to come out from underneath the covers when Alexander started off in search of the hot meal.

Padding through the aged structure of heavy cut stone and sturdy pine timber that had carried the Church through the so-called Dark Ages of Europe, acting as a bulwark against ignorance and heresy alike, he prayed the Lord would make their paths straight that day, guiding their plans to bolster the faithful and buttress against the rising tide of persecution.

Because after what had happened the day before, he flat had no clue what that path looked like.

Southwest of the City of Lights and just outside of Versailles, the compound was one of the last of the Order's secret outposts scattered throughout the Republic. He and the others chose to decamp there given its extensive library and research tools, which he hoped to use in service of their operation.

Originally a Cistercian female monastery built a millennium ago in the heart of the Chevreuse Valley in 1204 in the lineage of the Abbey of Clairvaux, the Order Remnant had refashioned the property and rebuilt the abbey for their own operational purposes, transforming it into a clandestine operation center that posed as a vineyard and working farm. Given the shortages experienced the past several years, with famines plaguing Solterra, the Republic had bought the ruse and left the farmers to their work. He could only hope the disguise continued to hold up to scrutiny.

Alexander continued following his nose toward the great hall where he figured breakfast awaited. He rounded a corner and there it was, ceilings vaulted high by solid pine beams with large wrought iron chandeliers affixed by modern light fixtures instead of the candles they had once borne. The center was commanded by rows of heavy wooden tables that were sparsely filled.

Ford sat at the end of a center table, looking like he was halfway through a plate of bacon and cheese eggs. Nia and Sasha weren't yet around, but Lucy and Rebekah were. He plopped next to his fellow Alkebulanan from the former African continent. Propping an elbow on the table and pressing his weary head against his fist, he yawned, longing for a full day of slumber. It was not to be.

"Morning, homefry," Ford said, taking a sip of black coffee. "No offense, but you look worse for wear. How'd you sleep?"

Alexander yawned again. "Fits and starts, thank you very much. And you?"

"Like a rock."

"Lucky you. But that's good, because we have lots of ground to cover today."

"No rest for the weary."

"Unfortunately not. But first things first."

Rebekah forked a scoop of eggs and held it up. "A plate of cheese eggs?"

"No, a pot of tea."

"Sorry to be the bearer of bad news, but..."

"You're joking..." he moaned.

"Sorry. But the coffee isn't half bad."

Alexander huffed off and grabbed a plate, filled it with the goodness he had smelled from his room, reluctantly filled a large mug of coffee, adding three cubes of sugar and a spot of cream, then sat down to fuel up for the day.

In searching for a safe house after fleeing the burning building that had apparently been a nerve center for the

Church's ancient enemy, Alexander was fascinated to learn about the history of the old monastery.

It had taken two decades to restore the original abbey complex to its former glory as a working monastery, but the complex was a sight to behold. Through floor-to-ceiling windows, the just-rising sun was beginning to dapple an expanse of rolling green hills outside with burnt orange light. Those hills were punctuated by apple orchards and vineyards that were eventually pressed into apple cider and fermented into wine, then sold to markets in Paris.

Three stories of rooms housed the ecumenical coterie of scholars and students dedicated to retrieving and preserving the vintage Christian faith. A large chapel had once held the daily prayer services, for both the abbey itself as well as the surrounding village community. Now it served as storage for the crops and bottles of wine. The largest of the sections was an original one, where they were eating breakfast, and under which they would later descend. For hidden beneath was the Archives, an effort Father Jim himself had taken pains to develop and cultivate, collecting the vast assortment of ecclesial documents and tomes from the Church's history into a digital, accessible vault.

Settling back down with his plate piled high with breakfast food, Alexander crunched first into a stick of bacon, salted and crisped to perfection. His weary brain drifted to the future, to the struggle that lay ahead—and some of Father Jim's first words he had given to Alexander when he invited him into the fray of things.

'All things worth fighting for demand sacrifice.'

He polished off his first strip of bacon and crunched into a second, not sure he had further fight in him.

"Whatcha thinking about, Alex?" Ford asked, throwing back a swig of coffee.

He swallowed, one end of his mouth curling upward. It wasn't often he called him by his first name. Homefry was usually his nickname, whatever that meant. It was nice to hear the personal connection for a change. Comforting, reassuring. Like he had a real ally in that fight Father Jim referenced.

Alexander washed the bacon down with coffee, a surprisingly light and caramelly drink that was already working wonders for his energy.

He answered, "Just something Father Jim had said a while back."

"And what was that?" Rebekah asked, turning toward him.

Lucy did the same, with Nia joining Ford's side now along with Sasha next to her, their plates piled high with food. Reeves made up the rear, plopping next to Lucy, his plate doubled that of the others.

That smile widened. His teammates, his crew. His family. Brothers and sisters in Christ, and in arms, waging war for the faith—for Ichthus and its survival. And for the gospel—for Solterra and its salvation.

Clearing his throat, he quoted Padre: "'*All things worth fighting for demand sacrifice.*'"

"'*Oof,*'" Ford said, shaking his head. "Ain't that the truth."

"Heavy," Reeves echoed with a full mouth.

Alexander continued, "He joined that with the equally heavy truth: '*All things worth fighting for demand a leap of faith. They're all fraught with risk.*' He went on to explain that when the early fathers of Ichthus traveled to the first ecumenical council at Nicaea, most of the Christian leaders came looking like the rearranged pile of goop I was worried about when he sent me catapulting the first time back into time."

Sasha laughed. "I remember hearing those same worries."

"And rightly so! Humans were never meant to zoom across the time-space—"

"*Nyet.* The space-time continuum," he corrected.

Nia jabbed an elbow into his ribcage; he yelped.

Alexander chuckled. "Whatever. The point Padre was making was that these early leaders of Ichthus—not just priestly overseers, elders, but lay ministers and deacons—they arrived missing arms and legs and eyeballs and pieces of their face and skull because of the immense persecution of Empire Rome."

The revelation settled hard at the center of the table, the group casting their gaze to their food and taking quiet bites.

Now he felt foolish, attending to his own plate. "Not the best of breakfast conversational items, I suppose. Especially after what happened to Kareema, to Father Jim..."

He trailed off, throat constricting with emotion and the same springing to his eyes.

Rebekah grabbed his hand and squeezed it with a smile, a sign of solidarity.

He squeezed back, then stuffed a bite of cold eggs into his mouth.

"I think the point you were making," Lucy said at Rebekah's side, "the point Cardinal Ferraro was making, was that they risked and risked big, all to contend for and preserve the once-for-all faith entrusted to them by Christ himself."

Swallowing, Alexander nodded. "'*All things worth fighting for demand sacrifice,*' Father Jim had said. '*The early fathers risked and risked big.*' I suppose it shan't be any different for us as well, the future Church."

Ford nodded. "Word."

"He was a wise man, a good man." Thomás Polanco settled next to Ford across from Alexander.

He asked, "Did you know him?"

Taking a drink of coffee, he nodded. "*Sí*. Cardinal Ferraro was the one responsible for aiding in my parish assignment, taking me in as a Defector and breathing new life into my bones."

Ford glanced at Alexander, recognition etched in his face. "The man did the same for me too."

"Really? A Defector, you are?"

"From the Legion."

"It is being more than that..." Nia muttered at the end.

Embarrassment flashed across Ford's face, his cheeks reddening and eyes falling to his plate. There had been lingering conflict between them the past months. Mostly her reacting to his past. Alexander wondered what that was about, and would have to watch it.

Ford answered, "Yeah, well, you might as well know I was a Purifier."

Polanco set his fork down at that revelation. "*De verdad?* John Mark Ford, is that right?"

"Right..."

"*Así es*. My contacts in the Capitolium told me about your Defection. It was quite the to do, given your work on Purity."

Polanco returned to his eggs, the scraping and pecking of his fork distinct in the settled silence.

Shoving the bite into his mouth, he went on, "I can tell you this much. Things are about to get far worse for Ichthus now that Neron is rising."

"How much worse?" Sasha squeaked.

"If you are a student of history, then you'll know." He pointed his fork at Ford. "I know you are, given your own designs for Purity, the ones unfolding now."

Alexander's veins went cold, an iciness flooding him. Did he hear that right? Had Ford helped craft the Republic's Purge campaign at some level?

"More than that," Polanco continued, munching on a stick of bacon now, "the earliest centuries of the Church offer sound instructions for what Ichthus is in for in the coming weeks and months."

Deflecting from Ford for a moment, Alexander pressed, "How so?"

He set down his bacon and crossed his arms, a mirror of Father Jim flashing in front of him. Like a sagacious guide, he was, offering his counsel. Alexander was thankful the Lord Almighty had placed this soul in their midsts.

Polanco explained, "The imperial persecuting campaigns of ancient Rome were monstrous. Palestine, Egypt, and Turkey saw the worst of it. Eusebius, the great Church historian, described the means and measure of such terror."

Downing a swig of coffee, he settled back again for an extended discourse.

"Crosses were common, where the martyr would die of hunger and dehydration. Bodies were scraped with seashells until they died. Women believers were often hung naked by a single leg from tree trunks. Other Christians were tied between two stout branches, bending them like siege machines until they were released and snapped back into their natural position, instantly tearing their body apart down the middle. Still others had their bowels and private members shamefully and inhumanly tormented, slit and torn and dismembered—even while the nobles and law-observing judges looked on, cheering the horrifying display! New tortures were continually invented, as if they were endeavoring, by surpassing one another, to gain prizes in a contest."

The table went silent and cold, Alexander and the rest processing what they were hearing—what had already unfolded in the lives of those closest to them.

"It was a brutal age," Polanco went on, "one that was

meant to dissuade anyone from joining Ichthus. Remarkably, Eusebius reported that most Christians remained steadfast, even willingly marching to their martyrs' grave."

"Didn't we capture some of these events?" Sasha said. "Polycarp, I am thinking, from one of your more recent jumps to the past."

Alexander flashed concerned eyes at Polanco, the man furrowing his brow in confusion. His time-jumping travels were a tightly guarded secret that had certainly helped Ichthus gird itself through witnessing the past up close. But who went and when, even how...that was not something Alexander was ready to let Polanco in on.

So he pivoted to a history lesson.

"Diocletian," he said, diverting Polanco's attention, "issued an edict mandating the arrest and imprisonment of the Roman Ministerium, isn't that right?"

He startled, giving his head a shake before nodding. "*Así es.* All the priests and lay clergy and the like. Because of massive overcrowding thanks to their unwillingness to bend the knee, a third edict was issued, allowing them to find release—provided they offer sacrifices to the Emperor. Those who did not were summarily executed."

"Egads, hombre," Ford said. "How long did this crazy last?"

Polanco answered, "A number of events of imperial intrigue too granular to cover ensued—power-plays between rival imperial powers and the like. However, it was eight years since Diocletian's first edict in 303, and the persecuting fires of the Empire had not abated. Upon his death, Maximinus, his successor, continued Galerius' reign of terror with his own round of persecution, instituting by imperial decree a new round of forced worship."

"The imperial cult," Lucy said, "requiring all men,

women, and children, even infants, to offer sacrifices to the Emperor."

"*Muy buena señora.* I see we have ourselves a Church historian on our hands!"

She blushed and pushed a lock of blond hair behind an ear. "I do have formal training, yes."

"As you alluded to, those who refused to cooperate with the imperial demands for allegiance were mutilated or slain. Many had their noses, ears, and eyes mangled or cut off. It wasn't at all uncommon for women to be stripped naked and whipped to death, even as they were marched through the streets."

The sight of Kareema suddenly flashed hot in Alexander's mind's eye. Her body torn and tattered, abused and desecrated with complete disregard for her dignity.

Bile rose at the back, sour and bitter, the memory threatening to rise until he retched.

Swallowing hard, he stood, knowing what they needed to do. Because if Polanco was right, that ancient history would soon repeat itself in the future present—which was surely evident in what they had already borne witness to at the reprogramming camp and in the recent broadcast of Father Jim's death—well, then they had work to do.

"Come with me." Shoving from the table, Alexander stood.

"Where's the fire, homefry?" Ford asked.

"We've got work to do."

"What sort of work?" Nia asked, unmoving.

"It's as Father Jim said: '*All things worth fighting for demand sacrifice.*' And I know how to fight."

Sasha scoffed. "But we are not being finished with our breakfast yet!"

"Breakfast can wait," Alexander replied. "The fate of Ichthus hangs in the balance."

'All things worth fighting for demand sacrifice.'

Polanco was right. A wise man with wise words.

Time to help Ichthus heed them.

CHAPTER 23

THE FAMILIAR SMELL of old paper and ink was dizzying to Ford. Knew those righteous smells from anywhere, like his very own BO, seen as how he'd been brought up proper on the stuff back home. Ma and Pops had been the learned type, cultivating a love for books when he was still in diapers. Had also been the hoarder types, gathering a nice size library of real books throughout their farmhouse.

America's former South wasn't just a hotbed of Noramericana hicks!

Paper had been banned after the Great Realignment, the Republic insisting deforestation had led to the calamitous climate crisis that sparked much of the wars from the Reckoning. They replaced it with those slate devices common across Solterra, believing technology was king, a generous bestowment from a generous Patron.

Ford, along with much of the polis, knew better. Figured it was one more way for the technocrats in the Capitolium to control the flow of information. So, to see so many volumes, so many books gathered together in one place—it was heavenly!

He breathed in deeply as the group followed Alex through the Order outpost. The mixture of paper and ink was a drug-addict high that only bibliophiles like him could appreciate. The dark walnut-lined walls, bookcases, and affixed burnished bronze light fixtures primed the senses even further.

"Just think about all that these walls have witnessed over the years," Polanco marveled, running a hand across a shelf sagging with ancient tomes. "I bet you they've got untold secrets stuffed away in these shelves."

"Quite the establishment, isn't it?" Alexander offered.

"How many books do you have in this library?"

"A million or so housed inside climate-controlled vaults beneath. That's where we're heading."

He whistled, chuckling to himself and shaking his head. "I've died and gone to Heaven..."

"We aren't aiming for them, however."

"We aren't?" Ford asked. "Where we heading?"

Alexander grinned. "You'll see."

They rounded a corner into a large, spacious foyer with high ceilings that took up the three floors of the building. At one end, a fire crackled and popped in a stone fireplace the size of a person, tendrils of spicy smoke escaping and mingling with the musty scent of old tomes.

A winding staircase rose through those stories; they didn't take it. Instead, Alexander led them down a nondescript hallway to a similarly nondescript door nestled at the center of the mansion—with something super familiar standing guard.

A keypad, like the ones Ford had installed across Ministerium properties when the entity was still a thing. Used his security know-how to bring Ichthus's security into the 22nd century. Only wished it had survived.

"What's this?" he asked.

"You'll see." Alexander slapped his hand against the black glass plate. It pulsed blue before glowing an OK green.

Then the doors parted to reveal an elevator.

Which sent his heart soaring into his throat.

"What's this, homefry?" Ford quickly asked, the others flowing past him into the carriage.

He motioned for him to enter. "An elevator, what else?"

Heat raced up his neck and sweat started beading at his forehead. Was never good with heights, or even closed spaces. The thought of falling however-many-stories down into Mother Earth sent the Grip reaching for his jugular!

"Ford!" Nia shouted. "Move it along, would you?"

He swallowed, hesitated, but inched past the doorway and just inside the threshold, scooting into a corner and bracing his hands against its cold metal walls. She filed in after him, then the doors closed. He closed his eyes. He thought he might retch, then and there.

Didn't take long to descend, gravity doing its thing to bring them down down down before throwing up a heavy groundedness that sent his stomach lurching up up up!

A ding announced their arrival, and the doors parted—revealing a room.

"We're here," Alexander said with a grin.

He led the way, Ford wondering where exactly *here* was.

Then he got it, a familiar sight from the years past.

It wasn't a large room, about the size of a modest two-stall magnacar garage, for those who could afford it. The walls carried metal shelving that were lined by books, from top to bottom, with a small metal table anchored at the center and a couch against one wall.

Ford stepped closer to one of the walls, an array of books stretching back to Ichthus's beginning all neatly placed—all *digitally placed.*

Titles ranged from *Against Heresies* by the early Church father Irenaeus to Saint Augustine's *City of God*, from the Medieval theologian Thomas Aquinas's *Summa Theologica* to the *Institutes on the Christian Faith* by the great Reformer John Calvin—which was an odd pairing! Then on to *Church Dogmatics* by Karl Barth and N.T. Wright's *Jesus and the Victory of God*, two of the greatest theologians of the 20th and 21st centuries.

He didn't spot any more recent titles. Then again, he was distracted by the unexpected sight.

Wasn't into such tomes, preferring earthly history than the Church's. Was also disappointed it didn't at all smell like he would've liked. Not the old library scent of dank must and pulpy paper and sweet ink, as one would expect from such books stuffed in a confined space. Fresh, sanitized air with traces of vegetation and fertilizer from up top hovered in the joint.

"What is this place?" Reeves asked, following Ford's moves.

"*Sí.* Where are we?" Polanco asked. "It is positively magical. Never knew something like this existed!"

Ford chuckled. "You're in for quite the surprise, hombre."

"And why is that?"

"Because these are the Vatican Archives," Alexander explained. "Well, some of it anyway. Though you can access the rest if you want."

Polanco snapped his head toward him with wide eyes. "*Qué dijiste?* Did you say the Archives?"

"That's right," he said with a grin.

"*Imposible!* They drowned in the sea when the waters rose from climate change. OneWorld News said so."

Ford said, "That's what the Ministerium *wanted* OneWorld News to report."

Alexander added, "And some of the precious manuscripts and documents and codices of the Church's past did unfortunately sink to the bottom of the Mediterranean when the seas rose. Thankfully, Ichthus transferred the most important and vast majority of them into safe harbor, where they're accessed now at the drop of a command."

"And now from anywhere in the world."

"That's crazier than a jackrabbit in heat!" Reeves exclaimed.

Polanco added, "Especially, since the Republic banned books!"

He was right. After the Reckoning, real books were hard to come by. Deforestation for paper production was a strict no-no that carried significant monetary and hard-labor penalties. So digital was the way the biblio-world went. Ford was one of many who suspected the Republic outlawed paper production for reasons other than merely environmental protection: Information was much easier to control when it was in ones and zeros rather than ink and parchment. Who needed book burnings when they could be evaporated with a simple command input from the Patron or an AI algorithmic command line?

Ford grinned. "That's the beauty of this here set up."

Alexander added, "It's all been uploaded into the Ministerium cloud."

"Digital?" Reeves said with surprise. "Looks as real as rain to me."

"It's right as rain, son," Ford corrected.

"Whatev..."

Polanco eyed the space some more, walking up to a wall, then muttering to himself before moving to another panel.

"It was programmed to look that way, apparently," Ford said. "Though, I'm more beholden to its analogue brethren."

The priest startled. "Programmed?"

Before he could explain, Alexander cleared his throat and announced, "Qoheleth, bring up everything you can from the writings of Eusebius."

Polanco startled. "Did you say, *Qoheleth?*"

Before Alexander could answer, a male Britannia-sounding voice echoed, "Granted."

Which sent the newcomer into a whole other startling fit.

The room instantly transformed into a selection of spine-out titles neatly arrayed across one of the walls.

Ford said, "Some fine Ichthus ingenuity, that there is."

Alexander explained, "The purported author of the Book of Ecclesiastes activates the artificial intelligence to collate the relevant sources."

"*Qué es?*" Polanco asked, taking a hesitant step to a wall.

Ford shrugged. "Books, what else?"

Alexander walked over to the metal table at the center of the room. He retrieved a familiar sapphire slate device before heading for the shelves of digital titles arrayed on one panel.

"Go ahead, touch it," Ford said, nodding to one panel, which was really a bookshelf full of titles.

The priest grinned now, then brought a hesitant hand up to the shelf. He touched the smooth-as-glass surface, face scrunching up in confusion at what happened next. The image instantly rippled with red, blue, and green perturbation, like a stone dropped in a pond until it evened back out into the faux library of books.

He yanked his hand away, giving it a shake.

Alexander laughed. "I recall being equally startled by the feeling, but look at this place. Ichthus has instant access to a billion-book digital archive from the storehouses of the Church's knowledge. Father Jim had originally built it for the Ministerium. We both carried forward the project to serve the Order of Thaddeus in its own faith-contending interest."

Polanco asked, "So we can retrieve any book we want?"

He nodded. "That's right. The digital archives have preserved knowledge of all sorts during these dark times. Not just that which had been contained in the Vatican Archives before it sank beneath the sea, but all books from every corner of the world."

"Just as before..." The priest eyed the room, taking in a measured breath before crossing his arms, a giddy grin playing across his face. "Of course, the Church has always been in the knowledge-preserving business."

"Just like the Dark Ages—"

"*Bah!* A misnomer if there ever was one."

"You sound like Padre," Ford said.

"The Renaissance was only made possible by the studious and judicious care with which Christians sought, discovered, and preserved the wisdom that God himself ordained his creatures to possess."

"This room," Alexander explained, "like more across Solterra, has secured the Church's knowledge base during these dark times on our very own sector of DiviNet—all thanks to Sasha, here."

He patted Sasha on the back; he grinned and puffed out his chest with pride.

"Like the original Vatican Archives, this one gives us access to nearly the entire storehouse of knowledge across the full spectrum of humanity. Using machine learning algorithms, it not only catalogs but cross-checks the vault of knowledge with other sources."

Ford handed Polanco one of the sapphire slate devices. "Look here, it's quite simple. You walk over to the shelves and search for your book. When you find it, simply tap once, then again for it to be instantly delivered to the device."

Alexander cleared his throat, then said, "Qoheleth, cross-check Eusebius's work against anything related to persecution."

"Granted," the male voice said again.

"Amazing..." Polanco marveled. Ford understood the feeling.

A *purr* sounded, indicating Qoheleth had worked its magic. The walls shifted again, transforming the shelves of books back into the original frescos except for a single section with an arrangement of books.

Alexander brought the sapphire tablet near a particular set of tomes that lined the wall on the middle shelf, the others surrounding it instantly dimmed while three remained brightly lit. He touched the middle volume, and the others joined the other books in dimmed darkness. He tapped it again, and it shone with an almost golden brilliance, a faint halo of rainbow light ringing it.

"All set," he announced, walking over to Polanco with the slate device.

Ford craned over his shoulder for a look-see. "Says here the first shot across the bow in the Empire's anti-Christian offensive was the intentional burning of the church in Nicomedia."

"That's right," Polanco said. "A town in Arabia-Persia, something Diocletian and Galerius observed personally."

Alexander read aloud:

[W]hile it was yet hardly light, the prefect, together with chief commanders, tribunes, and officers of the treasury, came to the church in Nicomedia, and the gates having been forced open, they searched everywhere for an image of the Divinity. The books of the Holy Scriptures were found, and they were committed to the flames; the utensils and furniture of the church were abandoned to pillage: all was rapine, confusion, tumult.

Polanco explained, "It was only Diocletian's fear of the city's total incineration that prevented the mob from setting the church on fire. Instead, the Praetorian Guard, the emperor's personal detachment, hacked away at the structure with swords and axes, leveling it in only a few hours. The next day the edict was published in town. While Diocletian originally had wanted his persecuting campaign's start to be a bloodless one, civil magistrates across the Empire had the authority to issue capital punishments, and many let the sword fall on Christians out of longstanding prejudices against Ichthus. The next eight years resulted in thousands of slain Christians. Another chronicler of the madness was Lactantius. Do you think..."

He tossed Alexander a boyish grin and cleared his throat. "Qoheleth, add Lactantius to the shelves."

"Granted," came the response.

Polanco chuckled, racing to one panel—snatching Ford's slate device along the way.

"Hey, no fair!" he protested.

The priest seemed to have gotten the hang of the particulars, retrieving one of the volumes and bringing it back to the group.

"Listen to this," he announced, quoting the text:

Presbyters and other officers of the Church were seized, without evidence by witnesses or confession, condemned, and together with their families led to execution. In burning alive, no distinction of sex or age was regarded; and because of their great multitude, they were not burnt one after another, but a herd of them were encircled with the same fire; and servants, having millstones tied about their necks, were cast into the sea.

"Golly," Lucy said. "Sounds like Church leaders were put through the wringer."

"A trial by fire, for sure. But they weren't the only ones. Eusebius was eager to recount the martyrdom of one of the palace attendants who happened to be a Christian."

"Palace attendants. You mean in Caesar's palace?"

"*Exactamente.*"

"I have that account here," Alexander said, holding up his own slate device. He read from it aloud:

A certain man was brought forward in the above-mentioned city, before the rulers of whom we have spoken. He was then commanded to sacrifice, but as he refused, he was ordered to be stripped and raised on high and beaten with rods over his entire body, until, being conquered, he should, even against his will, do what was commanded. But as he was unmoved by these sufferings, and his bones were already appearing, they mixed vinegar with salt and poured it upon the mangled parts of his body. As he scorned these agonies, a gridiron and fire were brought forward. And the remnants of his body, like flesh intended for eating, were placed on the fire, not at once, lest he should expire instantly, but a little at a time. And those who placed him on the pyre were not permitted to desist until, after such sufferings, he should assent to the things commanded. But he held his purpose firmly, and victoriously gave up his life while the tortures were still going on.

Finishing, he set the device down on the center table, the room growing silent at hearing these horrifying accounts.

"We need these stories," he said.

"Ain't that the truth," Reeves agreed. "Too bad we can't beam the Archives into every Christian slate device!"

"That's not a bad idea," Lucy said.

Ford shook his head. "No way. Too dangerous."

"John Mark is right," Alexander agreed. "It is dangerous enough that the Order has been safeguarding it on our hidden node on DiviNet. If they got a whiff of its existence, they would burn it all to the ground."

"Metaphorically speaking, of course."

"Right. But pulling the plug on a bunch of ones and zeroes is far easier than book banning and burning. But you are right, Ryder. We need regular Christians to access these stories. Up close and personal."

Took Ford a beat to get his meaning—then he did.

"Time travel..."

Alexander nodded. Face was serious, mouth thin and jaw set. "We need to go back."

"Alex..." Rebekah said, coming up to his side. "What about your head?"

"*Da, bratishka*," Sasha warned. "We are not knowing the effects of time travel, whether it is what is causing the headaches."

"I don't care!" Alexander took a breath, running a hand across his buzzed head. "Look, if the Republic is ratcheting up its campaign to martyr the Church, if the Antichrist has risen onto the Solterran stage—well, then we're going to need to prepare people with the stories of those who've gone through the persecuting fires before us from the last time Ichthus dealt with something of this magnitude."

"The Great Persecution," Lucy said.

He nodded. "And I think having a chat with Eusebius could give us some insight into those stories."

The room went quiet, contemplating his move.

"*Perdóneme*," Polanco said, clearing his throat and putting up a finger, "*pero*...time travel?"

"It is being *my* invention, by the way," Sasha said. "I can share more about it if you'd—"

"Doc..." Ford said with intervention. "Neither the time nor the place. But that's right, hombre. Us here are Ichthus's intrepid time travelers."

The priest gasped, putting a hand against his forehead. "*Aye yi yi*...I have heard tale about this! Even saw a video of someone being burned in the center of an arena."

Alexander frowned. "That was Polycarp."

Polanco's salt-and-pepper brows leaped for the ceiling. "Of Smyrna?"

He chuckled. "That's right."

"But I was thinking it was all make believe, just a dramatic presentation."

"Nope. As real as rain," Reeves said.

Ford huffed. "Right as—"

"From our time to the past," Polanco interrupted, "you can transport anyone—to Caesarea, perhaps, in AD 335?"

"That is being correct!" Sasha answered. "Using a highly sophisticated algorithm, the time-travel belt warps the local region of the space-time continuum by focusing the energy stored in the device onto a single point. Like folding a piece of paper and punching a hole through the center, bringing the two dots from two locations along the plane of the paper into one single phase."

"*Fascinante...*"

Alexander turned to him. "Curious, why Caesarea, circa AD 335?"

"Because, *mi hijo*, that is where and when Eusebius finished his magnum opus before his death a few years later."

He hummed knowingly. "His Church Histories."

"*Exactamente!* If you want to hear from the horse's mouth these stories of persecution you want Ichthus to see and hear, then that is where you go."

Alexander nodded, jaw set and eyes locked on the course ahead. He looked to Ford, confirming it all.

Didn't know what to think about it, this time travel business. He and Lucy had had their own bout of travel, and nearly bit the big one because of it. But if Alex thought it best, the Order Master, then that was that.

Ford had served Father Jim the best he knew how, and now it was Alex's turn to lead. Wouldn't say it out loud, but he'd do the same, executing on the operations he felt best to protect Ichthus and propagate the gospel.

Laying down his life if need be.

Nodding, Ford smiled. "Let's roll, homefry."

CHAPTER 24

THEY CAME for him in the middle of the night. Strong hands yanking Ford from his bed, faceless and without form in the darkness of slumber.

And now he was strapped to a bed not of his own, held by tight straps with a spotlight trained on his face, blinding and white hot, his brow sweating to beat the band. But that wasn't all of it.

A cheer arose, from all around. Rabid and riotous, bloodthirsty and braying, the voices growing and growing until—

He saw it, glinting in the light.

Sharp and searing, rising high in firm hands with a heaviness that meant nothing good.

And then it fell to Earth, to him—to his *head*.

Down down down it went, and up up up his scream rose until—

New hands grasped him now, joined by a voice calling his name.

"Ford..."

Could barely make it out in the midst of the swirling panic. Didn't matter a lick anyway, because—

The blade!

There it was again, the voice: *"John Mark!"*

Along with those hands that made not a lick of sense, which Ford paid not a lick of attention to because—

Blade!

A sharp and searing, glinting piece of metal falling toward his head, his neck, in firm hands with a heaviness that was about to connect in...

Three.

Two.

One—

The blade smacked into his Adam's apple, the hardness pressing in against his neck and choking him something fierce!

Sending Ford shooting straight up and crying out with pained fright.

Which was joined by another cry as he knocked heads with whoever had been calling his name.

"Oy!" the voice cried out.

Ford awoke to his own hands at his throat, sunlight pouring in through the small window above his small bed in his small room on the third floor of the Order outpost.

But what had called him out, grabbed him even?

Ford darted his peepers around, looking for the offending—

"Doc?"

Sasha was on the floor, rubbing his forehead. *"Da,* it is me. But you need to be paying more attention to what the heck you are doing!"

"Me? What the hot Hades are you doing here, coming into my room like that and scaring the bejeebers out of me?"

"I was checking in on you after you were missing breakfast!"

He stood, muttering some Muscovia curses under his breath and continuing to rub his head.

Ford sat and rubbed his neck, catching his breath after the terrorizing dream where he almost lost his noggin.

"What was that being anyhow?" Sasha asked. "Your hands at your neck, like you were choking yourself?"

He let his hands fall, an embarrassed heat rising to his face.

"Just a dream."

"Quite the dream, *bratishka*. What was it about?"

Thought of telling him, but what difference would it make?

He went with: "Falling to my death."

Sasha shivered and made for the door. "That is my worst nightmare, falling to my death. You better be coming quick, because breakfast is almost finished."

He left, but Ford stayed a moment to catch his breath, his heart still rapping a mean beat and panic racing through his veins.

Apparently, Father Jim's beheading had affected him more than he wanted to admit it. Just hoped his sacrifice was worth it, the memory of his martyrdom bolstering Ichthus's faith during these cray-to-the-Z times.

Speaking of which...he wondered how Alex and Rebekah were getting along.

It was agreed that the pair would jump to the past to retrieve the memory of the early Church's own martyrs and persecution, with Luciana Jane joining their jaunt across Europa as backup. No telling what they might encounter as the Republic ramped up the Purge against them Unfit kind. But Ford felt better they had backup if it came to it zooming across the continent.

Traveling by magnarail was always a risky proposition, and a long one. Planes had been outlawed thanks to Mother Nature's water breaking. The Republic claimed the ban was on the carbon-emitting fossil fuels that wrecked the atmosphere, though they themselves did employ aerialcrafts that were rumored to still run on the stuff. Either way, it was ultrafast magnarail lines or deep submergence vehicles. Modern Caesarea was on the coast of the Mediterranean Sea, but it was safer to get a magnarail ticket and a private carriage in some Podunk town and ride out the 2800-some miles to the landing zone. With stops along the way, with any luck they would reach the LZ in another morning from now, maybe more.

That is, if the Republic didn't throw their backsides in a reprogramming camp first and lop off their—

Ford stopped himself, his neck pulsing where he'd nearly lost his own head. Hoped it wasn't an omen, a foreshadowing of bad things to come...

He and his sidekicks, Junia Kaminski and Sasha Pavlovich and Ryder Reeves, had stayed behind at the Order outpost. Along with Thomás Polanco-Kolocovich, who was turning out to be way more than Ford had bargained for when they rescued him. Figuring out what to do with him, and who he was—now that was gonna be a challenge and a half.

That could wait. What couldn't was breakfast, because his stomach was starting to attack his ribs, he was so freakin' hungry!

Sauntering down to the mess hall, he'd expected to smell the oh-so-smelly goodness of frying pig and scrambled cheesy eggs. At least some fresh baked bread or cinnamon buns. Nada on all four counts. Did catch a whiff of strong black coffee on approach, along with a pinch of cinnamon, joined by some other nutty, mealy dealio, but that was about it.

Looked like most of the farmhands had already had their fill and gone off to work. The rest of his crew was already eating. But—

Did his eyes deceive him?

He padded through the vast hall, craning for a look-see, his peepers peeping nothing good.

"What the..."

Was that oatmeal? He hustled over to his crew, and moaned.

"No, not oatmeal..." he complained, spinning around for a look at the buffet and seeing nothing but a large cauldron of the stuff.

Sasha held up a plate. "They are also having some very nice berry muffins and an assortment of fruit."

"I don't want no fruit, or no muffins. Definitely don't want no slop. I want greasy pig fat wigglin' between my teeth and cheesy eggs!"

"Eww..."

Nia shrugged. "*Khorosho*. Then you will be starving."

Ford went to retort, but figured there wasn't any use. Instead, he moseyed over to the craft services table and scooped a bowl of oatmeal, dousing it with cinnamon, then grabbed an apple and a spare. Never knew when a piece of fruit would come in handy.

Sitting down, Ford chanced a bite of the slop. Not...terrible. Not satisfying either. It was gonna be a long day.

"Anyone hear from Alex yet?" he asked.

"Lucy rang a bit ago," Reeves replied. "So far, so good. Next stop was the target city, then finding a place to make the jump."

"That's right. They needed to jump from point A to point B across the—" he glanced at Sasha, throwing him a wink "—space-time continuum at the exact physical spot. Ain't that right, doc?"

Sasha chuckled and nodded. "Very good, cowboy. Space-time continuum, that is being right. You are also being right about the exact spot in space they are to be standing before they jump phases back in time."

"So tell me, if you wouldn't mind," Polanco said, chewing a bite of oatmeal. "How does it work?"

Sasha grinned and rubbed his hands together. "Leave that to me."

Ford gestured for him to explain, shoving another bite of oatmeal into his mouth.

The doc dove in: "Most people think of objects as having length, width, and height, right? Think of a book, with length and width, then the spine is being the height."

"*Sí*, an object taking up space," Polanco said.

"*Da!* But what most people don't realize is that the book also occupies a place in time. Which I am calling *phasement*."

He lifted his hand upward and traced an imaginary line downward.

Ford had heard this spiel several times. Still didn't get it. But it was fascinating. Crunched into his apple now and checked his watch, wondering about his crew down south.

"Which means," Sasha went on, "you can travel along this line down into time. When you are taking a book from the bookshelf, that's one phase. Then when you are placing it on the couch, that is being another phase in time. The fourth dimension is recording this placement along time in the past, just like the x, y, z dimensions record its occupancy of space in the present. We used to be thinking that solid, liquid, and gas were the only kids on the physics block. Not anymore. A new phase of matter called time crystals was discovered."

Polanco furrowed his brow. "What is this...time crystal, as you say?"

"A totally new state of matter whose atomic structure repeats through time as regular matter repeats in space—or even changes, which is where things get remarkable."

He stared back at him blankly.

Ford leaned over to him. "Don't worry, hombre. Sailed right over my head the first time I'd heard it, too!"

Sasha waved his hands in the air. "Let me try this. At the normal state of water, it's a liquid. Add energy to it, and you have steam. Reduce the amount of potential energy, you are having solid ice. So three states of matter and its placement in space. But a professor from California theorized that if you could move the atoms from their original position in some way, then it would break time-translation symmetry and transform its phasement as well."

"And it wasn't until the good ol' doc here—" Ford gave Sasha's back a good slap, "—that the technology finally got small enough to harness the time-travel capabilities of mankind into time travel belts our intrepid time traveler Alexander has used to jump along the time-space continuum!"

Sasha huffed a sigh. "How many times do I have to be saying it. Space-time continuum. Space-time continuum!"

"Same diff."

The doc scoffed but went on: "Anyway, as I was saying, in essence, a fusion reaction inside the time-travel device unleashes enough energy to open a wormhole in the space-time continuum—warping a local region of the continuum with an electromagnetic field."

"A wormhole?" Reeves asked, brow furrowing. "Is this guy for real?"

"As real as a hamster with wings..." Ford muttered, popping the finished apple core into his mouth.

Polanco asked, "And how does this...electromagnetic field work?"

Sasha rubbed his hands together again. "Well, the electro-magnetic field not only transforms the matter of the host into a new phase of matter that transcends the continuum, but also envelops them inside the warped region of the continuum, the wormhole—a thin tube of space-time that flattens the phases of history into a next-door region you can just zip into through to the other side."

He laughed, throwing his head back with delight. *"Increíble!"*

Voices suddenly arose outside the mess hall. Sounded like they were coming down from the front lounge at the entrance. At first hushed and rushed, but now growing into a panic that meant nothing good.

Nia must've seen his own growing concern, the Ukrainski chickadee grabbing her Scythe and making for the window.

Ford almost didn't want to ask, but: "Anything to worry about?"

"There is a dust cloud rising in the east."

"Sounds like the opening to a bad sci-fi DiviNet ebook. What're you—"

She spun toward him, lips thin and eyes narrowed. "A caravan of magnacars is coming fast for the compound."

Took a beat to get her meaning. Then he did.

"Shucky ducky." He leaped to his feet, hand going for his back on instinct and coming up empty.

Dang. Wished he'd brought his Blastgun down. At least Nia had her Scythe, the woman carrying that thing around like a security blanket. Also glimpsed a few guards on his way over, so that would have to do.

She was already making for the entrance when Ford did the same. How the heck they'd been found—and by whom they'd been found...didn't make a lick of sense.

By the time they made it to the front door, the caravan was screeching to a halt and doors to beat-up magnacars—sedans and trucks—were being thrown open. Voices outside didn't seem panicked or worried, so that was a plus. Even sounded happy to see who'd ever rolled up on them.

Nia reached the door first. She glanced at Ford before opening it, Reeves and Polanco close behind, with Sasha making up the distant rear.

Ford nodded, and she opened the door—throwing up a gasp before a squeal.

"*Dzhoshie!*" She threw down her Scythe and ran to greet the man, her son.

Heat raced up Ford's neck. Just what he needed. The caped crusader riding up on his backside and challenging him to a duel.

He took a breath and told himself to relax. Hadn't seen the man in over a year after he and his compadres left Blake Ridge Station, his home base. Apparently the dude had resurrected an old Order of Thaddeus special-ops unit and spearheaded the Resistance against the Republic's persecution. Ford had other things to worry about than to get caught up with that hooey. Although, now it seemed like the right move, given the Purge and now the Antichrist's rise.

A tall, broad-shouldered man dressed in black with long dark hair was greeting people, trailed by half a dozen other men and women. Looked like a rough bunch, too. With hard faces and visible scars, heads shaved short, even the women, and some men were sporting ponytails. Each one was bearing a weapon slung around their shoulders. Reminded him of Viking raiders he had learned about in school.

Sasha came up to his side. "Who's that?"

"*Joshie*, that's who," Ford replied with more bite than he intended.

"Ah, yes. Junia's son. What has he been up to?"

"Commanding SEPIO," Reeves answered, "if I recall."

Ford threw him a frown, nodding while Nia and her son continued yammering away.

"SEPIO?" Sasha asked, a brow raised. "What is that meaning again?"

Ford replied, "Stands for *Sepio, Erudio, Pugno, Inviglio, Observo*. An acronym and Latin for the word *sepio*, which suggests the idea of surrounding something with a hedge of protection. Apparently, it spelled out the mission of a para-military arm of the Order of Thaddeus from a century ago: protect, instruct, fight for, watch over, heed."

"What do they do?"

Reeves explained, "Well, what they *did* was surround the memory of the Christian faith itself with a hedge of protection. Its goal was to preserve and protect objects and relics of the faith, as well as the memory itself by retrieving the essential, funda-mental elements of the vintage Christian faith. But that was a long time ago. They're a legend among us Order Remnant type."

Ford snorted a laugh. "Before they went belly up, you mean?"

"What was happening to them?" asked Sasha.

"Something about it splintering into two separate bands, one that focused more on the intellectual defense of the faith, the other a sort of newfangled Templar knights taking a more militaristic posture to protect Christians and churches around the world."

"No no no no! We are not bloodthirsty mercenaries." A tall, brawny woman with two long braids down her back, the sides of her head buzzed short, and arms tattooed up and down, sauntered past.

Ford looked to Reeves for the 411 on that chickadee. He just shrugged.

"And who might you be?" he asked.

She spun around and looked him up and down, face hard and mouth turned down with a sneering frown. Crossing her arms, she answered, "Zeljka is my name."

"Zelda?"

"No no no! *Zeljka.*"

"It is from Vostokana," Nia explained, coming inside with Joshua, along with a few other men who were as large and tattooed as She-Zelda.

The woman explained, "People call me Z, and so can you."

Ford smirked. "Gee, thanks...Who are you and why are you here?"

"SEPIO, as you were saying."

Reeves whistled, grinning like a giddy two-year-old.

Ford said, "I thought you were the Resistance, as Joshua had said before."

Z nodded. "That is right. We are both. SEPIO is Resistance, Resistance is SEPIO."

"Glad we cleared that up..." Ford muttered. "Whatchya been up to all these months?"

"Fighting, that's what!" another man exclaimed, short and squat, a generous beard flowing over a generous gut. Was even wielding a Scythe, its head glowing red.

Joshua added, "Waging war against the Republic for the sake of our persecuted, dying brothers and sisters."

Ford said, "I thought James Ferraro said this wasn't the way. That Ichthus wasn't a Resistance but a Remnant, preserved during this time by the Holy Spirit and Christ himself to offer the world one last chance before all hell breaks loose."

"Yes, well, Ferraro is dead, and the Republic is murdering our own."

That didn't sit well.

He stepped closer, eyes narrowed. "Watch it, son, the way you speak of Padre. He isn't just dead. He was murdered. Martyred, as a witness to Christ, as an example to the rest of Ichthus."

Joshua sighed, his face falling. "I know. I meant no disrespect. We have business here, and not much time."

Ford rubbed his chin, an interesting turn to find out about what the Resistance had been up to the past year. Or rather, SEPIO. Had known about the lost entity of the Order of Thaddeus that had been something of a paramilitary arm of the organization. The project had been launched over a century ago to give some more muscular, intentional attention to defending the Christian faith in the face of growing hostility during the 20th and 21st centuries. Then there had been trouble, the group going rogue and later disappearing altogether.

But now, to see them all put back together again, and with business...He wasn't sure what to make of it.

He asked, "What sort of business?"

"I was told the Archdeacon had arrived."

Ford twisted up his face. "Archdeacon?"

Before Joshua answered, his face brightened into a wide grin, and he shoved past to embrace the newcomer.

That Polanco-Kolocovich character!

Sasha leaned in and whispered, "I thought he was being a Republic Senator."

Reeves added, "I thought he was a simple parish priest."

Ford trained his peepers on the lovebirds yakking it up, jaw set and brain whirling with the implications that somehow there was way more going on with this fella than the so-called simple parish priest had fessed up to.

And that Polanco-Kolocovich character was not at all who they thought—or bargained for.

"What the hot Hades…" Ford said, hustling up to the pair. "What is this?"

They ignored him, Joshua saying to the fella, "It has begun."

Polanco gasped. "The Two Witnesses. They are in place?"

"That's right, for several months now, they have been—"

Ford interrupted the debrief with a firm hand on Joshua's shoulder. Then he jerked him around, coming nose to nose with the fella who plucked his ever-living nerves!

The man scowled. "What are you—"

"I want answers, *Joshie!*"

Polanco stepped over now, putting up a staying hand. "I can explain."

"Then do it!" Ford snapped, peepers still trained on Joshua who didn't at all look like he was thrilled with the interrogation.

Before the priest or Archdeacon or whoever could get to his explanation, someone hustled up from behind.

It was that other character, Z, or Thor's wife or whoever. She handed him a slate device, face pale and pinched.

Took him a beat to register what he was looking at.

Then—

"Oh, no…" Joshua whispered. "Here we go."

"Here what go?" Ford demanded.

Joshua said nothing, hustling to the stairwell with his posse.

And leaving Ford with a whole pants load of questions.

CHAPTER 25

Ford was as hot as a hen in a henhouse with a fox runnin' around! Who did this guy think he was, this Joshua Kaminski fella? Comes barging into one of the Order safe houses like he owns the joint!

So he asked him.

Reaching the third level, hot on Joshie's heels, Ford called out, "Hey!"

Dude didn't turn around. Didn't flinch. Just kept walking down a hallway and veering into a large dark room with a bunch of broadcaster displays and workstations that gave Ford pause.

But just for a beat.

Because hot on his heels was him with the same beckoning call: "Hey!"

Same answer. Nada.

Joshie was fiddling with that slate device of his, punching at it with his pointer.

Which irritated the snot out of Ford. So he went back at it, asking, "Who do you think you are, barging into one of the Order safe houses like you own the joint?"

"I do own the joint," Joshua said.

"Come again?"

More pecking with that pointer of his until—

The screen transitioned into a wide shot of the ultra-modern seat of government on the former Azores archipelago in the middle of the Atlantic Ocean, zooming in for the dais at the center of a vast circular auditorium with hundreds of Senators in white standing at attention, clenched fists outstretched toward the center.

"What do you mean by that?" Ford asked, peepers trained on the massive broadcaster display zooming in now toward the main attraction.

"This is a Resistance outpost," he explained. "Well SEPIO's, the last-century outfit reconstituted under the auspices of the Order of Thaddeus."

That was new.

Ford whipped his head toward Joshie. "Does Alex know about this?"

He nodded. "It was his idea. What, you didn't know?"

Thought he detected a slight upturn to the corner of his mouth. Like he was relishing the fact Ford was left out of the loop.

His face fell. No, no he didn't. But he wouldn't voice it. No way, no how.

Thankfully, he was saved by the broadcaster, which threw up a whole bunch of cray-cray he wasn't prepared for—yet had seen before.

The room had filled now with the others, everyone gasping at what was displayed for all to see across Solterra Republic.

There he was, Neron Kaisar. The tall, lanky man with translucent skin and silver hair, eyes blazing. Standing tall and proud and smug at the center of the Senate—with the most terrifying, horrifying unbelievable of Beings surrounding him.

The ones that had haunted his nightmares since last year, when the bastard-born, divine-human hybrids emerged across Solterra—looking very much like what he had witnessed in the Neutral Zone.

A Watcher-spirit.

A Fallen One...

Standing behind that Neron character was something that looked like it was from another dimension. A hulking figure, with a bulbous head resting atop wide shoulders corded with muscle, skin rippling in scaly waves with an iridescent glow.

The Being was hideous, horrendous, something straight out of a Stephen King fever dream, his fave author from reading through Ma and Pops's library back on his peanut farm as a teenager.

Yet...

Yet there was something attractive about it. Enticing, even. As if it was what Ford had been waiting for his whole life—to give meaning and definition and permission to his identity as a man, as a human.

An Angel of Light. Come to save humanity.

A chyron banner beneath announced the event as a special session of the Senate convened by the new Patron, Neron Kaisar. He took a slight bow as the thunderous applause began to recede, bringing a fist to his mouth and clearing his throat.

All six of his fingers clenched together!

This was unreal...

The room quieted to nothing but nothing as Neron began to address the entire Republic.

"Last we met, Solterra," Neron intoned, "I promised you a revolutionary evolution to our peace, prosperity, and progress that would finally push the human race forward—No!" he interrupted himself, snapping his fingers and widening his eyes bulging with possession. "*Someone* to show us a new way forward. To show us a better way of living and being human by rising above the ignorance and bigotry, to progress our race forward by revealing to us the universal ideal in a way that makes sense to our 22nd century human condition, to restore it to its sublime, ancient purity."

The man pushed his silver hair behind his ears and smiled a menacing grin with closed lips that stretched from ear to ear. He looked like the Joker from the Batman comic books Ford had read as a teenager from his parents' vintage stash. Creepy as all get out!

"Today, Solterra will realize the full potential of the Republic of Heaven—becoming the firstfruits of what I promise will be a rich harvest for all humanity!"

A wave of clapping echoed throughout the vast white hall through the broadcaster. The room itself in the Order—or Ford supposed the *SEPIO*, or the *Resistance*—outpost was dead silent. Not a peep, not a movement, all peepers trained ahead for what lay ahead.

Which Ford sensed was nothing good.

"For centuries," the Patron went on, "Ichthus has peddled the myth that some sort of salvation was found in—" he paused, swallowed hard, face twisting up into an agonizing pucker "—the Christ, in He-Who-Shall-Remain-Nameless from henceforth. Believing his pitiful death on that Roman cross from time past did something for the world."

The man shook his head and smirked, his face twisting into a mixture of revulsion and eye-roll awe, his eyes inflamed with what looked like rage.

"No no no! Understand this, my fellow humans, salvation comes not through the Nameless One's death on the cross. We do not need saving from our sins! The entire human experience has been one of constantly emerging from what we have been into what we can *become*. Where we humans decided for ourselves what is right and good, true and beautiful. Our ultimate aim is the Republic—the Republic of Heaven, a realm populated by a race of supermen! The Homo Deus."

Neron leaned forward, that Basset Hound silver hair of his falling forward. He pushed it behind his ears, then crowed: "*God men...*"

There were several applauses to that line, Ford not knowing what the hot Hades the new Patron was yakking about.

"This I pledge this day," Neron went on. "I pledge to offer every person in Solterra the chance to tap into the natural energies, the natural Powers of the Universe in order to raise humanity up to a higher level of consciousness and usher in the Republic of Heaven. A realm of unlimited human potential across the planet, completely divorced from the silly, dead god's Kingdom of Heaven. Nay! Divorced from the Nameless One himself!"

More clapping, more cheering from the broadcaster, the Senators rising to their feet with fists raised in *For Humanity!* solidarity.

He continued, "What happens to the Kingdom of Heaven when the King is dead, the Nameless One from Ichthus's fables and stories—murdered at the hands of sensible adults? What else but the complete transformation of the Kingdom into a Republic, governed not by the whims of a self-centered, self-indulgent, needy Bearded Being in the sky. But by the enlightened ones grabbing reality by the horns and transcending it to greater heights of purpose."

The Senate quieted, Neron gripping the lectern now and the camera swooping around behind before spinning around for a close-up of his face.

Which sent an electric jolt skittering up Ford's spine.

Dude looked possessed, that's for sure. With eyes wide and blood-shot, cheeks flushed and lips pulled back into a menacing grin. Even detected a tremor to his mug. Creepy as all get out!

"The Republic of Heaven," Neron continued, "is a state of existence in our this-life reality when the collective humanity transcends their brutish nature and baser selves, while approaching the universe with curiosity and wonder and transcending the current human condition through enlightened reason—all of it will soon come to pass. It is full of all the possibilities and potential of conscious life lived on our terms, and enjoying the glory and the power and authority for all time, now and forever. The power to name and claim and deem what is good and evil in the coming Republic of Heaven. *Amen!*"

That got the Senators back to their feet, the men and women in white rising to clap and cheer.

"This day I pledge to make the Republic of Heaven a reality, in which Solterra is invited into the Übermensch—humanity emerging beyond itself as envisioned by the Germanian prophet Friedrich Nietzsche. Recall the words of the man who laid bare the reality of our religious world."

Neron cleared his throat, then boomed: "Have you not heard of that madman," he said, voice almost wistful as he stared into the camera, "who lit a lantern in the bright morning hours, ran to the marketplace, and cried incessantly: *I seek God! I seek God!*—As many of those who did not believe in God were standing around just then, he provoked much laughter. Has he got lost? asked one. Did he lose his way like a child? asked another. Or is he hiding? Is he afraid of us? Has he gone on a voyage? Thus they yelled and laughed."

Then one end of Neron's mouth curled upward, and he leaned in across the lectern, fixing it with a mad obsession.

"The madman jumped into their midst and pierced them with his eyes. *'Whither is God?'* he cried; *'I will tell you. We have killed him—you and I. All of us are his murderers.'"*

He shot straight, putting his hair back into place.

"'We have killed him—you and I. All of us are his murderers.'" Neron went on. "Oh, that Nameless Monster in the sky still pops his head up from time to time with those crazy religious fanatics. But through science and brute force, humanity has finally begun to transcend its baser religious selves, rising to become like gods—not merely knowing good and evil, but *deciding* what is good and evil. The Nameless One is dead in our hearts. Soon the Nameless One will be obliterated from Solterra—we will destroy him. Once and for all!"

A sinking feeling filled Ford's stomach, rising through him until it skated through his veins with a cold dread. This wasn't good...

"The Nameless One is dead," the Patron shouted. *"'We have killed him—you and I. All of us are his murderers.'* So how shall we comfort ourselves, the murderers of all murderers? Must we ourselves not become gods simply to appear worthy of it? There has never been a greater deed; and whoever is born after us—for the sake of this deed he will belong to a higher history than all history hitherto."

Raising a fist, closed and outstretched, six fingers glistering in the white light, Neron Kaisar shouted something Ford never expected in all his thirty-eight years on this Third Rock from the Sun to hear: "I am your Patron, I am your Antichrist. Today you are released from the shackles of the Nameless One! Today, in this hearing, you are given full permission to become all who you were ever meant to be. I will make it so. For I have come to wage war against the Nameless One in order to release you from the bondage of your captivity."

More rising, more clapping, more cheers and hoots and hollers from the Senate.

"But first—" Neron went on, voice rising along with his long arms, his long fingers—six of 'em!—outstretched for the room to quiet down; it didn't, he just shouted louder "—first, we must eliminate the stench of an invasive species from our midst. We must slay a pair of terrorists who have been waging war against our precious Republic of Heaven."

Nia asked, "What is that mad man speaking about?"

Before Ford could grunt a reply, something unexpected—and, quite frankly, unbelievable—happened.

There was a wavy shudder, a trick of the light it seemed—where shadow and sun rippled with an exchange of places, back and forth for a few seconds. Like a stone had been dropped into the center of his family farm pond, the glassy water rippling with perturbation.

Then Neron was gone. Just like that.

There one minute, gone the next—the dais was empty!

"What the—" Ford craned his head toward the broadcaster, rubbing his eyes.

"Holy cow!" Reeves echoed.

As did Nia: "*Kakogo cherta?* Where was he going?"

"He was disappearing," Sasha said in a startled rush, "that is where he was going!"

So he wasn't going crazy. They'd all seen it too.

Neron disapperating!

But how? And like Nia said, where was he—

Before he could finish the thought, the broadcaster switched things up to an outside aerial shot. By the look of it, some Tracker drone hovering over a city that looked far more ancient than anything Ford had seen in a real long time in the Republic.

There was a temple in the far right, a gold dome glinting

in the dimmed sunlight. A massive thing, by the look of it. Down below were massive stone walls and a stone courtyard, where hundreds of milling black dots were—well, they were milling! The Tracker came in for a look-see now, zooming real close for the action.

Where it was clear two figures were standing in the center of a massive crowd in the middle of that stone courtyard.

Ford brought a hand to his stubbled chin. "Where is this?"

"Jerusalem," a voice, low and bassy, answered.

It was Polanco. He asked, "How do you know?"

"*'Now when they have finished their testimony,'*" the Senator-turned-priest responded, "*'the beast that comes up from the Abyss will attack them, and overpower and kill them. Their bodies will lie in the public square of the great city—which is figuratively called Sodom and Egypt—where also their Lord was crucified.'*"

"What the hot Hades is—"

Reeves answered, "Revelation, chapter 11." He swallowed hard, his brown face losing some color and glistening with sweat. Looked like the man might blow chunks right there! "The Two Witnesses..."

Ford returned back to the broadcaster, recalling them biblical figures from Alexander's encounter a year ago—two prophets sent by the good Lord himself. The picture zoomed in for a proper look-see now, the figures wearing these weirdo burlap getups. Sackcloth, he figured, the proper biblical term.

Also recalled the reports he'd gotten through the year of all those two men had been doing across Solterra. Activity that'd been suppressed by the Republic but was known well enough by the Resistance and the Order Remnant. Their evangelism, their miracles, their prophetic work to convict the polis across Solterra of their sins and bring them to repentance. Had even heard rumor of some cray-cray goings on around them dudes.

Mobs forming and trying to take them out, but the two dudes making it out alive—mostly by roasting their backsides! So to see them there, in the Holy Land, waving their arms around and saying who-knew-what in high-definition color...crazier than a bare-naked bear in a berry patch, it was!

Except—

Wait a hot minute...

Something had just blinked in and out near the men. The shadows and sunlight folding in on themselves in a wavy exchange of places—reality itself rippling from a perturbation of some sort!

"Holybamoly," Sasha shouted with interruption. "*Smotri!*"

Ford saw it, his breath lodging in his throat from sheer disbelief.

And bowels growing weak from sheer dread.

A third figure had joined the two men. Tall and lithe. Whiter than a goose egg, with silver hair and wielding something that looked very familiar.

"Is that...?" Reeves asked, bringing a disbelieving hand to his mouth.

"*Bozhe moy,*" Nia whispered. "That is not being possible..."

"Is that—" Sasha echoed, swallowing hard before finishing his thought. "Is that...the new Patron?"

"Neron Kaisar," Polanco confirmed, a quiver in his voice betraying his self-assured steeliness.

Ford shook his head. Flat not possible. But there he was. He'd blinked out of the Capitolium and blinked back into the Holy Land!

"What's that in his hand?" Reeves asked.

"A sword," Ford said matter-of-factly, eliciting a round of hushed moans.

The Tracker drone came in for a closeup of the trio, the crowd clearly startled by the sudden appearance of the pale man—and the Two Amigos seemingly not having a clue about the sudden turn of things!

Wanted to scream at the Witnesses to turn around before it was too late.

And then it was.

In a flash, polished carbon steel sliced through Witness One, the tip jutting into his back and giving the camera a wink through his stomach.

The man's arms were raised with evangelistic appeal, and he lurched forward. The tip sliced farther out before twisting in a wicked arch and slicing backward—a disemboweling maneuver that did the trick. Entrails flopped down past the man's knees like bloated sausages, and blood spurted from his mouth before dribbling down his lips. Dude was a goner, crumpling to his knees before folding into a bloody, bowely pile.

And so was Witness Two.

Unlike his partner, the prophet knew it was coming, probably having heard and seen the dastardly deed done while preaching to the masses surrounding him. But instead of running, like any sane person, he faced his killer with raised pleading hands. Couldn't tell what he was saying, but it seemed to piss the Patron right off!

Face twisted up into a wicked scowl, lips curling back with jagged teeth gleaming white before his mouth opened into a roar while ramming that sword of his through the center of the prophet. Like his companion, Witness Two stumbled, feet faltering as Neron twisted the sword and yanked it out in a wicked scything motion that sent a stream of blood arching from the man.

It was over, just like that, the second witness joining the first in a pool of crimson.

After the deed had been done, OneWorld News went back to the Capitolium, where the Senate was still in session—men and women standing and cheering with rabid bloodlust. The wide shot caught the sudden reappearance of Neron Kaisar, the man's white robes and pale skin stained crimson, like he'd just slaughtered a pig.

Or two prophets of Jesus Christ himself...

Didn't seem to phase the Senators one bit, they were so possessed by their sycophantic subjugation. Though they did settle some, sitting down and giving the Patron their full attention.

Holding the sword aloft, Neron boomed, "I have freed us from the chains of the Nameless One, removing the blight of harassment from our midst!"

More chanting, more cheers, more rabid bloodlust.

Then he bellowed: "Long live the Republic! The Republic of Heaven—*For Humanity!*"

At this, the chamber rose to its feet again and started shouting the familiar refrain: *"For Humanity! For Humanity! For Humanity!"*

The SEPIO command center stood in grave silence, every last person saying not a peep, making not a movement nor a sound.

Ford's mouth ran dry. His blood ran cold. His mind ran ragged trying to make sense of it all. The Two Witnesses and their death—what the Good Book had to say about it and what it meant for Ichthus, for Solterra. Neron Kaisar and his crazy talk—not to mention his Houdini trick disappearing into some other dimension, only to reappear back into this dimension 5,500 miles away!

"What the hey-ho day just happened?" Reeves asked,

interrupting the silence as the broadcaster continued its crowing chant.

Polanco answered, "The events—the ones from the Apocalypse—they are unfolding in greater measure now. Far quicker than I had anticipated."

"What does this mean?" Nia asked.

"It means—" He faltered, then swallowed and continued: "It means the Antichrist has truly risen, and soon the last battle will commence."

"What does this mean for Ichthus?" Joshua said, glancing at his right-hand gal Zeljka, who shifted and nodded.

She added, "What does it mean for the Resistance, for individual Christians?"

There was an instant change in Polanco, his demeanor darkening, a fire rising in his eyes as his features hardened.

"The Dragon has finally stormed the stage of Solterra's history, and he will unleash the fires of hell itself across the Republic in a way that will make all other totalitarian persecuting campaigns look like child's play. Which means we must prepare Ichthus to stand firm in the faith, to remain vigilant until the end—even the *ultimate* end, a fate which is assured of us all—with the hope of ultimate victory."

No one said a word. No one needed to. And Ford understood it all perfectly.

The worm had turned something fierce.

With them at the center of it all.

They were the Church's last chance to hold the line, to remain faithful, to find ultimate vindication.

Against the Antichrist's rising.

CONTINUE READING SEASON 3

You've just finished episode 1 in the religious sci-fi apocalyptic adventure *End Times Chronicles Season 3*, the first book in the four-episode series, *Antichrist Rising*.

Think of it like your favorite Netflix, HBO, or Hulu show, where the story unfolds in installments. Each book can be read as a complete story with a beginning, middle, and end—but it ends on a cliffhanger that naturally flows into the next episode, fitting within a larger four-part tale.

Continue binge-reading the adventure by diving into the next episode now!

ANTICHRIST RISING • *Season 3*

Episode 1
Episode 2
Episode 3
Episode 4

Nobody should have to read bad religious fiction—whether it's cheesy plots with pat answers or misrepresentations of the Christian faith and the Bible. So J. A. Bouma tells compelling, propulsive stories that thrill as much as inspire, offering a dose of insight along the way.

Order of Thaddeus Action-Adventure Thriller Series

Holy Shroud • Book 1

The Thirteenth Apostle • Book 2

Hidden Covenant • Book 3

American God • Book 4

Grail of Power • Book 5

Templars Rising • Book 6

Rite of Darkness • Book 7

Gospel Zero • Book 8

The Emperor's Code • Book 9

Deadly Hope • Book 10

Fallen Ones • Book 11

The Eden Legacy • Book 12

Silas Grey Collection 1 (Books 1-3)

Silas Grey Collection 2 (Books 4-6)

Silas Grey Collection 3 (Books 7-9)

Backstories: Short Story Collection 1

Martyrs Bones: Short Story Collection 2

My Name's Johnny Pope • Collection 2

Joy to the Junction! • Collection 3

The Ties that Bind Us • Collection 4

A Matter of Justice • Collection 5

He Will Direct Your Paths • Collection 6

Find all of my latest book releases at: www.jabouma.com